The Arb

JON SMITH

BALKON
media

THE ARB

Published by Balkon Media

Paperback edition ISBN: 978-1-8384529-6-4
Also available in e-book format

A CIP catalogue record for this title is available from the British Library.

Cover illustration: @hoangtejieng
Cover design: Balkon Media

www.jonsmith.net

THE ARB

ALSO BY JON SMITH

FICTION

The Fifth Horseman

Destiny Can Bite Me (Fang & Loathing #1)

The Stakeout Diaries (Fang & Loathing #2)

Rewrite the Dead (Fang & Loathing #3)

YOUNG ADULT

The Arb

CHILDREN'S FICTION

Toytopia

NON-FICTION

Once Upon A Brand

Founder Mode

The Bloke's Guide To Pregnancy

The Bloke's Guide To Babies

Get Into Bed With Google

Google Adwords That Work

Smarter Business Start-Ups

Start An Online Business

Digital Marketing For Businesses

For Elena

CHAPTER ONE

The light sprinkle of rain against the car window was not something Sothea had ever seen before. It was delicate and timid, and seemed to hang in the air like a mist rather than fall. She squinted her eyes as the tiny droplets clung to the glass like inanimate insects, and tried to predict when the window wipers would swoosh them away. The wind was meek as well, the leaves of the trees fluttered flimsily, and the nature that surrounded them was bare compared to the lush dense abundance of the Cambodian jungle.

Back home she was used to the powerful, heavy rainfall that came for months at a time. The rain she knew formed with giant droplets that would fall suddenly and for hours, flooding streets with enough power and anger to uproot trees and carry stilt houses down mountains. Sothea was used to the thick, humid texture of the air, that was filled with the chirping sounds of insects and the bright and colourful skyborne calls of tropical birds. She had lived with ancient ruins in her backyard, built by a civilisation long gone, and even more ancient trees – massive venerable trees, with thick vines as far as the eye could see, below which stood bushes that took up every inch of ground and foliage so impenetrable that it took numerous men with machetes to clear. The English countryside was feeble in comparison.

The front passenger seat of the car was empty. At least physically it was. That was where Sothea's mother would ordinarily sit, and Sothea believed it was where her mother's spirit wanted to be, even now, when they were thousands of miles away from home in a foreign land where the rain had no courage. Sothea believed in those kinds of things, and most people would too if they had experienced what she had. She knew the world was blinded by what they could see, blinded by the privilege of what lay right in front of them. Most never cared to look past the tips of their own noses.

There had been an argument. Her father, who was driving in cold silence, had made a fuss over Sothea's refusal to sit in the front, and when he finally gave in, made another fuss about her not wanting their housekeeper, Ama – who had flown with them from Cambodia – to sit in the front either. Now all three of them sat in a tense and uncomfortable silence, a tension only made worse by the rain's near silent patter and the annoying squeak of the window wipers.

Sothea could still hear the phantom echo of the jungle wildlife in her ears. She wished they were still at home in their village. She wished that her father hadn't suddenly decided that they were all moving to England. Hadn't torn her from her heritage where she had been born and raised, and stolen her away to this weak land that couldn't even make up its mind whether it wanted to rain or not. Sothea strongly believed that a land was a reflection of its people, and that the people were a reflection of their land. If this was England, then she already knew what kind of humans lived here. And she despised them.

They had pulled off the smooth tarmacked surface of the

motorway, driven through rolling hills, and had been on narrow wood-lined roads for nearly twenty minutes. Sothea squinted as a slant of sunlight filtered through the grey clouds, and they slowly rolled to a stop in front of a giant black gate. It was gothic in appearance, with wrought-iron filigree embellishments and a signature pointed arch. Her father opened the car door in a huffed and tempered silence and got out. She watched him through her curtain of jet-black hair, and a small smile crept over her lips as he struggled to open the huge metal gate. She felt a dark amusement as she heard him cursing to himself.

"*Tsk*." Ama clicked with her tongue.

It was a Cambodian catch-all phrase – in this case, a sign of disapproval.

Sothea turned her head towards Ama and met the old woman's eyes with a piercing glare. Ama returned that stare with a look of fearless strength, and muttered a chastisement in Khmer. "Show some respect. He is your father."

The language had a light nasal quality, with very pronounced and distinct vowels, sharp, bright "ah"s and "ow"s defined and framed by gentle, aspirated consonants.

Sothea's jaw clenched and her lips pursed, conceding the fight as she folded her arms and turned back to the window. Even though she was being told off, it warmed her heart to hear Khmer spoken. Especially in this foreign land. Especially now. Whatever frustration she was feeling vanished in an instant as the creased skin of Ama's fingers slid across her arm and rested on the back of her hand. Sothea was eternally grateful Ama had come with them. The familiar feeling of the housekeeper's weathered, calloused hand on her skin was both comforting and calming.

"Sorry," Sothea whispered in Khmer.

"It's not me you should apologise to."

Sothea kept her gaze focussed on the trees and turned her

hand to interlock her fingers with Ama's. She loved Ama and Ama loved her. The old woman had been around since she was ten, coming on six years now. Sothea didn't see her as hired help, but like a grandmother. That was to say that Ama was very dear and close to Sothea's heart. Ama had become like blood to her. It was a sentiment that wasn't shared by her father, who had never been comfortable with a stranger moving into their house. It was another point of contention between them.

There was the sound of metal scraping and some self-congratulatory mumbles from her father, and Sothea looked up to see him pushing the large gates open. He jogged back to the car, closing the door instantly behind him, and engaging the gear-box. The tyres spun for a second on the wet earth before finding their grip and propelling the car forward, up the long, winding drive.

The rain, if you could call it that, had stopped now, and the grey clouds seemed to be blowing eastward, away from them. Sothea rolled down her window and looked up. Large scudding clouds sailed across the sky above her, with cracks of blue shining through, and already small grey-and-brown birds were chirping happily in the trees.

Sothea took in her first breath of the English country air and was taken aback by the crisp freshness of it. It carried with it the gentle sweetness of the flowers and herbs of the woods. Of course, she didn't know the names of the plants yet, but suddenly had a desire to learn where the smells came from. Ama and her late mother had always been keen herbalists, and she had followed in their passion. She knew every single medicinal property, herbal remedy, and other purpose for all the fauna and flora in Cambodia, and she was enticed by the prospect of learning an entirely new range of plant life here in England.

Maybe it won't be so bad here, she thought.

She found her heart responding to the tranquil tweets of the little birds. They were nothing like the open, awe-inspiring calls of the vibrant and colourful jungle birds, but they had their own unique charm. Sothea was, after all, both Khmer – through her mum – and English, through her dad. She reflected on the fact that she knew little to nothing about her Caucasian heritage.

The woods fell away as they drove, and the landscape opened into a large and slightly unkempt clearing. Right in the centre stood a large Victorian manor house. It was a perfect image of the time period in which it was built. Ama muttered something akin to awe under her breath, and Sothea found herself feeling the same. The manor house was stunning, but not only that. There was something else about it, something different, like it held a presence – a power even. It stood tall and majestic, despite the test of time, commanding attention with the intricacies of its architecture, designed with a puzzlement of turrets. There was a maze of large, projected windows framed in brilliant arches, along with porches and balconies on each of the three stories. The roofs were decorated with finials and confident crestings, with large chimneys that jutted out of the patterned roof tiles. On the upper stories, the roof was embellished with decorative trim, elaborate brackets, banisters, and spindles. All of this together made the house look mysterious, mystifying, and even romantic.

But as the car drove further up, the side of the house – which had been obscured only moments ago – came into view. It was not nearly as breathtaking, mainly because it was covered in scaffolding and blue plastic tarpaulin.

"You've got to be kidding me!" Sothea's father cursed. "What are they still doing here?!"

Sothea frowned and exchanged a glance with Ama, who shrugged, raising her eyebrows and looking up. Sothea smiled at the non-verbal commentary on the way her father was reacting.

She watched through the open window of the car as her father jumped out and yelled at the workers. She scanned the pinched and slightly red faces of the English men, and noticed a strange boy hiding in the shadows behind them. Their eyes met for a moment.

"You told me the repointing was finished weeks ago!" her father chastised them.

"We're a little behind schedule I'm afraid, Mr Bailey," replied one of the workmen.

"A *little* behind? You should have been done and gone. This isn't what we agreed."

"Cement. Timber. Even builder's sand. Can't get none for love nor money."

"Why am I only hearing about this now? You could have mentioned it when we spoke on the phone last week."

"Didn't want to worry you," the workman continued. "What with your big trip and all. Figured you had enough to worry about. And anyways, Big Phil said he could sort me out with some timber off a job that's gone wrong down Nantwich way. But it didn't happen."

Sothea's father turned to her. "Get inside."

He mumbled something in heavily accented Khmer to Ama and handed her a set of keys. She took Sothea's arm, guiding her out of the backseat and away from the scene, towards the wooden double doors of the front entrance. Sothea sighed and let Ama lead her.

"The people here are strange," she said in Khmer.

Ama gave her signature *tsk*. It was a million words in one.

Sothea stole one last frowning glance at the strange boy behind the scaffolding. He disappeared as they took the stone stairs up to the front door. It creaked as it opened, and a musty smell filled her nostrils.

Stepping inside gave Sothea a strange feeling. The house was dark and quiet, and yet it was as if a thousand spirits whispered in the walls. The entrance hall was grand, with beautiful dark herringbone parquet flooring. Intricate, unpainted woodwork framed every inch of space and a giant stairway unfurled in the centre of the grand hallway, rising fifteen steps before splitting into two wing staircases, carved in such a way that it resembled a wave curling over and crashing against a static shore.

Dust motes hung suspended in the air, as if a spell had been uttered long ago, freezing the tide of time in its place. Sothea reached out and rubbed the tip of her finger against the dusty wood, taking a deep breath and closing her eyes, letting her mind fill the gaps and spaces between her knowledge. An air current moved through the halls like a phantom, whispering to whomever would listen, and there was a gentle sway and rhythm to the creaking floors.

Ama gave Sothea a sharp pinch on her arm, and her eyes shot back open. The old woman gave her a pointed look. She took in a couple of deep breaths and tried to focus on the details of the house to keep her rooted in the here and now.

She quickly found that the house had a wildness to it, contrary to how sculpted and planned everything was. There were so many tiny details carved into the panels, arches, chandeliers, and ornate banisters that the eye had no place to rest. There were symbols, swirls, flower motifs, animals, and faces. Only the smooth parquet floor had escaped the carpenter's chisel. It made Sothea dizzy, remembering only one other place that made her feel like this – the sprawling temple complex of Angkor Wat. Ama seemed to notice and rested a hand on Sothea's shoulder, muttering a soft mantra in Khmer.

Sothea focused on the words as footsteps echoed through the hallway and her father's silhouette came to a stop at the base of the grand staircase. He pulled out a brass pocket watch and flicked it open. Except that the face of the watch was not a clock. Not a clock to tell the time anyway. Instead of numbers, there were sixteen depictions of the moon around the border, from full to new and back. There were three hands, the longest of which pointed towards the thinnest sliver of the waning crescent. Her father's jaw clenched and Sothea could see the worry in his features.

"Ama, please take Sothea up to the top floor. The attic. Follow the stairs until you can climb no higher," he said simply.

Sothea looked up at him, and he met her eyes with that distant gaze of his. Sighing, he approached her and brushed her jet-black hair from over her eyes, tucking it behind her ear. He stroked her delicate cheek with the back of his fingers.

"Don't worry," he whispered. "I will sort it out. Just go upstairs and get some rest. Settle in and I'll give you the tour once I've dealt with the builders."

Sothea's lips thinned into a narrow line, and she nodded.

"Come," Ama said sweetly in Khmer, linking her arm through Sothea's.

Once at the top of the stairs, they turned right and walked down the long length of a dimly lit corridor. There were no windows, and a narrow carpet muffled the tread of their footsteps. Sothea frowned and looked quizzically at the assortment of portraits hanging on the walls. These were all people she did not recognise, and yet scanning the small brass plaques under each painting revealed that they all shared the same last name. Her family name. Bailey.

Her ancestors on her dad's side. Her English heritage.

In addition to the family name, they all seemed to share a similar expression. A distant sombre haunting, as if a single spirit inhabited them all. Ama muttered some prayers in Khmer under her breath, obviously unsettled by the eerie silence.

There was a single door at the end of the corridor. It was worn and weathered with the varnish peeling to reveal the original wood beneath. Ama opened it and they were greeted with a wooden staircase, spiralling upwards to an unseen room above.

Ama indicated forward with her eyes. "*Laeng*," she whispered in her original tongue, before switching to her broken English. "Up."

With one hand on the wooden rail, Sothea slowly ascended the spiral stairs. Halfway up, grey light poured in through a frosted window, highlighting again the stagnant particles of dust that lingered in the silence. Every step creaked loudly, all the way up to the top, until they opened into a large attic room. At the far end was a queen-sized four-poster bed with dark-crimson curtains, and the ceiling slanted to a point with a single circular window in the centre. It was framed in wrought iron, and a strange symbol that slightly resembled an eye was also cast into the metal, forming the centre of the windowpane.

Sothea smiled. The room had been swept, dusted, and freshly painted. Something about the room welcomed her, like it had been waiting for her arrival. She ran her fingers over the quilted bedspread and couldn't resist sitting down on the bed to see if the springs squeaked. A moment later she was up again, exploring, opening each of the wardrobe doors and all the drawers, each as empty as the last.

Footsteps clunked up the stairs and her father appeared in the entrance a moment later, struggling to bring the two large suitcases up the narrow stairway, and then setting them down with a relieved huff. He pulled a handkerchief from his pocket and wiped the sweat off his brow before looking around.

"I had someone prepare the room before we arrived," he told her.

"I love it," Sothea said, reaching over to hug her father in what had become a rare act of affection.

"I'm glad." He kissed the top of her head and held her tight before she pulled away. "I was thinking that Ama could spend the first few nights up here with you."

Sothea looked to her excitedly.

"Just until we sort out some of the other rooms," he said, exchanging a quick glance with the old woman, who nodded and gave Sothea a little bow of respect. "Okay, why don't you unpack and I'll bring a mattress up for Ama?"

"*Tsk,*" Ama said, waving a dismissive hand. "Just blanket fine."

"Don't be ridiculous," her father replied. "The floor isn't soft like the bamboo back home. It also gets very cold at night, and in a house as old as this there will be a chill seeping through the cracks in the floorboards."

Ama let out a dismissive huff through her nostrils, but eventually she conceded, nodding. She didn't speak much English, but she understood everything. She spoke rarely and when she did, it was seldom in English, and never in sentences. More so single-worded observations or commands.

"I'm going to nip into the village and pick up some things for dinner," her father continued. "You hungry?"

Sothea nodded and her mouth began to salivate at the mention of food.

"Good." He turned to Ama and switched to Khmer. "The shipping container arrives tomorrow." He took a step closer to her and lowered his voice so that Sothea could only just make out what he was saying. "I will need you to unload the plants and get them into the greenhouse before sundown."

The old woman gave a nod.

Sothea's eyes wandered back and forth between them as they talked. Her heart stung a little that her father clearly wanted her to be kept out of the conversation and so she turned away, gliding softly over to the large window. She leaned to the side of it, staring out, so that if you were looking from down below you could only make out the faint pale outline of the side of her face. Her reflection was an ethereal white. Whiter than the peachy cream of the English, soft like moonlight, and yet not the kind of white to burn in the sun. As half of her face was illuminated by the thin rays of light cracking through the clouds, it almost seemed to shimmer, as if a small lunar aurora hovered over the surface of her skin.

"Sweetheart?" her father said. "What are you looking at?"

Sothea didn't turn away from the window but shifted her focus to watch as the workers packed up their tools for the day. The boy that had been hiding behind the scaffolding was hovering awkwardly, fiddling with his fingers. She frowned, and as soon as she did, his head turned, and he looked straight up to the eye-framed window. Sothea's father came to stand by her side.

"Those men. You're not to talk to them," he told her. "Let them get on with their work. They don't need you getting under their feet. They'll just use it as an excuse as to why they haven't finished."

He didn't wait for a response before turning and making his way down the stairs. Sothea watched her father leave with narrow eyes. She didn't like when he did things like that. Laying down the rules. Forbidding her from this and that. Managing her. Treating her like a child... Ama came to her side and laid a hand on Sothea's arm, but she yanked it free. She stormed to the other side of the room and pulled the crimson bed curtains closed, sealing herself in a cocoon and burying her face in the pillow. Her slender fingers squeezed the life out of it, and she threw curses to the wind with the sharp sting of her tongue.

Through her tirade, she heard Ama mutter a Khmer mantra of prayer and set to unpacking both of Sothea's suitcases.

Up on the scaffolding, the youngest of the workers – Gabe – had been the first to notice the car when it pulled up in the drive. He had turned and was about to tell the others, but his voice was cut off by his father before he even began.

"You wouldn't believe it. Got a tip on a horse. Warren said it was a sure thing. I knew something was off. Felt it right 'ere." He grabbed his groin and laughed with a crooked-toothed grin at his labourers, who were soaking in his story.

Hanging on every word was lanky labourer Jake, who ran his tongue along the sticky end of a Rizla as he expertly rolled a cigarette with one hand. And there was Vincent, a mountain of a man who had been his father's number two since they both dropped out of school and apprenticed as builders. He was lounging on the scaffold planks, taking an enormous bite out of the first of three pasties that would constitute his lunch.

"I said his tips weren't worth shit. So, what do I do?" Gabe's father turned to him and pointed at him with his cigarette, narrowing his eyes. "Take a guess."

"Umm..." Gabe's voice came out squeaky.

"Ah, for Christ's sake, boy. Why do you still sound like a little girl before her cherry's popped?"

There was a wheezing laugh from Vincent at that.

Gabe's dad laughed along at his own joke and pointed his thumb at his son. "Can you believe it? I wanted a boy, and the missus wanted a girl. God gave us half and half."

Gabe lowered his head and felt that familiar twist in his chest. His jaw tensed, as did his fists, and he watched silently as the car drove up the drive towards them.

"Psh." His dad waved his hand in a dismissive gesture. "Shouldn't 'ave asked you in the first place." He turned back to Vincent and Jake. "I'll tell you what I did. I downed me pint and put five hundred quid on 'I'll Have Another'. The sixteen-to-one outsider."

He soaked up their reactions, feeding off the laughter with the kind of amusement a con man gets when he's hit his mark.

"It's the horse's fourth race. Ever. Barely even left the stables. She only goes and wins. I slam down my pint, turn to Warren, and give him two of these." He raised both middle fingers. "You shoulda seen the look on his face."

Their laughter this time was interrupted by the slam of a car door.

"What the hell is going on here?!" shouted a voice from below up into the scaffolding.

"Ah shit," Gabe's dad cursed, and flicked his cigarette onto the wooden planks.

Gabe hid behind one of the scaffolding poles, peering out with one eye at the scene that followed. The words and raised voices merged into a milieu of mumbled noises, which Gabe felt more than he heard. He felt it like a texture in the air, a suffocating, syrupy, overwhelming mixing pot of emotions. His eyes flickered over to the car and that was when he noticed her for the first time.

Their eyes met and she held his gaze. Gabe had to look away from the scrutiny to break the contact. He couldn't help feeling exposed. It was unlike the looks he was used to getting. The looks he got from his dad and his dad's friends were dulled and blurry, like they only saw the surface, or only saw what they projected onto him. Even his teachers and the boys and girls in school barely gave him a second's notice. But her... It was like she had pierced every layer of him, like a needle passing straight to his core. It made him feel shaky and vulnerable.

When his father was packing their tools away, Gabe saw the girl's father in the attic window, but he could feel her there too, even if he couldn't see her. He felt that same piercing stare, like the soft touch of a white rose, surrounded by the strangle of sharp thorns.

The man drew the curtains over the window, obfuscating Gabe's view of them. It served to snap him out of his staring trance and the world came rushing to meet him, the all-consuming feeling of the girl's stare vanishing in an instant.

"Come on, you divvy," his dad said from the van. "Standing there with your willy in your hands."

Gabe shook himself out of his strange daze. He could hear his father mumbling to Vincent in the front passenger seat: "Honestly, I swear he's got only half a brain." Gabe ignored his father with a clench of his jaw.

He slid the side door to the van open and got inside, taking one last look at the veiled window before shutting the door behind him.

CHAPTER TWO

That night, the rain fell almost apologetically against the window of the old attic room. There was no sound of thunder, just the timid patter of raindrops, like a lost ghost tapping ever so persistently at the veil between worlds, wishing so desperately to be let through. This time of the month was always the hardest for Sothea to sleep. She lay awake in her bed, eyes wide open, staring at the strange shapes the shadows formed when there was no light to define them. On the other side of the curtains at the foot of her bed, Sothea could hear the rhythmic inhales and exhales of Ama as she slept. Sothea always envied how easily Ama could rest, how peacefully she could dream. The area around Sothea's tummy hurt, and her nails dug into her skin as she twined her arms around her belly and curled into a foetal position. It was like there was a thin-bladed knife inside her, stabbing, slicing with every passing second.

But Sothea was used to it. She did not let herself wince. She did not let herself groan, or even let any tears run loose. Instead, she stared dead ahead with wide-open eyes, playing mind games with the shadows that swam in the night.

R oughly three miles away in the village of Alderley Edge, Gabe was curled up on his side, staring at the soft glow of the teddy-bear night light plugged into the wall socket. He had relied on this very light to help him fall to sleep every night for seventeen years, ever since he had been born. It was a routine of his. He would stare at it with a soft gaze and its amber hue would begin to lose its definition, pulsing like a glowing orb, sometimes becoming so large that it consumed his entire vision. One of his favourite things to do was squint his eyes at it. The gentle diffusion of light would stretch out into several beams and he would make a game of shortening and elongating the length of them. Sometimes if he was really zoned in, he could pinpoint a speck of light and expand it into a circular droplet that resembled a cell, with unique pigments of light that would take on different colours of the rainbow.

He wore earplugs to sleep, and even still he could hear the muted mumble of the television from downstairs. No doubt his father had fallen asleep with a beer in his hand, like he did every night. As Gabe stared, he began to see images in his mind's eye of the girl from the manor house earlier that day. He saw her walking in the space between the beams of the night light. For now, he could only see the back of her. She moved as if she was made of air, floating gracefully like a dancer in the mist. She turned to him and smiled, and with that smile, she beckoned him into the world of dreams. The night light slowly faded away as his eyelids gently stilled and drooped over his pupils, taking him away to a world of his own making.

S othea rose from her bed at the crack of dawn, having not slept a wink. Her bare feet touched the cold wood soundlessly and she glided past Ama, slipping through the open door like a wisp and drifting down the stairs without triggering a single creak.

It was still early morning but the birds tweeted with bright and enthusiastic trills. Sothea sat at the top of the stone stairs at the front of the house in the chill of dawn, listening to the birdsong in just her nightdress. Only minutes passed by before Ama showed up behind her. Sothea must have woken her after all. She was wrapped in multiple layers of clothes, with her arms hugged tightly around herself. She brought with her a blanket, which she draped over Sothea's shoulders without saying a word.

"I don't think I'll ever be happy here," Sothea said in Khmer.

The rain had stopped last night, and the grey clouds had been blown away by the morning winds, leaving a glassy orange sky as the sun began to rise.

"But I can feel my ancestors," she continued softly.

"It is cruel," Ama replied in her own language, "to split one's ancestors in different lands. A body cannot be in two places at once, and so being close to one part of you comes with the loss of another."

Sothea frowned. "What if I want to lose parts of the past?"

"There is no escape, my child. We pay for the mistakes of our ancestors," Ama said sombrely. "We pay until the debt is gone."

Sothea sighed and looked down at her toes, scrunching them on the stone steps.

"Come inside out of the cold," Ama said sweetly. "The world might look a little better once you're dressed."

She turned and began to shuffle back inside. Sothea nodded

and stood to follow her, the blanket still wrapped tightly around her shoulders. But as she rose, she spotted something between the gaps in the forest trees across the drive. Her heart skipped a beat before she recognised the creature that stared back at her. A fox. It stood motionless, staring at her with black, vertical-slitted pupils. Sothea met the fox's gaze and stared back for a long time, taking in the bright orange of its fur, before bowing respectfully and turning to walk back inside.

The peace of the morning was soon swept away as the builders' van trundled along the drive of the manor. Her father was waiting for them on the steps with a list of overdue tasks before the workers had even climbed out of it.

Sothea watched from above as he spoke to them. "I want no one stepping foot in or anywhere near this part of the house, is that understood?" her father said sternly, pointing to a section of blueprints.

The workman nearest to him frowned but nodded.

"It is very important," he continued. "I have rare and important flora specimens coming in today that require very specific conditions. It is essential they are not disturbed."

Eavesdropping on the conversation quickly bored her and Sothea's eyes wandered in other directions. Towards the other end of the house, she saw two men jump-scare the youngest worker, the one who liked to hide. As a result, he dropped all the things he was carrying and raised his arms over his face, instinctively trying to protect himself. The men clapped their hands together and laughed. Their distant voices echoed to where Sothea watched from above.

"He's too easy."

"Hope you didn't wet your pants."

They left him standing there with his hands over his head. It took a surprisingly long time for the boy to lower them. Eventually he knelt and began picking up the tools he had dropped. Sothea stared like a hawk, sharp and focused. As soon as he was sure he had picked everything up, he stormed off, out of sight.

She frowned. Why did he let them treat him like that?

Her eyes honed in on a shiny piece of metal that still lay on the ground where he had been. She smiled and turned away from the window, descending the stairs and sneaking out of the side entrance of the house. Still barefoot, she walked over to the shiny object and picked it up. She was not sure what it was, but assumed it was a tool of some sort. She turned it over in her hands, inspecting it.

"Sothea!" Her father's voice came from behind her.

She turned abruptly, hiding the tool behind her back as her father approached her at a quick pace.

"What did I tell you?!" His hand seized her arm in a tight grip, and he pulled her back to the house. "I already have to manage a bunch of morons; I can't be keeping an eye out for you all the time too." He said it in that hushed anger that fathers are so good at – the dad whisper, a voice that can't be overheard by others but still packs a punch, full of tension and barely contained restraint. "Don't make me ground you," he continued, giving her a look that made clear it wasn't an empty threat. "There is an entire house to explore. Just... please. Stay inside."

He shoved her into the house and slammed the door shut behind her before storming off to follow the men, who had disappeared around the other side of the house.

Sothea's straight, black hair had fallen over half of both her eyes in the tussle, and she silently raged at her father through the closed door. Her fingers began to curl and tense, and a hot pressure built instantly inside her like a kettle rising to boil. The high-pitched squealing in her ears got louder and louder, and the stabbing pain in her womb returned as her blood pulsed like a heavy drum beat. The high-pitched squeal turned into screams, and just when the crescendo built to the point of bursting, there came the soft tranquil tone of Ama's voice. She was whispering a mantra like a soothing balm, the ancient Khmer pouring out of her lips like tranquillity transmuted into sound. Ama wrapped her arm around Sothea's and gently rubbed her back in calming circles.

The pressure inside her diffused. Ama's influence was like burning incense sticks warding off evil spirits. She brushed casually at the air around Sothea's body, as if she were shooing flies away or dusting off cobwebs. She clapped a couple of times and did a grasping-at-the-air-type motion, taking handfuls of invisible air and throwing them elsewhere. And, of course, she squeezed in a couple of signature Ama "*tsk*"s.

Sothea suddenly felt cold. She was still holding the tool she had picked up, but was now gripping it so tightly that her knuckles had turned even whiter than normal. She let out a deep breath and the last of the tension faded away. Her hands tingled, and she was light-headed, like the headrush that comes when you stand up too fast.

"Shh. Your baba doesn't mean to be like that," Ama said in Khmer, with kind beaming eyes. She took Sothea's head between her palms and brushed the hair away from her forehead. "He is a sleepwalker," she added. "Sleepwalkers don't know how they act until it's too late."

The term didn't properly translate into English. It was more of a concept, a way of referring to people who were acting in an unconscious way – sleepwalking through life – who believed themselves to be justified in their actions, without taking into consideration how they made other people feel or how their actions affected others.

"Come." Ama guided her towards the nearest room. "Rest in here, I'll make us some tea."

Sothea entered the room to discover that it was a library. It was dark and dusty, and heavy velvet curtains hung over the large windows. She could hear Ama humming away in the kitchen to the accompaniment of pots and pans clanking on the stove. Her eyes scanned the room. The bookshelves were lavishly ornate with hundreds of moulding leather-bound books. There were various corners and nooks with well-cushioned chairs, and a large rug in the centre of the room with nice, comfortable couches. She took a book from the shelf but quickly realised she was in no mood to read and placed it back.

Soon, Ama appeared at the door with two steaming cups and they took a seat in one of the reading nooks. The herbal infusion Ama had made helped return the feeling to Sothea's body, and the familiar nostalgic taste of Cambodian herbs made her feel warm and fuzzy inside.

"You need to get better at sneaking out," Ama declared matter-of-factly.

"Aren't you supposed to be watching over me? Running to Baba if I break the rules?"

If Ama was offended by Sothea's tone, she hid it well. She smiled as she sipped at her drink. "I will always watch over you. But what Baba doesn't know won't hurt him." She winked and stood up, patting Sothea's leg before she shuffled out of the library.

Sothea was staring at a small ladybird crawling over the surface of the window frame when she heard raised voices.

"You was the last one to have it, Gabe!"

There was a mumbled response that Sothea couldn't hear. She put her tea down quietly and crept over to the window, hiding behind the folds of the curtains and peering out with one eye.

The boy, who must have been Gabe, fumbled with his fingers and pointed to an imaginary pile of tools on the floor, trying to

speak but having a lot of trouble getting his words out. "Jake...
Knocked..."

Sothea watched him closely. It was like the words were getting
caught in his throat. Gabe raised a hand to his neck, which only
furthered her hypothesis.

"Oh, *'Jake knocked'*?" The other man mocked Gabe's voice
with a sharp edge. "Grow a pair of balls, son, and go find it!"

With that he stormed off, leaving Gabe standing and
muttering to himself with his head looking down at the ground
and his fingers twining in and out of one another in a nervous
tick. Sothea watched the other man leave with narrow eyes. He
was a sleepwalker too. Turning her attention back to Gabe, she felt
a pang of empathy. She had been the reason he had gotten in trouble. Biting her lip, she knocked lightly at the window.

Gabe's head turned. He wasn't startled; instead he met her
eyes with a deep sadness. Sothea raised a finger and mouthed the
words, "One moment". She rushed over to her chair and grabbed
the tool. Assured that the coast was clear, she slipped back to
unlatch the window.

"Hey," she said softly.

Gabe didn't reply.

"I'm sorry," she added. "I think I got you into trouble."

He frowned.

Guiltily, Sothea revealed the small tool she was still holding on
to, and stretched her arm out. Gabe stared at it for a long while
before eventually reaching out his own hand and taking it from
her. He still hadn't said a word, and it made Sothea feel uncomfortable.

"Your name's Gabe?" she asked politely.

He nodded.

"I'm Sothea."

Gabe met her eyes for a second and offered a sad turn up of his lips. "Nice to meet you."

"Why do you let him talk to you like that?" Sothea asked, leaning like a cat on the windowsill.

Gabe shrugged. "He's my dad. I'm not supposed to talk back."

"I talk back to my dad all the time," Sothea said with a sharp glare. "Just because he is your dad, it doesn't mean he is right."

Gabe frowned and ignored her. "How did you get the trowel?"

"I saw it, so I picked it up," she replied matter-of-factly. "I should go. Sorry again for getting you in trouble." She closed the window and dipped out of sight a moment later.

———

Gabe found himself standing in the same spot for a long time, just staring at the tool in his hand. Or that's what it might have looked like on the surface. His mind was processing a million thoughts at once. That was the thing about Gabe; he didn't quite know how to tone down his experiences. Memories of the last few moments continued to replay in his head through different angles and in quick succession. He saw the light flutter of her eyelashes over and over, the way she casually leaned up against the window. Her long black hair, and the way her eyes stared all the time, so focused, unwavering. Again and again and again.

Her voice sounded like glass chimes. The memory of it tinkled in his mind, and now he wished he had said more. A burning curiosity started to yearn inside of his gut and chest. He found himself walking, handing the trowel over to his father, ignoring the insults and laughs that came after, and continuing away from them until he was safely hidden under a large weeping willow tree. There, he sat against the trunk and hugged his knees into his chest. The long skinny branches of the willow drooped down, mirroring the fall of Sothea's hair, swaying gently in the wind. Cracks of sunlight would creep through the gaps, and when they did, sparkles danced in the air of Gabe's vision. The world went blurry, and he let the silence soothe him.

The bleep, bleep, bleep of a lorry reversing announced the arrival of the delivery truck. A look of relief flashed across Sothea's father's face, and he slid his chair back from the kitchen table and marched out of the room. Ama and Sothea followed.

The shipping container carrying all of the family's worldly possessions, along with her father's hand-picked specimen trees, plants, fauna and flora, had finally arrived, albeit half a day late. Sothea watched as he guided the delivery men and their pallets of greenery around the side of the building to the giant palm house that was connected to the manor's east side. It was so big that it should have looked out of place in a house – as her father had so proudly told her yesterday, its cylindrical centre could easily accommodate trees up to eight metres in height – but somehow it worked here. A wrought-iron frame supporting hundreds of panes of glass, it was surprisingly warm and humid inside, despite the cold weather. Her father had meticulously planned the layout down to the smallest of saplings, and he guided the delivery men to the exact spot he wanted each plant left, ready for setting into the earth.

Soon the air was filled with the strong bitter scents of the Cambodian jungle. Sothea stopped at each of the potted plants and herbs. She knew all of them by their Khmer names, thanks to

Ama's instruction. She knew why her father was growing them, and she knew that Ama was counting the minutes until she'd be able to spend her days in the palm house, tending to them and occasionally picking a leaf from this one and a berry from that one. Sothea knew what they were for and how they could be used to treat everything from tiredness to pain, melancholy to dizziness. More and more plants were arranged inside, and it wasn't long before the palm house felt alive and felt like home.

"I'll get this all bedded in this afternoon," her father said. "I'll leave the cardamom and lemongrass for you to plant, since you did such a good job at the villa."

Sothea nodded. "Of course!" She meant it. She'd enjoyed looking after her kitchen garden in the jungle. She could while away hours pruning and dead-heading, squatting next to Ama with her hands deep in dirt, feeling the earth between her fingers. It would be a pleasure.

"It's just—" But Sothea stopped mid-sentence, one hand on her tummy, as the plumber hobbled over. She stood back to let the man talk.

"All done, Mr Bailey."

"Excellent, Billy. Thank you." Her father patted the man on the back. "Let's see it in action."

Billy wiped his wet hands on his trousers and led her dad to a small silver console fixed to the wall. "Dead easy," he said. "You just need to turn it on there. The dial on the left controls the frequency."

Her father held a finger over the console and pressed the yellow power button. A small light turned on and what must have been about a mile of hose – laid over the floor, along the base of each of the vast planters, up the iron posts, and even the highest part of the palm house ceiling – suddenly became taut and burst into life, releasing a fine mist that soaked everyone and everything.

Sothea held a hand out, watching the beads of moisture form on her fingers. She smiled.

"Do you need me to fix anything up in there?" The plumber pointed to the door at the far end of the palm house, that led back into the manor. "What is it, some sort of wet room?"

"No," her father replied sternly, shooting the man a look. "I can handle that myself."

The plumber looked at him for a moment before shrugging and walking off to avoid the mist that had formed in the air. Sothea took Ama's arm and they too ambled away, leaving her dad to work his way through the rest of his checklist.

Lightning struck and dark storm clouds obscured the sky as night drew in. Sothea sat with her eyes glued to the attic window. The wind tore through the trees, howling wildly, and cracking branches in the space between thunderclaps.

Finally, she thought. England is showing some passion.

Despite the darkness and the weather, her father was still at work. Having planted the last of the new arrivals, he was now fixing thin sheets of metal to the walls and floor of the small room next to the palm house. Her dad had explained that it once housed the boiler used to heat the palm house during winter. But it had been stripped bare and now looked like a walk-in refrigerator. She watched as he stood with his hands on his hips for a moment, admiring his hard work. His clothes were soaked through thanks to his new irrigation system and there were streaks of mud across his cheeks and his arms. He fished out his strange moon clock, and again she saw worry in his face when he looked at it. Then he shoved it back in his pocket, seemingly more determined than ever to get everything finished.

That night, again, Sothea didn't sleep a wink. Instead of tossing and turning in her bed, she sat upright by the window nook, watching as the storm raged on. Ama had set up a small wooden altar and was conducting her own religious prayers to mark the coming of the new moon. The smell of incense was thick in the air. Ama came from a tribe of indigenous people in the uplands of the Ratanakiri province that don't define themselves as Khmer. She had been married to a Khmer man, once upon a time, and learned his ways and language, but always kept up her more shamanic traditions. When her husband passed to the next life, she had become a sort of medicine woman – a *Kru Khmer* – bringing the wisdom of her tribe into the lowlands, and healing many of the poorer people, who could not afford to go to hospitals in the city or afford western medicine. She healed not only physical wounds, but spiritual and emotional ones too.

Even in the height of the Hindu Era of Cambodia, when magnificent and grand temples such as Angkor Wat were carved from rock, Ama's ancestors had lived separately. Her tribe, for as long as history, had been viewed as savages, and still to this day experienced great struggles with oppression. But Ama had defied those struggles and become famous across the province. That was how Sothea's father had come to find her and convince her to join his household as a nanny.

Ama told Sothea that at first she had refused. The young couple who had asked for her help, James and Chantrea – Sothea's parents – seemed like a nice enough couple, clearly very much in love. But Ama wanted to help whole communities, not focus on one well-off family and their daughter. But then a ten-year-old Sothea had run into the room, straight across to Ama, and given her a big cuddle. Ama was suspicious at first that Sothea had been put up to this very convincing display of affection by her parents, and she was ready to leave the villa and return to her own village.

But then she had looked at Sothea, and Sothea at her. In that moment, Ama saw something in her eyes and knew, without question, that her place was at the side of this gangly little girl. She accepted the role on the spot.

Ama moved into the family's villa on the outskirts of Siem Reap and it wasn't long before she took Sothea under her wing and began to instruct her on the medicinal properties of the flora and fauna that grew with such abundance in the Cambodian countryside and jungle. After Sothea's mother died, Ama had helped look after her more and more. The older woman had been a great comfort to both her and her father.

Sothea listened now as Ama spoke to her spirits and wondered if those spirits could still hear her whispers and chants from thousands of miles away. The violence of the storm kept her enthralled, but an iron hot fear was beginning to grow deep in Sothea's heart – a fear that felt as familiar as her own name, and yet she still could not trace the origin. Her abdomen stabbed and clawed as the storm raged on, dulled only slightly by the comfort of Ama's chanting. It was a long night, and the ancient whispers got louder and louder, as though straining to take life.

CHAPTER THREE

Gabe overheard his father's phone call that morning. Mr Bailey didn't want them on site tomorrow and, in fact, they weren't to return until Tuesday. Gabe thought it strange, considering the man had made such a fuss about getting the work done quicker. Regardless, he felt all the better for it. Without the work, he and the rest of the crew had earned themselves a couple of days off.

Without delay, his dad had left for the pub, with no indication of when – or if – he would return, leaving Gabe to his own peace and quiet and the prospect of yet another dinner made from whatever scraps he could find in the fridge and cupboards. With the summer storm in full swing, he couldn't escape to his favourite spot on the outskirts of Alderley Edge, a small retreat in the woods that was elaborately wrapped up in the myths he loved so much. And so, he had no option but to indulge in his second-favourite hobby: reading.

Gabe had probably re-read this same book well over a hundred times. It was an old, out-of-print novel based on the legends of

King Arthur. In the story, it was said that there was a secret cave entrance hidden in the rocks, where King Arthur and his Round Table still slept in divine hibernation, slumbering until the age came in which they could rise again and lead mankind back to true honour. There was mention of portals to the realm of the fae and a secret well, abundant with magical properties. There was one passage in particular that Gabe had latched on to: "Should a wanderer of pure heart find and wake the sleeping King, a favour shall be granted upon him." As a young boy, Gabe had always hoped that he would be the one to find Arthur. If he had, he would have wished for a limitless supply of Lego, so he could build to his heart's content and never run out of bricks. As he grew older and things at home became more and more unbearable, he had only one wish: to become a sworn knight of the King and leave home forever.

He loved the stories with all his heart. When he was young, his mother had taken him to the small town of Tintagel on the coast of Cornwall, where he had explored Merlin's Cave and swum in the ocean over which the great sea priestess Morgan le Fay once cast spells bathed in starlight. To him, the magic in these stories was as real as the sea he swam in that day. That was to say that it inhabited the air of his world like a second layer of skin, like a dreamy ocean cloud hovering around every corner. When he then learned that the resting place of Arthur and his knights was fabled to be right here in Alderley Edge, he had thought his heart might explode with a mixture of pride and excitement. From that moment on, he was hooked. The stories were his solace and his friend. They were a rich tapestry of history, myth, and legend that offered countless possibilities.

Unlike most people, Gabe looked forward to mornings wrapped in fog. His head swam with tales of heroes who were suddenly taken by a silver mist, only to find themselves walking into another world once the mists had receded. Gabe read out loud in his bed, memorising the words, evoking the images clear as day in his imagination. If called upon, he could tell each story without pause, reciting every word perfectly, pausing when the commas slowed the pace and speeding up when the action took its place.

Unfortunately, it seemed like no one else cared about his stories. Most seventeen-year-olds, at least those that Gabe went to college with, had forgotten all about their imaginations. So, other than when he was working with his dad, Gabe spent all his time alone.

The rain beat heavy against the window and Gabe closed his book, moving towards the glass and looking out to the darkness. In the shadows, his imagination took full form, the empty night becoming a storming sea that kings and witches traversed on giant waves, sails coming loose and tearing free in the high nautical winds, and where frightening sea monsters emerged from the briny depths to lay havoc on the world above.

Much to his surprise, Sothea appeared in the folds of his daydreams. She glowed white, even though the new moon had left the night sky empty. She seemed to call out to him through the third wall of his mind, directly through the story, breaching the boundaries of fantasy and reality. As Gabe stared out into the dark night, he imagined what Sothea was doing, imagined her looking out of her own window.

In many ways she was just like him, he thought. She too seemed to always be watching, observing life through the lens of a thin pane of glass, one step removed. Never quite participating. Staring from afar.

Her image was what consumed his mind that evening too, as he drifted from the fragile plane of waking life into the deeper unconscious ocean of his dreams. And only there did he join her, atop the deck of a wavering ship that struggled with the tides and storms, their eyes ever seeking a stable land to anchor upon.

***

"Good work today," Sothea's tutor commented as he slipped on his overcoat. "I hope you will consider sitting the Further Mathematics paper next year. You have a gift for calculus."

"Thanks to your teaching," Sothea replied as she opened the front door of Bailey Manor to let him out. Idle conversation didn't come naturally to her, but she knew how to layer on the charm when it was required.

Her avuncular tutor beamed with pride and skipped down the stone steps to his car. She watched as he drove away along their expansive drive. A brief yellow blink of an indicator and the car turned left to join the main road, the noise of its engine soon lost.

She paused in the doorway. It was finally her weekend. Sothea had slipped into a routine. Power through the weekdays and the parade of private tutors who passed through the house, and then relax at the weekend with the freedom to spend her time as she saw fit. Although half of Saturday had already been lost to French literature and maths, she was determined to enjoy what was left of it. Taking in long deep breaths, inhaling and exhaling, she relished the fresh air in her lungs. The air in England the morning after a storm had a unique smell – fresh, metallic, and alive. Sothea liked it. If it were up to her, she'd sit on the front steps all day. But she'd promised to help Ama in the palm house and she had yet to plant her own kitchen garden.

Passing from the main house to the palm house required her to walk through two heavy metal doors. The moment she did, she was hit with a wall of incredible heat and humidity. This was what a summer should be like. This was just like the jungle back in Cambodia. It was perfect. The plant life clearly thought so too. It was flourishing in the temperature-controlled environment. Many of the specimens were already showing an abundance of new growth and looked like they'd been established there for years, not days.

Ama waved her over to a raised border on the far side of the palm house. The old woman was wearing her signature gardening gloves, which she'd brought with her from Cambodia and had been repaired with patches and stitches so often that Sothea wasn't actually sure there was any of the original material remaining.

Sothea approached slowly when she saw Ama's forehead creased even more than usual in concentration. She was using the finest of tweezers to extract the stamens of a particularly rude-looking plant.

"Don't even breathe," Ama hissed in Khmer, poised like a neurosurgeon as she went in again with the delicate tweezers. A moment later she was wearing an unusual facial expression. Unusual for her, at least. She was smiling. "Got it."

Ama dropped her prize into a stone pestle and sat back on her haunches, looking at Sothea properly for the first time since she had arrived.

"Was school fun?" she asked.

"Like being trampled by a water buffalo."

"*Tsk*," Ama reprimanded her. "I lost a cousin to a water buffalo once. It's not a laughing matter."

"Really?" Sothea was genuinely surprised. She thought she'd heard about all of Ama's extensive family.

"No."

"*Tsk*," Sothea chided, mostly to herself for falling for Ama's trick.

"Water buffalo are very big and slow," Ama continued, then switched to English, using one of her favourite new phrases. "You have to be a *silly sausage* to be caught by one." She poked and prodded Sothea with the tweezers before tickling her armpit.

"You're a silly sausage!" Sothea exclaimed, falling on the floor in laughter.

"Do you have everything you need?" her father asked, surprising them both with his presence.

Ama checked her pestle, counting the contents by pointing to each herb, berry, and leaf with her tweezers. She nodded. "We do."

"Good. Sothea, come with me. I need your help with something."

Sothea got up from the floor and followed her father through the palm house to his workshop.

"I know it's a mess, but there's a method to my madness."

A better name for her dad's workshop would probably have been "junk room". Sothea couldn't make head nor tail of it. There were sheets of stainless steel, toolboxes, piles of floor tiles, and lots and lots of timber all sawn to various lengths.

"I know this place doesn't feel like home yet," he continued. "But I promise that you'll be happy here. It needs a lot of work to bring it back to its former glory. But it's a good house. It just has a few scars that need repairing."

Sothea reached out to stroke the wooden frame of a mirror that her dad had dismantled and only partially sanded. She winced when a small splinter pricked her thumb, and instinctively put her thumb in her mouth to suck the tiny wound.

"Grab an end." Her father held up a large spool and passed a length of fencing wire to her. "Now walk towards the kitchen and tell me when you've gone forty-five paces."

Sothea did as she was asked and shouted "Okay!" when she'd walked the required distance. A moment later her father shouted for her to come back, and when she returned to the workshop, he had cut the wire from the spool and held the other end in his hands.

"Let's make a vine."

Sothea enjoyed the rest of the afternoon. Whenever a feeling of worry reared up inside her, she forced it back, distracting herself with planting and pruning. She had helped her father secure the wire across the diameter of the palm house between two iron pillars. Although it could be years until they saw their labour pay off, the sapling ivies and trailing plants now had something to support them. Spending time with her father and Ama in the palm house had reminded her of their time together in Cambodia – of better times without past regrets or present dreads.

Tuesday came sooner than Gabe anticipated, and he found himself excited to go to work. Not at the prospect of replacing cracked roof tiles, or repointing the crumbling brickwork, but because he might have a chance of seeing Sothea again. It sparked a joy and enthusiasm in him. At the back of his mind he knew they had almost completed the work on the house. But he didn't want to think about that yet, or what it might mean in terms of seeing her. He was going to enjoy each and every moment while he could. That was, until his father came to ruin it all.

"What's got your knickers in a twist?" he mocked. "Never seen you move so fast in me life!"

Gabe ignored him, getting in the van and sliding the door shut behind him. But his dad stuck his boot in the way and swung it back open.

"Hey, I asked you a question, soft lad! No respect..."

Gabe's jaw tensed. "Sorry."

His father scoffed. "Unbelievable. Just shutting the door on your old man. If it weren't for me, you'd be without a job, on the streets begging for pennies or selling your bum for a sausage roll and a can of Tango."

With that, he slammed the back door shut before jumping into the front seat, sending a jarring spike of emotions through Gabe's body.

"Useless prick," he continued. "Just my luck I get a son who spends all his time thinking about fairies."

Gabe was used to his father's slurs and insults by now. He told himself they didn't affect him, but the truth was that they did, and instead of processing them, they were just buried deep, shoved into the bottom of his gut, stewing in an unhealthy pot of repressed anger. And Gabe had been kicked out of college for that very reason. His anger. Something his father never failed to point out.

"You're a failure, you know that?" his dad said, adjusting the rear-view mirror to look at his son. "Don't got even half a brain to make it through school. You're lucky your old man has his own business. Able to give you a good job. And what thanks do I get in return?" He started the engine and began to steer out of the drive.

Gabe ignored him.

Vincent was standing outside his house a couple of blocks down and got into the front passenger seat. Soon the two older men were exchanging stories and laughing, insulting each other through jokes, as seemed to be so common in English banter. Gabe didn't understand it. He didn't understand why two people who insulted each other so much would remain friends.

Although, to be fair, Gabe himself had problems with tonality and sarcasm. He didn't get dry humour and took everything literally. So the banter between two mates just sounded like a toxic battle of two egos clashing. To be honest, in the case of his dad and Vincent, the reality probably wasn't so different. Take away the veil of humour and that was pretty much all it was.

Regardless of the words that his father had thrown at him, Gabe still felt excitement bubbling in him as they left Alderley Edge and drew closer to Bailey Manor. But as they turned off the main road and passed through the gates, the giddiness he'd felt on the approach evaporated. The van rolled to a stop and his father and Vincent got out, ignoring him as he followed them towards the house. He furrowed his brow. Something felt strange. He couldn't place it, but even though the sun was shining, it was like a heavy shadow sat over the manor. It twisted Gabe's gut every which way.

"Stop staring like a donkey and come help us carry the stuff over!" his father shouted.

Gabe did as he was told, only half-aware of the things he was doing, the other half deeply worried – though for the life of him, he couldn't figure out why.

The air was stale. There was no birdsong and the trees stood still, without a breath of wind moving through them. A rogue crow cawed, its harsh throat-rattle echoing eerily across the silence. Then came another. Gabe turned to where the noises were coming from and was shocked to see an entire murder of crows perched along a single branch in one of the large trees. He quickly turned away again lest they make eye contact with him.

He looked back at Vincent and his father. They didn't seem to notice anything, although that was no surprise. He knew for a fact that his father never saw past the tip of his own nose. Jake pulled up in his own van a second later and nudged past Gabe with a cocky sneer, taking a last pull from the dirty roach of his cigarette before flicking it to the ground and jogging to catch up with Vincent and Gabe's dad.

"Alright, gaffer! Alright, Vince!"

Gabe's compulsion towards hyperfocus made it impossible for him to look away from the smoking remains of tobacco and bleached paper as it cascaded across the ground in a small show of sparks. The collage of smoke, black feathers, and echoing crow calls swirled in the eerie stillness. Gabe half expected a crawling mist to creep in and the dark priestess herself, Morgan le Fay, to appear, thorny crown and all.

But as soon as the smoke from the discarded cigarette cut out, Gabe found himself standing once again in the light of day. And that was when he felt it. He looked up and saw Sothea at the edge of the upstairs window. She stared down at him with half-open, distantly glazed eyes. It was a profound difference from the sharp focus and unyielding attention he had seen from her before. She was wearing a pearl-white night dress, and her crow-black hair fell straight down in stark contrast against her white skin. For the first time he noticed how long her hair really was. It went well past her stomach and ended just below her hips. One of her long and slender arms was wrapped around her belly.

Gabe couldn't say how long they stared at one another before she suddenly turned and disappeared into the blanket of shadows behind her. There was the crunch of gravel ahead and Gabe turned to see the owner of the manor, Mr Bailey, striding over to him. His hair was dishevelled, revealing a deeply receding hairline, and he looked as if he hadn't slept in days. Deep bags, the colour of bruises, encircled the lower crescent of his eyes.

"Gabe, right?" he said with the non-committal attitude of exhaustion. It was curt and tossed out indignantly.

Gabe nodded, somewhat fearful of the man.

"Where's your father?"

Gabe pointed in the direction his dad had gone, and Mr Bailey walked off after him without another word. As soon as he was out of sight, Gabe looked back up to the windows, hoping to catch another glimpse of Sothea. He couldn't explain the feeling she gave him. It was like his entire body filled with a phantom force. It made him want to grow strong like the knights in his story. It made him want to draw a sword – preferably embedded within a stone – and charge into battle. There was an over-whelming feeling of attraction, as if she were a siren, calling him into the ocean tide.

But much to his dismay, he could not see her now. And he did not see her for the rest of the day. He was constantly distracted, finding his eyes searching the many windows of the house every few seconds.

"Ouch, you knob!" his dad shouted. "You hammered me bloody thumb!"

Gabe completely forgot about the tasks he was helping with, inspiring a long string of curses and insults from his father, which just blurred into a foggy mass of colour and muted mumbles. The only clarity Gabe got was from the sharp definition of the glassy paned windows, and the ornate framing that surrounded them.

There was a heavy sulk in his chest when he finally got in the back of the van at the end of the day. There was nothing more left to look forward to now. Gabe leaned up against the metal of the van's interior, the vibrations of the wheels against the driveway reverberating in his skull and bouncing his head every so often. But Gabe could hardly feel it beneath the soft cushion of his beanie hat. His heart and his mind were consumed with only one thing. And just like that, Gabe realised he was smitten.

It was a new sensation, one he had never felt before. And he had been in the presence of many girls before. To be honest, he had never paid them any attention at school, nor had they paid much attention him. He was seventeen and this was the first time he'd fancied someone. Ever. It was a swirl of contradicting feelings, and with no good role models in his life to look towards, he turned to his stories.

That night, he read about men traversing treacherous terrain solely for the purpose of finding an extremely rare flower, and cradling it like an infant child on the perilous journey back, just to hand it to the one they held dear. He read about honourable kings and gallant knights and the quests they endured all for the name of love. Then he fell asleep to the stories blending into his dreams.

———

For the rest of the week Gabe continued to look out for Sothea, but she never appeared in the windows. Sometimes he thought he caught a glimpse of her, but it would turn out just to be a reflection in the glass. On Saturday morning, the last working day of the week, Gabe decided to take a bouquet of flowers – a mix of roses he found growing in the gardens near his house. He hid them in his coat, despite the thorns that pricked at him every now and again as the van jostled up the country drive.

When they paused for their mid-morning break, he withdrew from his father's group and snuck to the part of the house where he had seen Sothea most often. He looked up to the large circular window with the wrought-iron eye and was dismayed to see that the curtains had been drawn closed. But a magical feeling was bursting in his heart. He rushed to the western wing, where some scaffolding still stood, and climbed with haste to the tiled roof. Traversing it carefully, he made his way to the roof above the circular attic window. Using a piece of string attached to the rose stems, he slowly lowered the crude bouquet and tied it to the rain gutter, so that it dangled right outside the window.

He felt a strange exhilaration in his chest as he quickly made his way back to the scaffolding and down to where his father and the other workmen were eating. As he settled in the shade, hidden behind them all, he saw Mr Bailey approaching. For a split second, Gabe worried that the owner of the manor had seen what he had done, and fear began to course wildly through his bones.

"Mr Bailey. What can I do for ya?" Gabe's father said, standing up and brushing off the crumbs on his pants.

"I owe you an apology," Sothea's father said. "I've let my frustrations get the better of me. I shouldn't have shouted at you all like I did. I was hard on you last week and for that I'm sorry."

"Apology accepted," Gabe's dad said, a smug smile spreading over his face.

But Mr Bailey raised a hand. "Please let me finish."

Gabe's dad cleared his throat and put his hands behind his back, obviously holding himself back from spewing a few personal resentments at his employer. If Gabe was being honest, he felt a little joy at seeing his dad submitting. God knows he never gave that privilege to anyone else.

"We don't need to dwell on the past," Mr Bailey continued. "I promise I won't, but moving forwards I need to know that you're going to stick to the schedule. I don't want you to lose focus, and I expect day-to-day progress reports."

"Sure thing, Mr Bailey," Gabe's dad said professionally.

"Good. I'll leave you to finish up the rest of the day." With that, Sothea's father strode off back to the house.

"*Sure thing, Mr Bailey,*" Vincent mocked, slapping Gabe's dad on the back.

"*Yes, sir, Mr Bailey,*" Jake mimicked.

"Shut your cake hole." Gabe's dad sat down in a huff. "Posh prick. They're all the same, ain't they? Bunch of stuck-up twats."

Gabe didn't even realise he was smiling. But his dad caught it.

"You find that amusing? Come here." He got up and raised his hand. "I'll give you a smack around the head and see if you enjoy it then."

Gabe's eyes widened and he got to his feet, running as his dad chased him around the trees. Vincent and Jake laughed and cheered him on.

"Get him!"

"Boy deserves a good wallop!"

The father-son bonding moment ended with Gabe holding the back of his throbbing head, and his dad sitting back down to his lunch, satisfied with having taken some power back. But despite the bump Gabe was sure would form, he felt good. The fact that he had left those roses outside Sothea's window gave him a nervous excitement.

The day drew on and all Gabe could think about were the multiple ways in which Sothea might react to his gift. For as many good scenarios that he could imagine, a larger handful of bad ones were conjured as well – like Mr Bailey finding them first, or Sothea telling her father and getting him kicked off the work site.

Luckily, there were no more visits from Mr Bailey, and when Gabe was helping to pack up the van and able to steal a glance at the attic window, his heart thrummed in his chest. The flowers were no longer there. And they had not fallen either, for there was no evidence on the ground below.

Right before he got into the van, he took one last look up at the attic, and all the breath in his lungs was stolen as he saw Sothea standing between the cracks in the curtain. All Gabe could think to do was raise a single hand. Sothea gave him brief wave in response, offering a little smile before she disappeared back behind the curtains.

But that little smile made Gabe feel like he was on top of the world. It made him feel like he had climbed the highest mountain and slayed a raging dragon. He replayed that moment over and over again in his head on the drive home, and it was all he thought about for the rest of the night.

Sothea withdrew from the curtains after collecting the roses while Ama was downstairs grinding down some herbs in her large pestle and mortar. She had not thought once about Gabe in the last few days, but knew instantly somehow that the roses had been from him. It gave her a warm feeling in her chest, one that spread down to her gut and the rest of her body. She felt her cheeks flush, and the urge to dance.

In Cambodia there had never been anyone around. She often saw some boys her age, but they stayed well away from the house and if they ever saw her, they quickly looked away. Sothea had never received attention like this before, and now that she had, it brought with it a whole mixture of emotions.

The first thought that passed through her mind, however, was of the implications if her father found out she'd defied his instructions and ventured outside. She knew she had to hide the roses. She went to her bed, planning to hide them under her pillows, but quickly decided against it, not wanting to squish the delicate petals. She soon discounted more options, since she also had Ama to worry about. She loved Ama, and Ama loved her, but Ama's loyalty was to her employer – Sothea's dad. If Ama told her father... Well, that couldn't happen.

Eventually she settled on the large fireplace in the room. She managed to attach them up within the chimney flue, knowing that it would not be lit, for the elusive English sun had finally made an appearance and was in full summer heat. Sothea willed herself not to think about it for the rest of the day, trying her best to hold her composure in front of Ama. When she heard the men packing up to leave, she dismissed Ama by requesting some tea, and rushed to the window just in time to catch Gabe leaving.

The spark of something kindled in her chest when her eyes met his. Surprisingly, it made her smile. But the smile was followed by a frown, and then a rise of heat growing to a flush in her cheeks. Suddenly shy, she withdrew from the window. She was confused by the emotions. They were scary and yet she found them strangely intoxicating. She was almost embarrassed by them. And yet...

She made her way back to the window, but Gabe had already gotten in the van, and Sothea watched as it vanished behind the trees down the drive. There was a sense of yearning in her blood – a yearning for the rest of the weekend to pass quicker, so that Gabe would return. It had been a long time since Sothea had looked forward to something. The last few years in Cambodia had become mundane and repetitive, filled with long hours of boredom and isolation. When her father had announced they were moving to England, it seemed like he was expecting her to jump for joy. Instead, she had further retreated into herself. She had practically given up on ever feeling happy again. Now there was a semblance of excitement inside her. It was a feeling of hope.

She returned to her bed just as Ama came up the stairs with her tea. She shuffled slowly over to Sothea's bedside and put it down on a coaster. When Sothea met her gaze, Ama raised her eyebrows, giving her a cheeky and knowing look. Sothea looked quickly away.

Damn it. How did Ama always know everything?

Sothea kept waiting for her to say something, but no words ever left her mouth. Not even a disapproving *"Tsk"*. Instead, she retreated to the old rocking chair she had brought up from downstairs, and set to her embroidery, humming and rocking slowly back and forth. Not long after, the sound of Sothea's father's footsteps sounded in the stairwell, and he appeared in the doorway. He gave a little knock at the already open door and stepped inside.

"Hey, sweetheart," he said softly. "I was wondering if you wanted to join me for some tea this evening."

She didn't reply immediately, taking a sip from her cup to make clear she was already having some.

"I've made some sandwiches for us," he continued. "I know that these last few weeks have been hard on all of us. But now that it's over—"

"Okay," Sothea interrupted.

"Great." Her dad's mood seemed to lift a tad, but the tiredness in his voice was still evident. "I'll just get it all set and call up when I'm ready."

Sothea offered him a thin-lipped smile of approval – a smile that wasn't really a smile, but more of a peace offering. He nodded and turned, making his way back down the stairs. Ama sighed, put down her silk embroidery, and made her way to the armoire. She picked out a summery white dress with yellow daisies on it.

Sothea cringed. "Ewww, not that one. It's for little kids."

"*Tsk*. You look beautiful in it," Ama replied in Khmer. "Just put it on to appease your father."

Sothea took in a deep breath and sighed it out. "Fine," she replied, putting down her tea and making her way to the edge of the bed.

Ama set the dress to hang on the beam of the four-poster bed and indicated with a flick of her hand and a small *tsk* for Sothea to turn around. Ama took Sothea's long black hair in her hands and set to brushing it with an old ivory brush she had brought over from Cambodia.

"You know your baba is a good man at heart," Ama said as she brushed gently through some of the knots.

Sothea nodded slightly. "I know." She heard the fragility in her voice as she said it.

"He just wants the best for you, but sometimes what he thinks is best is not always the truth."

"He wasn't as strict before Mama passed away," Sothea said. "He used to be... more fun."

"*Tsk*. Men need women," Ama replied. "Women live through their hearts." She tapped a couple times at the place on Sothea's spine directly behind her heart. It sent a little shiver through Sothea's body. "Men live through their heads." She gave Sothea another couple of taps on the top of her head. "Men think everything can be solved through thinking. But..." Ama drew out the last word as she began to brush at a particularly tough knot in Sothea's hair. "Sometimes knots only come undone with a gentle touch, and a little bit of intuition."

The brush no longer stuck in her hair. It ran smoothly through it, the knot unravelling as easily as a leaf gliding in the wind.

"Your mama would have wanted you to spend some time with that boy."

Sothea's heart jumped into her throat. "Ama, shh!"

"Come now. What your baba doesn't know won't hurt him." Her voice cracked with love.

"I don't even know if I want to spend time with him," Sothea said in a tense whisper.

"Well, you never know until you try..." Ama said, drawing out the last word again with a mischievous smile on her face. "That one is special," she added. "Not like other men. He uses his heart *and* his head."

Ama finished Sothea's hair by tying it up in a typical Khmer style, pinning it back so that it was out of her eyes, but letting it fall flat down her back at the same time.

"There. All done," she said proudly. "Now turn around so I can see."

Sothea did as she was asked.

"Wow. Too pretty. Maybe we should put it back down so the moon doesn't get jealous," Ama teased.

Sothea blushed and gave Ama a hug. "Thank you for coming with me. To England, I mean. I know you didn't have to, but I don't think I would be able to do this without you."

Ama smiled. "I gave birth to three sons. They have all gone off and started their own lives. Don't tell them this, but I always wanted a daughter." Ama winked and gave Sothea a small pinch on the cheek. "Come now. Let's go help your baba downstairs."

Sothea nodded with a true smile and led the way to the ground floor dining room.

Wrapped in legend and folklore, thousands had once flocked to the town to touch history. But Alderley Edge had changed a lot in recent years. The surrounding area attracted the rich and famous and the small town centre had reinvented itself to accommodate. Gone were the small independent shops, and in their place were trendy cocktail bars and boutique designer outlets. Gone also were the societies and clubs for people with an interest in the esoteric. Years ago, the town gossip would have been about witches and covens. There'd be talk of magic, and the legends and myths of Cheshire. Farmers would regale anyone who would listen with colourful accounts of strange footprints found on their land. Fortune-tellers would set up shop on market day, predicting the gender of unborn children or foretelling bright futures for anyone who crossed their palm with silver – or a fifty-pence piece if you didn't have sterling to hand.

For Gabe, who had no interest in sneaking into pubs and no friends to do it with, the town centre was the last place on earth he wanted to spend his spare time. So most Saturday afternoons he took himself off on his bike to the Wizard Tearoom, a small café in nearby Nether Alderley. It was about the only place on the planet where Gabe felt accepted for who he was.

Not only did the staff accept his interest in Arthurian legend and the arcane, they positively celebrated it. Sometimes they even encouraged him to share his encyclopaedic knowledge of the local area and its lore with visitors from out of town. He wasn't usually comfortable speaking to strangers, but somehow found the strength when the topic was so close to his heart.

The café was Gabe's safe space. An oasis. His retreat from the conflicts of home and college. If he mentioned faeries or magic here, he wasn't mocked or slapped around. Quite the opposite – sometimes grateful tourists would buy him a coffee.

Gabe put down the book he'd brought with him after he found himself reading the same paragraph for what must be the twentieth time. There was only one thing on his mind, and that was Sothea. She consumed his every thought and he found that he missed being close to her, even if they weren't able to speak or see each other. Knowing she was near afforded Gabe an inner peace. The sooner the weekend was over, the sooner he could return to Bailey Manor. He laughed to himself. He was actually looking forward to going back to work.

"Gabe?"

He looked up to see Polly, a Saturday waitress just a few years older than him, standing nervously by his table.

"Hello," he said.

"Hi. Yeah. Sorry to ask, but we've got a couple in the other room asking questions about Castle Rock. Would you mind?"

Gabe welcomed the distraction and was quickly introduced to Walt and Marlene, an older couple from Arkansas. They were under the impression that Excalibur was embedded in a nearby stone and Walt was determined to have a go at pulling it out. His great-grandfather had apparently emigrated from York, so he figured there was a small chance he was the one true King of England and that this heroic action would prove it, one way or another.

Despite the revelation that there was no sword waiting for Walt's strong arm, the couple's spirits weren't dampened. They were so enthralled by Gabe's knowledge they left him a £100 tip for thirty minutes of storytelling and paid his tab. He'd only gone there for a bit of peace and quiet and slice of cake.

Buoyed by his good fortune, this time when he picked up his book he was able to plough through a couple of hundred pages. It was only when the staff began to put the chairs on the tables and started brushing the floor near his feet that he realised they were closing and he took himself home with a lot more money in his pocket that when he'd left.

CHAPTER FOUR

On Sunday morning, Sothea watched as her father drove away. He had informed her over breakfast that he had to take a trip to a supplier for a few bits and pieces to finish off his own interior renovations. There had been non-stop hammering, sawing, and welding all weekend, and Sothea's ears were still ringing with the clank of metal on metal.

If she was being honest, she was genuinely relieved. There was a part of her that never quite felt comfortable around her father. Since her mother had passed, he was always watching her, always checking in to see where she was. On weekends especially. It was rare that an hour ever went by without him calling to her and asking how she was doing. It was overbearing. Claustrophobic. It made her resent the attention. Why couldn't he just leave her alone?

As soon as he left, Sothea and Ama went to inspect the room next to the palm house that he'd been working on. They were greeted by a reinforced steel door. Sothea knew before she even tried the door handle that it was locked. She'd have to satisfy her curiosity another day.

Today was the first time since they had moved to Bailey Manor that her dad had left her on her own. She decided to take the opportunity to explore the grounds. Her father had forbidden her from exploring the woods, despite her pleading on multiple occasions. He was worried that she would get lost and that he would have to come and find her.

"Let's go for a walk." Sothea tried her luck, expecting a stern reproach from Ama and another reminder that she was forbidden from leaving the house.

"I thought you'd never ask," Ama responded, smiling like a naughty schoolgirl and taking their coats off the hooks.

Together they explored the small deer paths that wove through the dense woods behind the house. Ama had a great eye for herbs and medicinal weeds and would point them out to Sothea as they passed them by. Ama didn't know the names of many of them but had enough knowledge to be able to distinguish between them based on their petals and leaf structure. She gave little tips as they walked along, uprooting certain plants and separating their various parts – roots, stems, leaves, buds, and flowers.

At one point they sat on the ground in a patch of different plants, and Ama picked one and held it out for Sothea to smell. Sothea's nose wrinkled.

"Ugh, that smells like rot."

"Well done," Ama told her. "An unpleasant odour is a bad sign." She threw it aside. "Poisonous. Avoid plants with milky sap, fine hairs, spines, or shiny, waxy leaves, and umbrella-shaped flowers. If you are not sure about a plant, then rub it on your inner forearm." She proceeded to pick a yellow flower by her side and did the test. "See. No rash." She handed it to Sothea. "Smell."

Sothea did it hesitantly. "It smells strong..." she observed.

"Pungent. But it feels good." Sothea wasn't sure how she knew it, but she did.

Ama nodded. She stuck her tongue out and tasted the petal, then proceeded to chew on the root. "Good for inflammation." She chewed a little longer. "Good for skin also."

"How can you tell just by tasting it?" Sothea said, slightly in awe.

"Ancestors," she said nonchalantly.

"What do you mean?"

"We have many ancestors. Over many, many thousands of years they have learned the way of the world. They are with us in every gesture, standing behind us since the beginning of humankind. Teaching us, if we choose to listen. Their knowledge is inside." She tapped on her chest as if it was the most obvious thing.

Sothea frowned and picked up the root of the plant, placing it her own mouth. She chewed a couple of times before cringing at the bitterness of it. She spat it back out, her mouth full of the taste of soil and dirt. "Ewww. Gross. It's horrible."

Ama laughed, still chewing on the root, amused by Sothea's discomfort. "Bitter is good," she said. "You young people are always eating sweet." She waved her hand dismissively. "Bitter is medicine. We come from the earth, and the roots connect us with the ground. The fruits we pick are gifts from the land, and the flowers are reminders that the universe is one big pattern. And, of course, the herbs keep us healthy and strong."

Sothea smiled. Ama returned the smile and gave Sothea a gentle pat on her cheek before standing up with ease, her old limbs still fluid even though she was well over seventy. She clasped her hands behind her back and continued to walk. Sothea got to her feet as well and fell into stride with the old woman, her bare soles making contact with the warm earth. Sothea rarely wore shoes, if ever. She liked the feeling of direct contact with the ground.

Ama hooked her arm around Sothea's and together they walked through the woods in silence, two women without a care in the world, taking a long loop before returning to the manor.

It was a beautiful sunny day in the English countryside. Much colder than what Sothea would usually recognise as summer, but wrapped in her heavy coat, it was very pleasant indeed. At times like this, she wondered what she would do if she was allowed out and had friends. For a while now, the only friend she'd had was Ama. Her dad hadn't even given her a phone or a computer to access the internet. She was completely isolated, and didn't even really know what she was missing out on. She only had the faint memories of what it was like before. Before her mother died.

In Cambodia, until Sothea was eleven, she had attended an international school. Her dad had always wanted her to follow the British school curriculum, but never really explained why. She had blurry dreamlike images in her mind of playing with other kids, fragments of memories of learning in a classroom. But everything before that age was inconsistent and patchy, like it was from another lifetime, another world.

Ama and Sothea sat outside in the garden now, sipping on tea and watching as flocks of tits and finches chirped and chased one another from tree to tree. Eventually the sun began to set, and Sothea left Ama to nap, which she liked to do around the early evening. The sky turned a deep orange, tinting the clouds a cotton-candy pink, before eventually dipping into the dark pastel tones of dusk.

The past few weeks had been monotonous. Already there was a routine – study, eat, sleep, repeat. The thing with isolation was that it often drove Sothea into a slump where she barely had any urge to leave the bed, let alone her room. She had found some distraction through stealing glances at Gabe, but it did little to relieve her terrible boredom. Today's walk in the woods had given her a taste of freedom and adventure, and it had invigorated her.

As evening set in, she began to wander around the giant manor house, exploring every room, switching on lights that hadn't been used in years. But as she wound through the empty hallways, she began to feel a nausea churning in her gut. At first, she ignored it, passing it off as hunger, for she hadn't eaten much besides a pear that morning and the few little petals and roots that she and Ama had tasted in the woods.

All of a sudden, Sothea found herself stumbling and felt as if the floors of the corridors were moving of their own accord. Fear began to take hold inside her heart. She quickly made for the closest window, stepping into a room that had no light. The furniture inside was all covered in dusty white sheets, and the paintings were faded and barely recognisable. Her slender fingers gripped at the edges of the windowsill, pale and slightly aglow with the last sliver of silver light from the waxing crescent moon.

No, she thought. Please, not now.

As her eyes found the pale moon low in the night sky, her pupils gorged to twice their size. For a long, stretched-out moment, it called to her, made her heart drum to a dissonant beat. She ripped her eyes away from it and called out Ama's name, stumbling to the ground before quickly picking herself up and forcing her body back to the hall. The dim lighting in the corridor made the shadows come to life. They reached out to her like sharp-nailed claws, and in her head, she began to hear them whisper.

She shook her head and honed her focus, taking one step forward at a time.

"Ama!" she called out again.

But her voice felt as if it were muted or muffled through a

thick pillow, a million miles away from her own ears. Tears began to stream from her eyes, and a violent dizziness overtook her senses. The walls swam back and forth, the floor wavering. With her next step she crumpled to the ground, overwhelmed by the world shifting around her. She could see the shadows moving, even from the ground. She heard distant sounds that shouldn't belong, and memories of her mother came streaming through her mind.

There were footsteps.

Heavy footfalls.

She saw boots.

Her father's legs.

He lifted her up and held her in his arms. A glimpse of Ama's face made it through the blur of her vision. In that moment, Sothea knew she was having an episode. She was suddenly grateful for her father's return, for the fact that he was always checking up on her. That he hadn't given up. That he hadn't abandoned her. She felt herself sobbing, repeating the same words over and over again: "I'm sorry."

The drum beat in her heart grew to head-breaking proportions, thrashing and writhing in her blood, turning silence into screams and casting the shadows into life. Eventually her mind couldn't hold it all, and the panic and fear inside her gave way, plunging her into an ocean of unconsciousness. Every sensation faded into nothing, and the world went black.

S*othea*, said a faraway voice. *Sothea, wake up.*

"Mama?" Sothea replied.

She found herself standing in the darkness, with a single spotlight illuminating only a small circle around her. She had been to this place many times before. There was nothing around her, just an endless expanse of nothingness, broken only by the light shining into the void.

Sothea.

It was her mother's voice again, as if calling from a distant realm, cracking through the darkness, breaking Sothea free from the prison of the night.

Her eyes slowly opened to the sound of birds singing. As her foggy brain adjusted to the light of morning, she winced at a throbbing pain in her temple. It was hot and sharp, with a dull beat, hurting every time her heart pumped blood around her body. Fluorescent lights shone with a buzz from above.

The floor was cold and formed of sheets of stainless steel. Sothea tried to breathe. She writhed on the floor; her body twisted and convulsed. Very quickly she began to panic. She could still barely focus, seeing double, triple, as the world spun around her.

"Baba!" she shouted. "Baba!" Her voice tore through the air like the whistle of a boiling kettle.

It was the last thing she remembered before passing out again.

CHAPTER FIVE

James sat on a hard metal chair outside the locked door of the room next to the palm house. His head hung low, bloodshot eyes staring blurrily at the ground. He had yellow foam earplugs shoved deep into his ears, and a pair of construction ear defenders over those. He could never handle it when his daughter screamed. It shattered his heart into a million pieces.

Only when the sun was well over the horizon did he unlock the door. He took a deep breath and entered the room. Sothea was out cold, lying on the floor in one corner. He cursed when he saw the mangled sheet of stainless steel that had been wrenched from the far wall and, behind it, the twisted frame of the small window on the far side of the room. Broken glass lay on the floor. He'd foolishly thought his attempt to seal the only other exit to the room would be enough. He had failed miserably, and he was furious with himself. Now there was a gaping hole in the wall and clearly the room was far from secure. He calmed himself; he would rebuild and strengthen the fortifications, but not now. His face set in stoic resignation, he carried Sothea up to her bed in the attic room and tucked her in, wiping away her sweat-plastered hair to plant a kiss on the side of her temple.

"Forgive me," he whispered into her ear before turning to leave.

Ama stood behind him with her hands clasped, meeting his eyes with a sorrowful nod. James wanted to go to bed, but he didn't allow himself that privilege. He had to get more supplies. Last night proved that he hadn't been prepared enough. He got in his car and sped off along the drive. As he drove, he went over the list of things he would need to get from the local hardware store, but he barely made it a mile before he saw a group of people huddled in the road ahead and the flashing lights of parked police cars. James's jaw clenched and he slowed down to a steady crawl.

There was police tape drawn across the gated entrance to Crowley farm. Dozens of other cars were parked up against the side of the narrow country road. Townsfolk stood ashen-faced on the tarmac with hands over their mouths, staring at something that James couldn't quite see yet. His heart was beating quicker than ever. He glanced up at the rear-view mirror. Thick beads of sweat dripped down his face. He realised his hands were shaking and his leg was taking on a nervous twitch.

"Get it together, James," he chastised himself, gripping the steering wheel even tighter.

He pulled out a handkerchief from his coat pocket and wiped at his brow, parting his hair away from his face and over to one side. This was the only way into town, and there was not a chance that anyone would be able to pass through until the mob of townsfolk cleared out of the way. As he turned off the ignition and pulled up his handbrake, some heads turned his way.

He steeled himself and got out of the car to see what it was that everyone was looking at. The odour was overpowering. It wafted through the fields like a haze, thick and heavy in the heat of summer. James had to hold back his revulsion as it filled his nose and mouth. He stepped closer, feeling with every step he took that he was drawing nearer to some unavoidable destiny. It was silent, except for the odd buzz and chirp of the police radio, and the officers trying to communicate back.

James took one more step forward and finally saw it. A herd of cattle brutally slaughtered. Cows torn open, guts flowing out, intestines trailed in long strings, interlocking with the guts of the others. About two dozen of them, linked together in a maze of hollowed carcasses, entrails, and blood. He realised now that people had their hands on their faces for more than one reason. Shock was the first thing that slammed into his body and mind. Cold, dreadful shock. He felt the heat literally draining down his arms and slipping out of his fingertips.

"Oh, God." They were the only words that came out of his mouth before nausea bloomed in his stomach. He leaned forward, feeling as though he was going to be sick, though nothing came up.

When he lifted his head again, one of the nearby police officers finished writing something down and placed a small notebook in her breast pocket. She brushed her long auburn hair behind her ear.

"I know it doesn't look like it right now, Frank. But there's a way through this." She patted an older man on the forearm.

"But my cattle, Kath... They're me livelihood."

"Stay with a friend for a few days," she said. "We'll sort this."

"I can't, can I?" The man was twiddling with his flat cap, which looked well beyond its expiration date, and gestured at his flock with a shaky hand out towards the fields. "Sheep still need looking after."

James realised he was staring and turned away from the old farmer. He felt his leg twitching and shifted his weight onto it to make it stop. He resigned himself to hanging around until the horde of townsfolk moved on. He leaned over, hands on his knees, to try and settle his stomach. Then he heard the crunch of loose gravel, and his eyes darted over to see two black boots walking his way.

"James Bailey?"

He sighed and looked up to meet the detective's eyes for a split second, offering her a solemn nod.

"I'm Detective Sergeant Hughes," she said. "Word around town is that you've been restoring the old manor house?"

Again, James just nodded in reply.

"You wouldn't happen to know anything about this, would you?" Hughes asked, pulling out her notebook and nodding in the direction of the slaughtered cattle.

James shook his head. "I was just going into town to do a bit of shopping."

Hughes sighed. "Well, I'm sorry."

"For what?"

"You've not been here three weeks yet and then this happens. Not a great first impression. I can assure you this is the most interesting thing to happen here for a hundred or so years. Although I suppose 'interesting' isn't exactly the right word..." Her voice trailed off. "I just don't understand what could be capable of doing something like this."

"You and me both," he replied, before adding, "I lived here as a boy. It was the old family home. Before my father gambled away all his money..."

D.S. Hughes gave him a pitying look and sighed, putting her notebook back in her pocket again. "I've asked everyone to clear off," she said solemnly. "So, the road should be clear soon enough."

James nodded.

"Please, if you hear anything, don't hesitate to call." She handed him a card.

James took it and slipped it into his shirt pocket.

"I'll see you around," she said, before turning and walking back towards her car.

James closed his eyes. The images of the mutilated cattle came rushing in the second he plunged his eyes into darkness.

Feeling lightheaded, he opened his eyes again, and the contents of his stomach rose quickly to his throat. James coughed and shoved the nausea back down, forcing his bile to remain where it was, and spitting out the small amount that had passed through. It was enough to burn at his throat. He strode back towards his car. He could feel the questioning eyes of the townsfolk on the back of his head as he walked away from them and could tell they were all curious to size up their new neighbour, but this was neither the time nor the place. James was grateful for small mercies; he certainly wasn't in the mood for small talk.

He opened the car door and got in, putting the keys in the ignition, and resting his forehead on the wheel. He was so tired. Letting out a string of curses, he turned the keys and set off. He couldn't wait any longer. He rolled right up to the crowd of gathered people that stood ambling in the middle of the road. With no more patience in his bones, he honked his horn. Dozens of untrusting and glaring eyes shot him dirty looks, but James ignored them and honked again.

Muttering amongst themselves, they eventually moved out of the way and he sped away from the scene.

—

"Why have we stopped?" Gabe asked.

Up ahead, he saw P.C. Taylor in her uniform and D.S. Hughes standing next to their car, which was blocking half the road. His dad and Vincent were in the front seat of the van and he was in the back, straining to look beyond them at whatever had caused the standstill. That's when he beheld the mutilated cattle strewn across the field and a cold shiver ran down his body. A wave of nausea lurched in his stomach. He pulled back and managed to open the side door just in time to hurl his breakfast out onto the road.

After spitting out the last of the vomit, he took some deep breaths to try to steady himself. He felt cold and light-headed, and he hated vomiting. It was such a violent and frightening experience. Not to mention it left his throat feeling sore for days.

With the door open, he caught a little of the conversation between the police officers ahead of them, even with Vincent and his dad swearing loudly in the front seat.

"You've got to feel sorry for Mr Bailey," Hughes said to her partner.

P.C. Taylor sounded as surprised as Gabe was to hear Sothea's father's name mentioned. "How so?"

"Man lives barely a mile away. I'd be nervous living in that big old house on my own at the best of times. Don't know what I'd do if I woke up with that in my backyard."

"Maybe you could offer to guard the place for him. Of a night," Taylor joked, chuckling to himself.

"Leave it out," his boss responded. "I don't fancy him. I just genuinely don't understand how anyone could feel comfortable living in that great big manor house. Can you imagine the electricity bills?"

"He's probably minted. Sits there burning fifty-pound notes

to keep warm," Taylor said. "Play your cards right and you could be lady of the manor."

"I'm sure Mrs Bailey would have something to say about that!" Hughes laughed.

"There isn't a Mrs Bailey. She passed. So you're alright there. I heard he has a daughter though—"

"Come on, soft lad!" Gabe's dad shouted back at him. "It's only a bit of blood and guts!"

The two police officers spun around to look at him.

"No one teach you lot how to park?" Gabe's dad yelled out of his window, gesturing at their police car. "You should give yourselves a ticket!"

P.C. Taylor rolled his eyes and made his way over to the van. "Keep it moving, Mark. Or I might have to start asking some awkward questions about what colour diesel you're driving around on."

Gabe didn't hear his father's response. As he wiped his mouth with the back of his sleeve, his eyes were instinctively drawn back to the carnage at the side of the road. This time though, he thought he saw movement in and around the bloodied and cleaved carcasses. And he was right. Between the ribs and spinal columns, lungs, and many stomachs, there was what could only be described as a carpet of worms.

"We're taping the area off," Taylor said to his dad. "It's best you move on now."

The rest of the locals who had shown up were starting to disperse and get into their cars. Gabe sat back in the seat and pulled the side door closed to block his view, wishing he hadn't got out of bed that morning. But as the van started to crawl forward, D.S. Hughes approached them.

"Hold on a sec," she said. "You still working up on Bailey Manor?"

His dad hit the brake and nodded in response.

"What's he like, Bailey?" she asked.

"Usual snob. Keeps himself to himself. Bit of a temper. Pays his invoices on time, mind. I'll give him that, so no complaints from me."

"Who else is in the house?"

"An old dear, foreign-looking. And his daughter."

Gabe's ears perked up as Sothea was mentioned again.

"Yeah," his dad continued. "Little slip of a thing. Barely leaves the house, from what I've seen."

Gabe quickly moved up to the front of the van and appeared between the two seats. "Her name is Sothea," he said, the words coming out of his mouth very quickly. "Is she okay?"

Mark turned back to him with furrowed eyebrows. "How the hell do you know that?"

Gabe looked down. "I've seen her around."

He could feel D.S. Hughes eyes on him for a long moment.

"So what was it?" Vincent said from the passenger seat. "A big cat?"

"It would have to be a bloody sabre-toothed tiger to do that," P.C. Taylor replied. "But we're not ruling anything out."

"Christ..." Gabe's dad said, shaking his head. "I'll keep my eyes peeled for a depressed woolly mammoth and a walking sloth too!"

"You do that, Mark. Anyway, thank you for your time." DS Hughes saluted him sarcastically and walked away, Taylor following behind her.

Still shaking his head, Gabe's dad pulled the van forward slowly past the badly parked police car. A couple of minutes later, they were at Bailey Manor.

"I honestly don't know how we're going to work after seeing that," Vincent said as they got out.

"Man up," Gabe's dad told him. "Probably just a rabid dog or somethin'."

Vincent looked over his shoulder into the woods. "I wouldn't want to come up against whatever it was down a dark alley, I'll tell you that."

"You'd be lucky to come up against anything in a dark alley with that face," Gabe's dad replied, laughing so hard at his own joke that he started coughing.

Gabe slid open the side door and got out of the van, carrying a bag of supplies under his arm. He purposefully set them down in view of the attic window and, under the guise of sorting the equipment, he let his eyes wander upwards. The blinds to Sothea's window had been drawn closed.

"Hurry up, slowcoach!" his dad called out over his shoulder. "We ain't getting paid for overtime!" Then he turned to Vincent. "Best finish this up quick. Bloody sick of working at this place now."

Gabe was distracted all morning. Once again, he continuously found himself sneaking a look through the windows, hoping to catch sight of Sothea. It wasn't until lunch that his constant monitoring paid off. He was sat underneath a tree on the front lawn when he saw movement in one of the lower windows. His heart began to beat quicker in his chest as Sothea's pale outline appeared. She was wearing leggings and a crop top. The sun was shining directly into the window, and Gabe noticed how strangely the light acted around her skin. It was like the surface of a hot desert, as though the air turned liquid and moved in wafting currents around her. He watched her for a moment, trying to make sense of her slow but deliberate movements. And he realised that she was dancing. It was quite possibly the most beautiful thing he'd ever seen in his life. She paused for a moment before suddenly casting her arm straight out, fingers intricately twisted as she continued to dance to an unheard tune.

Gabe set his sandwich back down in his lunchbox and excused himself, telling his father he needed to go to the bathroom.

"You're bloody seventeen. You don't need to announce to the world every time you need to take a piss," his dad replied, not even bothering to look over at him.

Gabe smiled silently to himself, knowing he'd got away with the simple ruse. He walked slowly away, keeping up the pretence, even though all he wanted to do was run. He eventually turned a corner, rounding the other side of the house and stepping out of their view.

He broke into a sprint and almost ran right past Sothea.

He stopped in his tracks and turned back around to look at her through one of the open lower windows. He stood with his mouth open, not wanting to alert her that he was there – partly not to startle her, but mainly because he didn't want to interrupt her dance.

He wasn't sure if it was his imagination or if she was simply so beautiful that she glowed. Her skin was radiant and pure like a moonbeam let loose into the mortal world.

She held her hand out in one dance pose. And then another. Her fingers pressed together, twisting into the elegant moves. She stepped forward into a new position, one leg raised, her toes curled up.

It was faint at first, but the traditional music she was moving to soon grew in volume. Gabe had never heard anything like it.

Bolder now, more confident, she started to dance in earnest, stepping around the piles of books on the floor, through the shafts of light, kicking up the dust, and moving over to the largest pool of light seeping in from the open window. It was like a spotlight on her.

Gabe was mesmerised, easily imagining her not trapped in a stuffy English library but made up with stage make-up, and in full costume in the centre of a dance troupe performing classical ballet on a stage. Gold and red costumes, elaborate headdresses, and jewels. He imagined a painted backdrop behind her. She danced in perfect step and in perfect unison with the other female dancers in his mind. The orchestral music swelled...

Then suddenly she froze for a moment. Absolutely still. One foot and one arm were raised and she stared up at them, motionless in the timeless pose.

"Ahem." Gabe coughed to announce his presence.

It startled her out of her trance. She looked about her as if she didn't know where she was. Then she spotted him.

"Gabe!"

The music cut out abruptly with a loud scratch as she pulled the record player needle across the vinyl.

"It's rude to spy on people," she said.

"I'm sorry. I just wanted to see you. I wasn't spying, I just..."

He trailed off as he noticed she was smiling, wrapping a shawl around her shoulders.

"It's okay," she said. "It's just that I haven't practised much recently. Too many mistakes."

"I thought it was perfect."

"You have nothing to compare it to. Trust me, I'm an amateur compared to the girls at the Royal Ballet."

An awkward silence came over them, Gabe standing outside looking at Sothea in the library and Sothea returning his gaze.

"Are you okay?" he forced himself to ask, meeting her eyes.

They were so striking, attentive and penetrating. Gabe was normally quite a socially anxious person. At school and during his first and only term at college, he had barely been able to string together two words to save his life. But with Sothea... She had a way of seeing him that made him feel like *himself*. She looked past everything that other people always seemed to trip over or picked out to make fun of him. There was none of that with her.

"You look like you've seen a ghost," she said with a little smile.

It made him blush, but he did not avert his gaze. He noticed the colour of her eyes now. They were a deep chestnut, soft, warm, and inviting, but with a sharp intellect behind it all. Gabe frowned. He could have sworn they were a different colour. Granted he had only ever seen her from afar, but in his head, he had always imagined they were light. Now that he thought about it, "light" was the only adjective that came to his head. He couldn't recall an actual colour.

"I had to see you," he said. "I've been thinking about you a lot."

As soon as the words came out of his mouth, he felt suddenly vulnerable. As though he had said too much.

This time it was Sothea's turn to blush. Her pale cheeks flushed pink, and her lips pursed into what looked like a held-back smile. She turned her head away to look down at the ground. "Me too, actually."

Gabe felt his heart flutter. "Really?"

She nodded.

Silence filled the air between them again. He had never been in this sort of situation before, and he didn't really know what to say. But after several heartbeats, Sothea finally spoke.

"Why did you ask if I was okay earlier?" She looked up at him with a serious frown, searching his eyes for answers.

"Have you not heard?" he said.

Her brows furrowed deeper as she shook her head.

"Something attacked Frank Crowley's cattle last night. Absolute carnage."

"Frank Crowley?"

"One of the local farmers. His land borders the forest." Images of mutilated guts flashed in Gabe's mind as he said it, and he nearly threw up again. He had an incredibly vivid imagination, and a very detailed picture memory. The images in his mind were clear and bright as if he was seeing it all in front of him again.

A murder of crows flew over them, cawing at that moment. Their dark raspy gurgles echoed in the clearing.

"It was horrible," Gabe added. "There were dozens of them dead. And worms..." His voice trailed off.

When he looked back at Sothea she was looking down at the ground with wide perturbed eyes, her face crinkled in disgust. Gabe felt her emotions like a second skin, and without thinking, he reached a hand through the open window towards hers. Their skin made contact, and there was an instant spark. Sothea pulled away in shock, backing away from the window, holding the part of her hand where he had just touched it.

Gabe was equally as shocked. Her skin had been stone cold. It reminded him of when he picked up cold meat from the butchers.

"I-I have to go." Sothea ran away from the window, leaving it open, curtains starting to billow in a gentle breeze that wafted through it.

"Wait! Sothea!" Gabe called out after her.

He couldn't just let her go. He had to follow. So, without thinking, he jumped in through the open window and began to search for her inside the house.

CHAPTER SIX

A strong wind gusted against the old stilt house in the middle of the jungle. The wooden window blinds that were secured into place outside rattled as the wind threatened to unhook them and send them flying off at any moment. Sothea lay cuddled into her mother on a mat that rested on the bamboo flooring. Her mother was sat up, gently running fingers through Sothea's hair.

"There is an old legend amongst our people," her mother said softly in Khmer. "One that has been passed down through stories from family to family."

Sothea was nine years old, and her ears were wide open as she soaked in every word her mother said.

"A long time ago, there was famine and drought in the land. Farmers didn't have enough food to feed their children and their animals were close to starving. The King did not know what to do. Every day, thousands of people would turn up at his gates begging for help. His daughter watched all this from the window of her palace, even though her father did his best to keep the troubles of the outside world away."

Sothea painted a picture in her imagination as she listened – a golden palace with tall, pointed spires and sharp slanted roofs.

"Apsara was a beautiful princess, and she wanted so desperately to help her people. She could see their suffering, feel their pain, and Apsara knew that she could do nothing to help them while she was locked away inside. So, one night, she ran away into the jungle that surrounded the palace. The next morning, her servants found the bed empty and told the King that she was missing, but by that point she was already too far gone.

"You see, legend had it that a witch lived deep in the jungle. A witch with incredible powers. Once, Apsara's father had tried to locate this witch. He had sent his finest soldiers from the ranks of his personal guard, the bravest and strongest men he had. But only a few of them returned, and those who did had lost their minds, raving about a monster."

Sothea's mother waved her arms mimicking the guards who had been struck down with a madness. Sothea cuddled in tighter against her.

"Apsara didn't know where to look for the witch, and the jungle was a wild, vast place, full of dangerous animals. But she had something her father's men didn't. She knew how to follow her heart, and she trusted it beyond all things."

Sothea frowned and touched a hand to her own heart. Her mother shifted on the mat, acting out the part of the princess.

"On her first night alone in the jungle, Apsara decided to go to sleep at the base of a tree. But she awoke just a little later to the sound of growling. Her eyes shot open, and she found herself face to face with a tiger! Instead of running, Apsara reached out and stroked the tiger's head, before placing her own forehead on the ground in respect. In return, the tiger raised her front paw. Apsara noticed the tip of a sharp thorn embedded into the soft pad and set to work removing it. It turned out that this wasn't just any tiger. This tiger

was called Khala, and she ruled the jungle. Khala was touched by Apsara's kindness and bravery."

Her mother stroked the back of Sothea's hand, keeping her eyes fixed on her daughter's enthralled gaze.

"Apsara told Khala about her mission to find the witch of the jungle and Khala agreed to help her. You see, the drought was affecting her jungle as well, and it was her duty to care for the jungle and all the creatures that resided there.

"Together they travelled in search of the witch. And as sunrise came, they found her hovel. Herbs hung from branches in little bundles and a circle of salt surrounded her hut. The witch saw Sothea approaching on Khala and came out to greet them. She looked to be nothing more than an old woman and she walked only as far as the edge of the salt circle, pausing to bow at both Khala and Apsara.

"Apsara told the witch of the problems in the Khmer Empire, and that she needed a spell to make the rain fall. The witch looked at her with sad eyes and told her such a spell would only come at an extremely high price. Apsara was no stranger to wealth, of course, and she told the witch that she would pay whatever was demanded for the rain to fall once more. The witch nodded solemnly and allowed Apsara to step into the boundaries of her home."

Sothea's eyes were wide open, and her imagination was wild with fantasy.

"But it was not gold or spices, nor silks or fabric that the witch wanted," Sothea's mother continued. "It was sacrifice. And when Apsara heard this, she merely nodded. The princess would do anything for her people, even if it meant giving her own life. The spell was cast, and the witch drew a knife from thin air – a curved knife with a golden handle. With one smooth gesture, she cut off the princess's head.

"In an instant, dark clouds gathered and rain began to fall

heavily from the sky. All the inhabitants of the Empire, be they rich or poor, peasant or prince, began to rejoice at the palace gates. The rain fell and fell and never stopped for two whole months. The drought had ended and the paddy fields flourished. Once again the children of the Kingdom could eat, growing strong and healthy.

"Even though the King's people were happy, he was not. It had been months and he still had not seen or heard from his daughter. He mourned her loss, fearing that it was his sheltering of her that had driven her away, and worrying about the fate that had befallen her in the jungle.

"Then one night, as he lay awake, he saw his daughter's face in the hollow window across from his bed. Overjoyed, he ran to it, arms out ready to embrace her. However when he reached her, he stopped dead in his tracks. What he saw was not his daughter, but a monstrous spirit who had stolen his daughter's face.

"This creature was phantom white, with only a head, its hair floating as if suspended in water. Where her shoulders should have been there was only a spine, and her organs hung from it, intestines trailing low in the air. The King screamed and his guards came rushing in, but it was too late. The shock had caused the King's heart to stop. As they rushed into the room, they saw the monstrous creature hovering over him.

"Weapons raised, they charged it and chased it away into the jungle. Little did they know that the creature was their lost princess, Apsara. Her sacrifice had been to accept a curse, and whilst the kingdom received heavy rain for two months every year, the selfless princess was bound by dark magic to haunt the night for an eternity."

When Sothea's mother finished the story, there was a long silence.

"But Apsara was good, right?" Sothea said. "Even though she was a monster. Why did the soldiers hate her?"

"*People are afraid of what they don't understand,*" *Sothea's mother replied. "Every morning Apsara transformed back into her normal self. But she knew she could never return home, especially not after the guilt of her father's death. She moved far away to the very north of the country, and eventually married a man. He never knew of her curse and every month, when she knew she would transform, she hid herself deep in the jungle. But soon she became pregnant, and legend says she passed the curse on to her child. Apsara made the ulti-mate sacrifice, and the Khmer people hunted her and her descen-dants from that moment onwards. Sometimes, my dear, the world is cruel and unfair.*"

It was perhaps not a story that most mothers would tell their nine-year-old child, and it stuck with Sothea for countless nights, keeping her awake and sometimes giving her nightmares. It was what she thought of when she stood over her mother's grave, when the rain fell and her father piled dirt over a coffin.

CHAPTER SEVEN

The inside of Bailey Manor was dark and dusty. Other than the one Gabe had climbed through, most of the windows were draped with heavy curtains, which remained drawn. It took a moment for his eyes to adjust as he stumbled through what seemed to be a library, narrowly avoiding furniture covered in white sheets.

"Sothea!" he whispered loudly.

But there was no reply. He had an all-encompassing feeling of being somewhere he was not meant to be. The hairs on his arms stood up and a cold shiver passed through his muscles. He quickly glanced back at the open window, contemplating for a moment climbing back through it, but he steeled his nerves and turned towards the large double doors at the entrance to the room. He slowly took another step forward. The floorboards strained hauntingly, the creak echoing off the high ceilings in the vast room.

Gabe crept out of the doors and found himself in the large entrance hall with a massive staircase in the middle. There were multiple doors in every direction, including the space beneath the stairway. For a long moment he was overwhelmed by choices, then a sound from above him alerted his senses.

He bit his lip and ran across the space between the room and the stairway, feeling for some reason that if he lingered for too long, something would snatch him up and eat him. He had read countless stories of old houses like this, haunted by the spirits that lived in them before. He wasn't going to take any chances. He quickly made his way up the creaking stairs, following the sound he had heard just moments ago. He took a left when the stairs parted and once he reached the top, he found himself on a long landing.

He stopped dead in his tracks. The landing stretched out ahead of him, and the strange lighting distorted his perspective in such a way that he couldn't really tell how far it extended. It seemed to breathe, the end drawing closer and farther away at the same time. Before he found the courage to take another cautious step forward, he glanced over his shoulder and jumped when he saw a face staring back at him.

His heart tripled its pace in his chest, until he realised that the face staring back at him was his own. A large, stained mirror with ornate gold framing hung on the wall. It was tarnished and unclear, making his face appear ghostly. There was also a single crack down the glass that split his eyes off at odd, fragmented angles.

He shook his head and took a moment to calm his nerves. Come on, Gabe, get it together. He had heard the line in movies many times, and the characters would say it right before doing something brave. He could be brave too. He took in a deep breath and began to walk through the hallway. There were at least a dozen doors lining each side of the wall, and some of them were open.

A breeze blew through them in cross-currents that made a

high-pitched wailing sound. The phantom wind grazed over the back of his neck like slender fingers, and he had to fight against the urge to turn around again. Ghosts aren't real. Ghosts aren't real. He repeated the mantra to himself as he walked. His dad had said that to him many times when he had woken up screaming in the middle of the night as a child. To be honest though, he still didn't believe it.

King Arthur himself had dealt with spirits and ghosts on many occasions. And through those stories, Gabe had learned that most of them just needed encouragement to move on, a reason to let go of the things that still anchored them to the corporeal plane. Often, they would send Arthur on a quest to retrieve a part of themselves, or an artefact that they had lost and could no longer retrieve. As Gabe thought it over, he imagined that he could do the same. Maybe ghosts were only scary because they were misunderstood.

His secondary school English teacher, Ms Watson, had once sat him down and told him something similar. Noticing that he tended to prefer his own company and seldom hung around with the other children at lunchtime, she had tried to encourage him to make friends by joining in their games. He told her that he had tried. Numerous times. But it had only resulted in laughter and name-calling. On occasion, it had even ended with a punch to the face.

Ms Watson explained that they only hurt him because they were intimidated by the fact that he was different. And that being different was good. She had let Gabe take home a very rare and old copy of a collection of Arthurian tales, hand-stitched into a worn leather jacket. He had finished it in a single night and handed it back to her the next day. She winked at him and told him to hold on to it. It was his most safely guarded treasure to this day. He kept it wrapped in a scarf at the bottom of his underpants drawer – a place where he knew his dad would likely never go snooping.

With a little more courage, Gabe found himself standing a bit taller. Now it didn't matter if a ghost showed up. He would simply ask them how he could help. Ghosts were probably used to people running away from them. Maybe all they wanted was a friend. Just like him. He would be a good friend if anyone, or any ghost, gave him the chance.

He had almost walked the entire length of the landing and still he had not seen or heard any sign of Sothea. But there was one door that stood out amongst the rest. It was right at the end of the hall, covered with cracked and peeling paint, and it was slightly ajar, letting a crack of light in amidst the darkness.

His hand reached out towards the door-knob and hovered above it. For a second, he debated whether he should enter, but then something inside him made up his mind. It was a feeling. A feeling like home before his mother died. Warm, like belonging. And deeper still, Gabe felt a reverberating twist of emotion, one that made him both sad and full of hope at the same time. It made his entire body tingle, and compelled him to place his hand on the handle.

He slowly opened the door and made his way up the spiral staircase behind it, passing the stained-glass window that diffused the sunlight into small diamonds of red and orange and yellow. Sothea was across the room when he reached the final step, staring at the doorway. She looked at him with wide, pain-riddled eyes, and yet there was longing. Her fingers were clasped tightly together and they simply stared at one another in silence.

Then, as if animated by a courage not his own, Gabe closed the distance between them and hugged her. He felt the jolt of her body against his as she reacted first in shock, and her arms just hung loosely at her side, before she was able to let go of the strangeness of it and give in to the warmth he was offering her. She wrapped her arms around his waist.

Gabe felt his tension melting away. He couldn't remember the last time he had been hugged; his father had certainly never done it. Sothea was cold. There was no getting past that fact. But she filled him with an inner warmth. A light scent swirled from the top of her head, a gentle fragrance like jasmine in the wind.

Slowly, the moment came to an end and Sothea pulled gently away from him, glancing up to stare into his eyes.

"Gabe... You shouldn't be here."

"I couldn't help it," he replied.

"If Ama were to catch you up here..." She walked away from him towards the window. The window that Gabe looked up to every time he arrived.

He was captivated by her. She held the room with a poise that bent the light around her, pulled attention to the pale slender nakedness of her arm, the way her hair fell lightly over her eyes, and how – every now and then – she would brush it back, tucking it behind her ear, only for it to fall loose a moment later.

"I want—" Gabe was cut off by the sound of a car door closing.

Panic seemed to seize Sothea as she looked down at the driveway. She quickly shut the curtains and turned back to him.

"You must go! My father's home!"

Gabe panicked now. He couldn't quite explain why he'd searched for her inside the house. If he'd known in advance that she'd be at the very top of the building, with only one way in or out, there was no way he would have climbed inside. He made instantly for the staircase.

"No!" Sothea grabbed his hand and pulled him back. "He will be coming that way."

"Then where do I go?!"

"Uhh..." Sothea was pacing frantically, looking around the room – at the armoire, the space beneath the bed, and back at the window. Her eyes darted towards the fireplace.

"There!" She pointed, pushing Gabe towards it.

"A fireplace?! How am I supposed to hide in there?"

"Just get in. There isn't time!"

He could already hear her father's footsteps approaching from the creaking floorboards a level down. He ducked instinctively as she pushed him into the giant fireplace, just in time for his head to miss the hard stone mantle.

"Now what?" he whispered.

"Up!" she mouthed, pointing up the flue.

Gabe had no idea how he was going to climb a chimney, but he looked up anyway. His jaw practically dropped when he saw what was inside. The interior was lined with thick vines, vines that spiralled all the way to the top. Growing from those vines were leaves and flowers. White roses. Were they the same white roses he had picked and given to Sothea? Gabe didn't have time to question it, as he could now hear footsteps climbing the steps to the attic. He grabbed a vine and began to climb, disappearing just as the door opened.

Her father seemed to sniff at the air.

"What have you been doing?" he asked Sothea suspiciously.

Gabe didn't hear her muffled reply as he focused on climbing the chimney full of roses. He winced as a thorn pressed deep into his palm, drawing blood as he pulled it free. The rose vines were thick, some larger than the circumference of his forearm. He had never seen anything like it. The crude bouquet of roses he had picked for Sothea had come from his neighbour's bush, and that was how he had seen them growing every other time in his life. He had heard of climbing roses, but never seen them before. Nothing like these. These looked like they'd been growing here for years.

As he ascended towards the light at the top of the chimney, his leg rustled up against a bunch of leaves. He paused, cringing at the thought of Mr Bailey looking up the chimney to find him hanging there. So, trying to move as quietly as possible, he continued upwards until he managed to climb out of the chimney – not without enduring a series of cuts and scratches from the sharp rose thorns. His heart was beating frantically, and he trod carefully over the roof, doing his best not to make a single sound. He snuck onto the scaffolding on the opposite side of the house just as his father and Vincent were approaching.

"There you are!" his dad shouted up. "Been bloody looking for you everywhere!"

"Sorry," Gabe responded. "Was just getting a head start."

"Head start? Doesn't look like you've done a bloody thing. Honestly, sometimes I wonder why I bring you on site at all..."

Gabe ignored his father, picking up a can of paint and proceeding to set the brush to the rendered wall. He focused instead on the way the paint dripped from the brush, the thick glob that stuck to the edge of the can when he scraped the brush against it. Despite the hasty escape, he had an altogether wonderful feeling inside of him, which made painting all the more relaxing. He had hugged Sothea. And she had hugged him back.

He was in a daze as he applied the paint in smooth, even brush strokes, unlike the way Vincent and Jake usually slopped it on haphazardly. He felt as if he were floating on a cloud, held for the first time by a girl he liked. It was a magical feeling, and for most of his life he had been searching for magic in the real world. Magic he could touch, magic he could feel and believe in.

The day went by quickly from that point on, and soon it was nearing five, by which time his father was already packing up and loading the van. Gabe was itching to see Sothea again. He felt as if another day was way too long to wait. He found a small resentment forming in him as he walked behind his father. A resentment towards her dad. Why couldn't he just let Sothea be? Maybe it was a thing fathers did, because he knew how much his own father did to limit and demean him. He would have to wait for the days where Mr Bailey went off in his car to truly see Sothea without interruption. He only wished he didn't have to leave at the end of each day.

He wanted to soak up every second of his time in her presence. He already missed the strange coldness of her skin, and the fact that despite its temperature it still made him feel warm and cosy. He looked up to her window as he left, but Sothea wasn't there. He was disappointed but understood her situation. With great longing, he turned away and got into the van, sliding the door shut behind him.

Sothea could hear the van doors closing from her room. Ama was brushing her hair in silence at the foot of the bed like she always did. Sothea had to use every ounce of her will not to run to the window when she heard the builders packing up. Just thinking about Gabe made her lips start to quirk upwards into a smile. She couldn't explain what emotions had run through her body when he hugged her. She got hugs from Ama, but they never felt like that. He felt like the comfort of a favourite book, of being tucked up, cosy by the fire with a pot of tea. And warm. So warm. But she could not allow him inside the house again. Her father would never forgive her if he ever found out... Well, she didn't want Gabe to get hurt because of a decision she had made.

And she didn't think she'd be able to sneak outside to see him any time soon either – at least not while her father was around. He had told her about the dead cows Gabe had mentioned, and made clear that it was too dangerous for her to leave the house. Between that and his suspicion that she had been hiding something when he came up to her room earlier, she was sure he would be keeping an even closer eye on her than usual.

Anyway, she also knew something Gabe didn't. It was a secret that would make him turn and run in the opposite direction if he ever found out. It was what kept the people in her village in Cambodia whispering. It was the fear she saw in the men who walked by. Sothea knew something was wrong with her. She had a way of hurting the people closest to her. At least that was what her father always said.

But what if her father was wrong? What if she was different?

CHAPTER EIGHT

Sundays were a day of religion and relaxation in England. That was what Sothea had been taught this week by one of her tutors. Her dad had filled her weekdays with home-schooling, starting at eight in the morning and stretching to the later part of the afternoon. He'd brought in specialist tutors from across the county to instruct her. She even had school on Saturday mornings, and she was exhausted by the end of the third week.

The novelty of England had long passed. She had a routine now, and Sunday was her day to do nothing. Sleep in, stay in her nightdress, read, potter around in the palm house with Ama. It was bliss, and without doubt Sothea's favourite day of the week. This Sunday got even better when her dad came into her room with an apologetic look on her face.

"I'm so sorry, pumpkin. I know I promised we'd make a start on the library today but I've found a carpenter near Birmingham who specialises in restoration. I want to take a look at his studio."

"That's okay. I'll be fine."

He had nodded, and then after a pause added, "Remember, you're not to leave the house."

"Yes, Baba," she had replied demurely.

It was all an act, of course. One that he had bought surprisingly, earning her the response, "That's my girl" and a kiss on the top of her head.

She had stolen glances at Gabe all week, observing him when her classes were done, watching the way he would stop his work and look up at the many windows of the house. It made her smile, because she knew what he was doing. He was looking for her. The smile quickly disappeared though, as she realised that nothing would come from it. She would hide before he got the chance to spot her.

Whether it was the electrifying encounter with Gabe, or simply that she felt more comfortable with her new surroundings now, Sothea finally felt inspired to pick up a book from the extensive library. She had tossed one of the dust sheets from a large armchair on the floor in a heap and sat reading with her legs dangling over the edge of it. After some time, she looked up from her book for no reason in particular.

She had a sense for things out of the ordinary – one she had apparently earned from her mother. And something felt different in the air. She closed her book without marking the page. She had already read it a dozen times and knew roughly where she had left off. Spinning her legs around, she got up slowly and drifted towards the window, following the trail of a whim twisting in her chest. Slowly drawing the curtain back, she quirked her head at what she saw.

A fox. The same one as before.

It stood right at the edge of the woods, staring directly at her. Sothea stared back at it. It was a creature she had never seen before she arrived in England, and so it had a strangeness untarnished by preconceived notions, mythos, or bias.

She unlatched the window and opened it slowly, letting in a warm summer breeze. The birds were silent, as was the wind, even though she felt it brush against her cheeks.

"Hello." She waved at the fox.

It seemed to acknowledge her with a gentle drop of its head before turning and walking back into the brush. Sothea frowned. She had wanted more from the interaction. Immediately disobeying her father's orders, and without a second thought for the worry she might cause Ama, she jumped out of the library window, her bare feet coming down on the smooth gravel with a crunch.

She bounded after the fox, free as a bird, chasing it into the trees. She caught sight of its tail and ran in its direction. But it was elusive, soundless, and fast. Sothea ran as she tried to keep up with it, jumping over logs and avoiding sharp brambles. She scuddled under a fallen tree and clambered over a large boulder, jumping down once she got atop it. She moved like the wind, twisting and twirling. She ran until all sign of the fox was gone, and she was left breathing heavily in the middle of the thick foliage.

She cursed. The fox had outmanoeuvred her. But when she turned to head back, she realised a daunting fact. The trees were dense all around her, and no matter which way she looked, she couldn't recall the route that had brought her here. A tingle of fear riddled her bones. She was alone and she was lost.

"Ama!" she called out.

There was no response. When she looked up, she couldn't even make out the sun through the canopy of the trees.

She called out again.

This time when no response came, she began to worry. She took a stab at a random direction and began to run, calling out

Ama's name. She grabbed the bark of a tree, using it to help lever her around a corner, and suddenly she collided with something. She hit it hard and fell back onto the ground dazed. There was a groan, and then a rustle of leaves.

"Ouch!"

Sothea looked across from her to see Gabe in a similar position, holding a hand over the spot where they must have clashed heads.

"Gabe?"

"Hi," he said, offering her an awkward wave.

"What are you doing here?! How did you know where I was?" Sothea stood and offered a hand to help Gabe to his feet.

"Well…" Before he could finish his sentence, Sothea was against him, her arms squeezing tightly around the upper part of his waist. Gabe might have been taken by surprise by the sudden burst of intimacy, but he seemed to return it enthusiastically.

She pulled away from him and looked up with beaming eyes. She was so happy not to be alone in the forest anymore, and absolutely delighted that she had literally run in to Gabe.

"I know what this must look like," he said. "I swear I wasn't coming here to stalk you or anything. I mean, if I had seen you, I would have been happy…" Gabe stopped himself for a moment, as if to get his thoughts in order. "I was on my way to the Wizard's Well when I heard your voice," he managed to finish. "What are you doing out here?"

Sothea blushed a little at the fact that he must have heard her panicked shouts. "I was following a fox, but I got a little lost."

"Oh, right. Your house is that way," he said, pointing, and brushing over the first part of her answer as if it was nothing out of the ordinary.

"Oh. Thanks," Sothea replied.

He shuffled his feet. "Unless you wanted to come with me?"

Sothea had to work to restrain her enthusiasm, but when thoughts of her father returning to find her missing entered her head, her face quickly turned into a frown.

"You don't have to," Gabe quickly interjected. "I know you don't even have shoes on, and—"

"No. It's not that. I like being able to feel the ground beneath my feet. I just… " She paused, not quite sure how to explain it.

"It's… it's my birthday today," Gabe said. "It would make me really happy if you could."

"Happy birthday!" she said.

"Yeah. Thanks."

They looked at each other. She wasn't sure what they should do next.

"How far is it?" she asked eventually.

Gabe grinned. "Really not far at all. Just a twenty minute walk that way. I'm surprised you haven't found it already."

"Uhm… okay," Sothea said hesitantly. "As long as I am back before sunset."

"Why sunset? You aren't going to turn into an ogre, are you?" Gabe joked.

Sothea looked at him with a confused scowl.

"Ogre?" he prompted. "No? You know how they transform at sunset? Never mind. I'll just lead the way then."

For a good while the two of them walked in silence. The initial awkwardness was palpable.

"So, what's a wizard's well?" Sothea said, finally bringing the intolerable silence to an end.

"Not just any wizard's well. The most famous and powerful of them all. Merlin."

Sothea looked blankly back at him.

Gabe raised his eyebrows at that. "You don't know who Merlin is?" he asked, turning to face her.

She shook her head innocently.

"He is only the greatest wizard ever to set foot in the British Isles."

"Wizard?" she asked.

"Yeah, you know. Magic. Sorcerer."

"Oh. In Khmer we call them *abathmob*." She frowned. "Is he a good wizard?"

"Yes. He played a big role in helping King Arthur on his quests. Of course you must know who Arthur is?"

Sothea didn't. She stared blankly back.

"The sword in the stone?" Gabe asked. "Excalibur? The Lady of the Lake? Avalon?" He raised his eyebrows again when Sothea shook her head, but he seemed excited to be able to tell her about him.

"He is the last honourable King of Men. Or so the legend says. There was a time when kings were servants to their people. A time where a king would go to any lengths to ensure his kingdom prospered. Arthur was one of them. Merlin found him as a young boy and recognised immediately what a great leader he would become."

"What happened to him?" Sothea asked curiously.

"That is where the legends differ, but the oldest tales maintain that Arthur never died. It was said he went into a deep slumber, a breathless hibernation, suspending his body in stasis and never aging, and that he would wake only when the world was once again ready for him to return. All the knights who followed him refused to live in a world where he was not King, and they joined him in this slumber. It is part of the legend of the Wizard's Well. Look we're almost there!"

Gabe pointed and as Sothea followed his finger, she saw a clearing with ten large stones arranged in a circle. Weather-worn and covered with moss, they had clearly been there for centuries.

She frowned. "That doesn't look like a well."

"It both is and isn't," Gabe replied cryptically. "I was doing some reading and found that there is more than one type of well. It seemed the druids and language of Arthur's time also referred to wells of energy. There is no water here, but apparently, if you know how to activate the stones, the centre will open. Kind of like a portal. They created these earth wells not to draw water from the ground, but to draw energy instead. Some call it mana."

Sothea approached it slowly and stared wide-eyed at the air in the centre of the stone circle. There were sparkles there, like shimmering stars dancing and twirling in a cylindrical current, rising towards the sky. She had never felt, or seen, an energy so soft and peaceful. In awe, Sothea reached her fingers towards it.

"You see it too, don't you?" Gabe asked.

Sothea was shaken out of her trance and was almost surprised to see Gabe already standing next to her. He was looking up at the air as well.

"My dad said I was mental when I told him. That I had banged my head as a baby and had been seeing stuff that's not there ever since," Gabe continued. "But I always knew it was real."

"What is it?" Sothea tried to touch the sparkling energy with her fingertips, but it passed right through her like ether.

"I wish I knew. Come on," he said with a small smile. "This isn't even the best part."

Sothea followed him reluctantly, not wanting to leave the tranquillity that cloaked the atmosphere around the stones. The birds and insects seemed to match the same low pitch and frequency of the energy she felt so deeply in her bones. Seeing that she could barely take her eyes away, Gabe smiled and took her hand. She didn't flinch, but let him pull her away, deeper into the woods.

They walked in a peaceful silence towards what looked to be a large mossy rock face. Water was trickling out from the rock, and a large tree stood above it. As they got closer, Sothea got a new angle on the rock face, and she could see a shallow, hollowed cave. Gabe let go of her and cupped his hands under the trickle of water, letting it pool in his palms. He splashed his face and drank from it before stepping aside and letting Sothea do the same.

The cold water gave her a rush of energy. It was clean and fresh and rejuvenating, making her feel like the sparkles that were twirling in the air.

"This place is incredible, Gabe."

She ducked down and peered into the hollow chamber in the stone. It didn't go back very deep, maybe just four feet, but Sothea felt as if there was more to it. It was a feeling she couldn't explain, like it was an entrance way into a subterranean world... a world of magic. She just couldn't quite see it.

"I used to sit in there for hours," Gabe said quietly, as Sothea crouched and waddled inside.

She turned and looked up at him. "Why?"

Pain flashed across his face. "Just to get away from things."

He took a step away from the cave again and Sothea followed him out, meeting him in a silent solidarity and taking his hand. Gabe's eyes went to hers, searching. She offered him an empathetic smile and he squeezed her hand a little tighter as if to say, "Thank you".

"The legend says that a farmer trying to sell his horse met a strange old man who carried a staff with a gemstone infused in the top of the wood."

"A wizard?" she guessed.

"Yes," Gabe replied, leading Sothea further along the rock wall. "The wizard offered the farmer a large sum of gold for the horse, and led him through the forest, and further still, to this very place. The wizard stopped right here."

Gabe pointed and Sothea was surprised to see the face of a man carved into the stone.

"The wizard took out a wand and touched the rock. It slid open as if by magic and revealed a pair of iron gates, which flew open with a thunderous crash!" Gabe mimicked the sound with a large gesture, which made Sothea jump. "The wizard beckoned him inside, and despite the farmer's better judgement, he followed the old wizard into the cave. They went down, deeper and deeper, until they reached a huge cavern. It took a while, but once the farmer's eyes adjusted, he saw that there were over a hundred knights in shining silver armour, all standing to attention, but fast asleep. Next to each knight was a white horse, just like the farmer's own. All except for one. A man lay sleeping in the centre of the cavern, and he was different from all the rest. He wore a simple silver crown and had no armour on at all, just a plain white tunic.

"'With your horse, these men are now complete,' the wizard said, gently guiding the farmer's horse to the centre of the cavern, where it nuzzled the sleeping form of the man in the crown and lay down next to him.'"

"Was that King Arthur and his knights?" Sothea asked. "What were they all doing there?"

"Well, the farmer asked that same question and the wizard said, 'There will come a day when I will wake these horses and men. They will arise and descend upon the plain in the last battle of the world'," Gabe said, changing his voice to sound old and wise. "The wizard then took the farmer into another cavern, which was full to the brim with a hoard of treasure. There was gold and silver, and precious jewels, piled in large heaps. The wizard pointed to the treasure and instructed the farmer to take all that he could carry as payment for his horse. The farmer did so without question, and when he was done, and his pockets were brimming, the wizard led the farmer out of the caves. The farmer stepped out into the night, and when he turned around to thank the wizard, he was gone, and the iron gates had vanished."

Sothea reached out with one hand, grazing her fingers over the rough, mossy stone face of the wall. She felt a small spark of electricity tingle at her fingertips and instinctively pulled away.

"Do you think they are really in there?" she asked, turning to read Gabe's expression.

"Yes," he said resolutely, clearly with no doubt in his mind. "I just wish I knew how to open the gate."

"Why?"

"Because I would join them."

Sothea felt the pain in his words and her brows furrowed. She gripped his hand a little tighter.

"I never felt like I belonged in this world anyway," he continued. "Nothing makes sense here. It never did. And the more I see of it, the less sense it makes. But this..." He put his hands on the stone and closed his eyes. "This I can understand."

"You're right," Sothea replied. "I don't feel like I belong here either. But maybe some legends are best left untouched..."

Gabe seemed to take that in, though he didn't show much sign of a reply.

"Besides," she added, "I need you here."

That got Gabe's attention. He turned away from the wall to face her, and suddenly he seemed to stand a little taller.

"Then for you I will stay," he said, in a tone that sounded like he was taking a vow.

Sothea blushed and entwined herself in his arms, resting a head on his shoulder.

The moment didn't last long before Gabe, with some reluctance in his face, said, "It might be time to start heading back."

Sothea suddenly grew worried, as if she had completely forgotten about that detail, like she had been whisked away to another world, and suddenly been plunged into the cold pool of reality. But she didn't want to get in trouble – or worse, get Ama in trouble.

They raced back through the woods with a spring in their step and smiles on their faces, vaulting fallen tree-trunks and hopping from boulder to rock to avoid the brambles and dense bushes. Gabe led and Sothea followed.

They reached the edge of the clearing that surrounded Bailey Manor just as the sun was starting to set.

"I shouldn't have stayed out so long," Sothea said, with a nervous jolt of energy. "I hope Ama isn't worried."

She stepped out into the clearing and was so preoccupied that she almost didn't say goodbye. But her heart stopped her, and she turned around to see Gabe standing between the trees with a sad expression on his face. She bit her lip and ran to him. She wrapped her arms around his neck, hugging him tight, before pulling away and meeting his eyes with a hawk-like stare. Then she kissed him passionately on the lips and ran away, back to the house.

Ama was waiting for her at the front door, and ushered her inside with anxious eyes. Sothea couldn't tell if Ama had seen Gabe at the edge of the woods or not. She started formulating a complicated excuse to explain how she'd bumped into him on her walk, but Ama didn't ask, and Sothea was grateful not to have to lie.

CHAPTER NINE

Gabe was still in a daze, paralysed with the euphoria of his first kiss. There was no combination of words adequate to describe the feeling, and he cherished the secret like a precious gem. He'd been dreading today. His birthday. And not just any birthday, but his eighteenth. Birthdays always made Gabe think of his mother or, more accurately, reminded him that she wasn't there. He'd woken up knowing there would be no cake, no candles, no present...

And it had turned out to be the best birthday ever. In the slants of sunlight cast through the canopy of trees, Sothea had looked absolutely radiant. She had looked like a princess, royal in her grace and elegant poise. He'd told her that he had wanted to join the sleeping men in the story, but her presence made him feel more like a knight already – with someone to protect right in front of him.

He didn't think that he would ever lose the grin from his face, which – if he was honest – was beginning to hurt his cheeks. As he heated up frozen fish fingers in the kitchen to celebrate, he tried to tune out the loud bickering of his dad and friends that echoed incessantly through the open door that led to their small back yard. Gabe tried to ignore it, but little bits slipped through – meandering drunken conversations that never came to a conclusion, voices talking over one another and rising in volume when they weren't being listened to, shouts and arguments and impromptu bursts of song when one of them recognised a lyric or two from a tune on the radio.

The oven timer went off and Gabe pulled out his dinner just as his dad and his rabble of friends moved on to a different topic.

"I reckon it has something to do with that Bailey bloke," said a woman's voice.

Gabe's ears perked at the mention of the surname. His eyes darted over to the back yard and he approached the open door, positioning himself so that he could hear better but couldn't be seen.

"All I'm sayin' is that he shows up, doesn't say a word to no one, and not a week later it's like a scene from the apocalypse. Right on his doorstep!"

"He's a wrong 'un, that's for sure." Gabe recognised Vincent's voice as the one replying now. "Don't reckon he sleeps. Looks like he's practically risen from the dead 'alf the time…"

"What do you think he's doing all night?" another female voice interjected.

That was Sue speaking. He hated Sue. She was an evil, spiteful woman who had been spending more and more time at their house over the past few months.

"No idea. It's the daughter I feel sorry for," his dad replied, taking a swig of his pint and then spitting.

Gabe's jaw clenched at the mention of Sothea.

"You should see the poor thing," Jake added, presumably to Sue. "She's pale as a ghost and never sees the light of day. I've only caught sight of her once or twice. Doesn't go to school. Has a load of private tutors. He probably thinks he's better than all of us. Doesn't want his daughter mixing with real people!"

"Now that's not right," Sue said.

"Or she's got problems in the head. That's why he keeps her locked up all the time."

Gabe could no longer hold back his anger. A force like the wrath of titans burst through his muscles and he slammed through the door into the garden.

"Shut up! All of you! Shut your mouths!"

"Oh, not again," Sue said, rolling her eyes as she tapped the ash from the end of her cigarette. "Mark, don't you have a leash for this one?"

Gabe's dad stood up slowly and stared at him, pointing a thick finger at his face. "Who the bloody hell do you think you're talking to?!"

Gabe couldn't stand the look of that finger. He grabbed it and yanked it backwards in a way that no finger should bend.

"Jesus!" His dad let out a blood curdling scream and grabbed his hand. He looked at his disfigured digit in horror. "You broke my..."

His face distorted into the wrinkles and scowl of a monster. With his one good hand he punched Gabe square in the nose, sending him stumbling backwards, clutching at his face. Blood began to gush from his nostrils, but his dad showed no sign of stopping. With the flat of his foot, he kicked Gabe hard in the chest, sending him sprawling to the floor.

As Gabe struggled to stand, he saw Vincent try and fail to get up from his rusty sunchair, his weight and an afternoon on the beer making him topple back into a sitting position. Jake was the one who finally intervened as his dad began to pummel him with his one good hand. The other hung by his side, the index finger bending out at a disconcerting angle.

"Mark, stop it!" Jake said, trying to pull him back. "That's enough. You'll kill him!"

But Gabe's dad was big – not with fat like Vincent, but with the muscle that came from a lifetime of manual labour – and Jake couldn't hold him back on his own. Given the size difference between the two of them, Gabe thought he managed to put up a decent fight, taking many blows to the back of the head but sending more than a few back in return. His father screamed at him, and Gabe kicked and bit back.

"Pshh." Sue rolled her eyes and took another drag of her cigarette. "Like father, like son!"

Eventually, Vincent managed to get up out of his chair and with a combined effort, him and Jake pulled Gabe's dad off him. Gabe scrambled backwards, his face bleeding profusely and already starting to bruise. Adrenaline coursed through his body, but even still his nose pounded with a familiar searing pain. It was not the first time someone had broken it.

"Oh, you've done it now, you little turd!" His dad bared his teeth in a demonic grin, blood staining almost every inch of them. "You've done it now!"

But Gabe didn't stick around to hear the rest of what his father had to say. He got to his feet and ran up to his room, tearing a backpack from his closet and shoving it full of books, clothes, and his childhood security blanket, cursing all the while. He thundered down the stairs and out the front door, slamming it so hard behind him that the frosted glass above the door-knob shattered.

He grabbed his bike and set off into the night. Tears streamed down his cheeks as he rode. He hated his father. Why did his mum have to die? Why couldn't it have been his dad? Furious and distraught all at once, he wiped the tears from his face with the back of a bruised hand. He stood up and began to pedal harder. He rode hard and fast, passing a group of former classmates.

"What's wrong, freak?!"

"You know you've got red on you?"

"Must be on his period! Weirdo."

Gabe kept pedalling to the sound of their laughter dying off in the distance. They threw their half-empty energy-drink cans after him, though luckily none hit their mark.

He wanted to put as much distance as he could between himself and the housing estate where he lived. But as the adrenaline began to wear off, he came to the realisation that he had nowhere else to go to. He gritted his teeth and kept riding, taking the turn that veered towards the forest surrounding Alderley Edge. If this world wouldn't have him, he would go to the only other place that would.

When Gabe got to the dirt path that led to the Wizard's Well, he hopped off and began to walk his bike up the steep hill. He wound his way through the trees. It was difficult going, with the spokes of his wheels catching on exposed tree roots and scrub. The moon was veiled by clouds, and it made it hard to see, resulting in his T-shirt constantly being caught on thorns and brambles.

He eventually made it to the top and threw his bike and bag down, forgoing everything and heading straight to the hollow in the rock. He ducked inside and brought his knees in close to his chest, the pain in his head and especially his nose still throbbing. The cave was slightly damp, but he didn't really care.

He began to rock back and forth, his fingers scratching an itch on his leg and picking at the frayed threads of his jeans. He rocked until exhaustion overtook him and his head began to sink into the space between his knees. Covered in blood, some his own and some his father's, he was eventually swallowed by the sweet relief of unconsciousness, ushered away on the tides of night to a faraway place where his father wasn't, where old kings of honour ruled the land, and faerie folk mingled in and amongst the trees.

Gabe stirred suddenly in his sleep. His eyes darted open to a strange half-light and a creeping mist, curling like long, wispy fingertips into the small hovel in the rock. A cold dampness hung in the air and as he exhaled, the fog of his breath blended into the hazy air. He shivered and crawled out of the cave in a dreamlike daze. The ground was completely covered in mist, and he couldn't see his feet as he stumbled through it, arms wrapped tight around his torso in a pathetic attempt to keep himself warm.

He was still half-asleep and didn't immediately find it odd that his nose no longer hurt, or that the pounding in his head he had been struggling with since the fight was gone. The forest was silent. Not a flicker of wind passed through the trees, and not a single bird or insect chirped. He wandered through the fog until he reached a clearing in the trees that looked out on the rest of the wilderness.

The tops of trees poked out through the veil of glowing mist, or that was what Gabe thought initially. Upon closer inspection, he realised the things poking up were not trees at all, but stone spires. Gabe frowned, rubbing his eyes to make sure he wasn't hallucinating, but sure enough, there they were. As the mist swirled below, he could also make out towers and crumbling archways – the remains of what looked to be a castle.

That was not possible. He had been to this particular spot in the forest a thousand times. There were no ruins. He had to squint as he looked at the mist, because it was almost luminous, glowing in a faerie fire. At first, he thought it might be the reflection of the sun, but when he looked up at the sky, all he saw was grey cloud.

He took a step forward, then stopped when he saw a shadow amidst the strangeness of it all. No. That was hair. Long black hair floated through the mist, which cleared as a figure passed through it.

"Sothea?" Gabe muttered.

He rubbed his eyes again to be sure they weren't playing tricks on him, but the female figure was still there, still moving slowly through the fog. Pulled towards her by a strange impulse, Gabe began to descend the steep hill face. It was closer to a cliff than a hill, and he would have had trouble descending it on a dry day, but even as he began to slip and slide on the moss and dew, he did not question his decision.

There were a couple of moments when he almost lost his footing – a move that would surely have killed him, if he had fallen. But he didn't think twice about it, merely adjusting his footing and continuing onwards. As he got closer to the bottom, the sound of a rattle began to fill the air. No. More like a child's rain stick, like thousands of tiny stones cascading endlessly. It was pervasive, and seemed to be coming from every direction at once.

Then, from within the texture of the sound, Gabe began to hear voices. Hushed whispers at the fringe of his hearing. They were spoken quickly and in a language he did not understand. His eyes darted to the left, then right, and he spun around as the whispers moved around him.

"Who's there?" he called out, no longer able to see the figure he'd followed down the hill.

As soon as his words touched the air, the voices stopped all at once, and Gabe couldn't shake the feeling that there were eyes watching him from within the mist, as if a thin veil were separating him from them. He stumbled forwards, his hands outstretched, and jumped as his fingers met with something hard. He staggered away from it, but when nothing jumped out to attack him, he tentatively reached his hand out again.

Stone.

He lay his palm flat against it – solid, tangible, real. He took in a deep breath and closed his eyes, needing a couple of moments to centre himself, ignoring the fact that he had wandered in the mist and had no idea of which way he had come from. When he opened his eyes again, he was shocked by what he saw.

The mist had cleared directly in front of him to reveal a large stone archway. Multiple archways, in fact. He stood at the entrance of a large arching tunnel, and felt dwarfed by its size. The archways on either side of it decreased in height and width, and Gabe could now see that they formed the support for a bridge above them. He heard hoofs, hundreds of them, clattering over cobbles high above him.

Then, inside the tunnel, he saw a light. It was brief and bright, pulling his attention towards it for a second before it went out, submerging the tunnel once more into an all-consuming darkness. From inside came a voice, an ethereal hum. Gabe took a step forward, and as his foot passed over the threshold, it merged with the shadows themselves. He quickly pulled it back, staring at the line the shadows made at the entrance of the archway. It was a perfect line, not the gradual diffusion of light one might expect. He stretched a hand over it and was shocked to see half of his arm disappear.

Inquisitively, he slowly pulled it out, watching as it grew back into form as if by magic. He gazed at his hand in disbelief then back into the dark tunnel. A part of him knew there was nothing like this in or around Alderley Edge. A part of him still believed that he was dreaming, but another could not fight the urge to continue further.

He took one step in.

Then another.

And another.

There was no adjustment for his eyes to make. It was simply black. Not the black of the sky at night, nor the black of a television when it's switched off, but the literal absence of colour. An absolute darkness. And that was all. The humming too had stopped as soon as he had stepped fully beyond the border, and the only sense still active was the feeling of stone against his fingers as they grazed along the wall.

There was no sound, no sight. He could not even feel the ground beneath his feet. And yet he continued to place one foot in front of the other. The deeper he went, the less he could comprehend. At one point he realised he could no longer feel his fingers. But it was not only his senses that began to dissolve, it was the thoughts in his head too. He felt like he no longer knew who he was, no longer knew his own name, and yet, he could not stop walking. The deeper he went, the more he unravelled. Undo and unknow, until there was nothing but the black void.

CHAPTER TEN

abe, a voice said. *Gabe.*

He still could see nothing.

Gabe.

That was his name. His mind reached towards the sound of the voice. "Mum?" he replied. The sound of his own voice echoed in his head.

Gabe! The voice was louder now. *Gabe, you have to get up!*

This time it no longer seemed to come from inside him. He stirred, and vision began to fill his senses once more.

"Gabe, quickly! You must get up before my father sees you!"

He looked around, disoriented. "Sothea? What? What are you doing here?"

"What am *I* doing here?! You are the one in my room!"

Gabe frowned and looked around. Sure enough, he could make out the familiar four-poster bed, and the large circular window that he looked up at every day when he arrived for work. He was lying on the floor and Sothea was crouching down next to him in a pearl-white nightgown, looking more stressed than he had ever seen her.

"It's nearly eight in the morning! My dad will be up to check on me at any moment!" she urged with hushed impatience.

Gabe stood up quickly. A little too quickly. The room began to swim, and the edges of his vision swirled with stars. Sothea had to grab one of his arms to stop him from toppling over.

"You can't just come through my chimney unannounced!" Sothea chastised him under her breath.

"Chimney?" He turned to see a trail of dust and white rose petals leading from the fireplace to where he was standing.

Sothea suddenly stood back, after noticing the dried, crusted blood on Gabe's face and the backs of his hands. "What happened to you?"

He self-consciously turned away from her, realising how frightening he must look.

She rushed across the room to her armoire, rifling through a drawer of clothes until she found a T-shirt. She then pulled some flowers from a vase, throwing them onto the floor, and approached him again.

"Hold still," she whispered as she dipped the edge of the T-shirt into the water in the vase. She held his chin and dabbed at the blood on his face, cleaning his wounds.

"Who did this to you?" she asked.

Gabe remained silent.

"You can tell me. It's okay."

He turned to look at her then, tears in his eyes. "I got into a fight with my dad."

She continued to dab, taking care as she wiped around his nose. "I'm sorry."

"Me too."

He tried, but he couldn't hold the tears back. If Sothea

noticed, she didn't say anything as she continued to wipe away the blood and grime from his face. He watched her through glassy eyes as she worked with a singular intensity. His entire body, mind, and soul rejoiced at the care and attention this girl, who he barely knew, was showing to him.

"Thank you," Gabe mumbled.

The moment was interrupted by the sound of heavy creaking, and the thud of booted footsteps climbing the stairwell to Sothea's room.

Her eyes practically bulged out of their sockets in fear. "Quick! You must go now!"

She pushed him towards the fireplace, but it was too late. The door swung open and her dad walked in to see Gabe clumsily trying to duck under the ornate wooden mantlepiece. Sothea took a step back from him, dropping the vase, which clattered on the floor and spilled red-stained water across the floorboards. There was a moment of disbelief on her father's face, like he was trying to fathom whether what he was seeing was real or not. Then his features filled with a cold rage. It was not the kind of rage Gabe saw in his own father, full of red and distorted features. It was dark and calculated, emanating from his eyes.

He took a step forward, but as he did, Sothea jumped between them. She spoke quickly in another language.

Her dad turned on her with seething anger, but she stood fast despite the intensity of it.

"He knows exactly what he's doing!" her father spat back in English. "Let me past."

"No, Baba."

"I'm warning you," her dad said, stepping closer, one arm pushing her aside.

Gabe was still in a daze, but that seemed to shock him out of it. "I knew you were hurting her," he said, his fists clenching.

Mr Bailey shook his head. "Oh, you have no idea what I have done."

He grabbed Gabe's throat and sent him hurtling towards the stairs.

"No! Baba! Stop!" Sothea screamed, pulling at his arm.

Gabe instinctively caught hold of the banister as he fell to stop him from continuing down the stairs and breaking his neck. He stared down, face inches away from the steps, breathing heavily.

"Get off of me!" he heard Sothea's father yell, and turned back to see him trying to shake her free.

But Sothea clung to him like a strangling vine and refused to let go. In all the commotion, Gabe heard more footsteps on the stairs and turned to find himself face to face with the older woman he'd seen around the house. She met his gaze and quickly gestured for him to get up and follow her. She disappeared back down the stairs without attracting the attention of Sothea or her father. But even as Gabe began to run, he came to a stop halfway down. He couldn't just leave Sothea here. He turned back around and stormed up the stairs again, leaving the older woman at the bottom rolling her eyes.

"No! Run, Gabe!" Sothea shouted when she saw him coming back. "I'll be fine! Just get out of here!"

In that moment Gabe didn't know what to do, but he didn't have much time to decide, because her dad had broken free.

"Run!" Sothea said one last time.

This time Gabe heeded her words, because the look of fury in her father's eyes had gone from vengeful to deadly. There was a thundering of footsteps as both men crashed down the stairs. The woman at the bottom stepped back quickly as Sothea's dad jumped from two steps up and tackled Gabe in mid-air. They hit the landing in a twist of limbs, and Mr Bailey managed to get the upper hand and pin Gabe to the ground.

But he thrashed furiously, and her dad couldn't hold him down for long. Gabe dodged a punch at the last second, and her father's fist pounded straight into the floorboards. Gabe scrambled to his feet, slipping a little on the threadbare rug and careened down the long flight of stairs that led to the front door.

He didn't dare look back until he was already out of the house, and when he did, Mr Bailey stood in the open doorway brandishing a silver candlestick in one hand and his phone in the other.

"You better run, boy! Better run far! I'm calling the police!"

As Gabe jumped through the brush and disappeared into the woods, he heard her father's voice again, but it wasn't directed at him this time.

"Police, please. As soon as you can."

Gabe kept running.

Sothea stood watching at the window as her father spoke to the two uniformed police officers on the driveway. The lack of breeze meant that every word they said carried perfectly clearly up to her vantage point.

Her father had told them the whole story, and even embellished on some of the details, portraying Gabe as a dangerous predator. The male officer, who had introduced himself as P.C. Taylor, stood taking notes as the female officer, P.C. Quinn, gawked up at the grand building.

"This isn't the first call that we have had about the boy," Taylor told him. "His father called up last night. He's wanted for assault. We already have a couple of patrols out looking for him."

"I want him locked up," her father said darkly. "I will not have anyone intruding on my private home and terrorising my daughter."

"That will depend on the courts, but he's known to us. Has a bit of a record," P.C. Taylor replied. "Bit of a mentalist. Autism, the quacks think. Wouldn't say boo to a goose most of the time, but prone to bouts of rage. It all really started acting up when his mother passed away."

"I don't need his life story," her father said coldly, and Sothea felt a pang in her chest. "Just put him in handcuffs and make sure the little pervert never sets foot up here again." He turned to leave but just as he did, P.C. Quinn spoke up.

"Actually, Mr Bailey," she said, "we're going to need to take a statement from your daughter."

She pointed to the window that Sothea was looking out of with her pen. Her father turned and looked up, and Sothea quickly ducked behind the curtain.

"Don't you think she has had enough for one day?" her father said, through barely contained anger. She was sure he knew she had been listening now.

"Well—" P.C. Quinn started.

Her father interrupted her before she could continue. "That will be all, officers. You've got enough to go on now. Sothea's not in a fit state to speak with you, given the trauma she's just endured."

Sothea scowled. The only trauma she'd endured was watching her father attack Gabe. She wanted to talk to them. Wanted to tell them to leave Gabe alone. But at the same time, she knew that spending time with him was wrong. Dangerous. It was her fault that he was in this situation.

There was a long, uncomfortable pause before P.C. Taylor said, "As you wish, Mr Bailey. We'll be in touch if we need anything else. Bye for now."

The front door slammed – presumably her father coming back inside – and so Sothea risked another glance at the driveway. The officers were walking back to their car, exchanging a look that gave her the impression they didn't see everything exactly the same way her father did.

For Gabe's sake, she hoped she was right.

Gabe pressed himself flatter against a rock as the voices approached through the brush. He recognised P.C. Taylor as one of them, but didn't recognise the female officer with him. They stopped nearby, and the female officer sighed.

"I'm not sure I trust him," she said.

"Neither am I," Taylor replied. "But sometimes it's not our place to pry."

"What do you mean? He called us. We're only the bloody police. He expects us to do all the work and doesn't even have the decency to give us some respect."

"Respect is earned, Quinn." Taylor replied. "It's too early to push now. I have a feeling that this won't be the last time we hear from Bailey anyway. Maybe we should station a car nearby, just in case Gabe makes an appearance again."

"I don't get it," Quinn said. "He's had a couple of breach of the peace charges and some outbursts in school, but that was a few years ago. Why break into Bailey Manor?"

"Isn't it obvious?" Taylor said. "A tenner says the daughter's having a little secret romance."

Gabe felt himself flush. He wanted to start running again, but he couldn't risk making any more noise now. He just wished he didn't have to hear them talking about him. About Sothea.

"No?!" Quinn sounded incredulous. "With Mark's lad?"

"Two oddball teenagers," Taylor responded. "Did you see her? She's like Wednesday bloody Addams. Seems like a perfect match to me!"

"So, what are we gonna do when we catch him?"

"I hope it doesn't come to that," P.C. Taylor responded. "I feel sorry for him really. He's smart, and he wouldn't have lashed out against his dad without being provoked. Hopefully the kid's already skipped town. There's not much left for him here anyway. Hasn't been for a long time."

There was a short silence before Quinn asked, "Shall we get out of these bloody woods then and get ourselves a cuppa?"

Taylor laughed and Gabe waited for the crunch of their footsteps to disappear completely before he dared move again. He was really in trouble now. There was no way he could return home. Everyone and their grandmothers would have gotten wind that the police were looking for him. Alderley Edge was a small town, one where everyone knew each other's business. Like living in a goldfish bowl. Everyone knew his face, and he didn't doubt for a second that they would pick up a phone and call the police as soon as they saw him. He had already been to the police station multiple times. He had been let out on warnings because he was underage.

But he was eighteen now, which meant he would be treated, in the eyes of the law, as an adult. He had to leave. The nearest main-line train station was in Wilmslow, only an hour or so's walk from where he was. But... No. He couldn't just go. Not after he had somehow ended up in Sothea's room. How was that possible? His memories of last night were now clear in his head. Not like a dream, but fresh and lucid. He had walked through that tunnel and the next thing he knew, he had heard Sothea's voice. Something had called him to her last night.

It was magic. Gabe was sure of it. His heart began to swell. He had been to the well in the woods a hundred times and he knew that there were no structures like it in this world. *This* world... That was it. He dug through his memory for old stories. Yes. There was a legend about a traveller who had wandered upon a strange mist. In the story, he had walked through it and into another world: the realm of the fae. Gabe struggled to remember the rest of the details. Something about love, something about...

"Ugh!" He grunted with frustration.

His mother had told him that story when he was little. It was the only time he had ever heard it. Right before... Gabe picked up a stone and threw it. He wished she was here. None of this would have happened if she hadn't left him. His teeth clenched. She wasn't here anymore.

But Sothea was.

And he had now seen the way her father treated her. She was in danger, and it was his fault somehow. He still didn't quite understand why the mists had taken him to Sothea, but maybe it was because he needed to help her. Gabe felt a protective urge rush through his blood, and he thought about King Arthur.

"What would you do?" He closed his eyes, asking the question to the ghost of his hero.

Free her, a voice whispered in his head.

Startled, his eyes snapped open. Magical mist, hallucinations that felt real, and voices in his head too – he'd obviously been beaten more severely than he'd thought. Maybe everyone was right and he was a bit crazy. An oddball, just like P.C. Taylor said. Either way, Gabe had two choices now: run as far and for as long as he could with next to no money and certainly no plan, or... listen to the voice in his head.

He stood up with newfound resolve. It was settled. There was no doubt that Sothea was being held prisoner, and it was possible that her father was hurting her at this very moment, punishing her for his presence in her room. Hadn't the police just said that even they didn't trust him? Gabe had seen the anger in Mr Bailey's eyes. He had first-hand knowledge of dads with anger issues and he didn't wish for anyone to be on the receiving end of that level of rage.

Gabe felt the anger of injustice swelling in his veins. "Don't worry, Sothea," he whispered. "I *will* help you escape."

He wanted to race back to Bailey Manor and barge in, right at that moment, but his trail was still too hot. If he tried to go now, there was no doubt they would both get caught. The police would be back in minutes. So instead he began to run to his safe space in the stone circle, the spot where he was convinced King Arthur rested to this very day. His quest would have to wait. First, he needed to prepare.

Sothea sat anxiously in her room with Ama by her side. She had no idea what her father would do to her now that everyone was gone. At least Gabe had escaped. That much made her feel a little better.

Sothea reached out and took Ama's hand. "I did what you said, Ama..." she whispered. "I followed my heart. But look where that got me. Everything's gone wrong."

Ama smiled and brushed her hand lovingly. "You did the right thing," she said calmly in Khmer. "Don't worry. There is still time."

"Time for what?!" Sothea stood up and began to pace. "Baba will never let me out of his sight now. You know what happened last time he caught me disobeying him."

"*Tsk*." Ama looked at Sothea with serious eyes. "That was a long time ago. You have something you didn't have then." She said it as if it was the most obvious thing.

Sothea frowned. "Aren't you the one who is supposed to calm me down? To protect the world from me?"

Ama stood and took Sothea into her arms, hugging her tightly. "I did not come here because your father asked me to," she said softly. "I came because I love you."

Sothea had not expected that. She felt Ama's warmth, felt her love, and she surrendered to its glow. She leaned her head on Ama's shoulder and let the tears come loose.

"I'm scared, Ama. I don't know what to do. I can't live like this anymore. But I can't control what happens when I..." She turned her head away. "I am cursed."

"Oh, my sweet petal. You are not cursed. You are a woman now. You have more power than you think." Ama pulled back to brush away the tears from Sothea's face. "There are no urges too large, no desires too monstrous that your heart cannot overcome them. You think you are a victim, Sothea. You are not. You are larger than all of it. Only one thing will bring you to yourself."

Ama pressed her palm into Sothea's chest, and she felt it tingle with a warmth that spread around her entire torso and to her limbs.

"Remember this when it all starts to crumble around you," Ama said.

Sothea threw her arms around the older woman's frail body. "Thank you. I don't know what I would do without you."

"Just hold on a little longer," Ama said, giving her a pat on the back. She pulled away and met Sothea's eyes. "This will be hard, but you will make it through."

She stepped back, and just as she did, familiar footsteps began to sound up the stairs to the attic room. Sothea clenched her jaw in anticipation, waiting for the rage to smother her. But when her father appeared in the doorway, there was no anger or malice in his features. He looked tired and frail, but above all he looked grief-stricken.

His eyes went to Ama first. "Could you please give Sothea and I a moment?" he said in broken Khmer.

Ama nodded. As she brushed past on her way out, she slipped something into Sothea's hand. It was soft, but Sothea didn't dare look at it. Not while her father was standing there.

Once Ama was out of the room, her father closed the door and turned his back to Sothea for a long moment. Then he turned around and walked straight up to her. She was anticipating the worst but, instead, he hugged her.

She was stunned and stood frozen, her hands limp by her sides. She had broken the rules but was not being punished?

"I'm sorry," her father said, pulling away and wiping tears from his own eyes.

That disturbed Sothea even more. She had only seen him cry once before. And that was when Mama had... Sothea closed off the memory before it could arise.

Her father sat down on the edge of her bed in silence. He reached into his pocket and took out his strange little moon clock. His fingers rubbed the metal casing and then he clicked the lid open and closed. Again and again, without even looking at it.

Sothea stayed quiet, worried that saying the wrong thing might bring out the anger she had expected.

Then, as if waking from a daze, her father opened the moon clock once more and looked at the hands on the clock face.

"I had to do it," he said, with obvious regret in his voice. "If that boy had been hurt... I would never be able to forgive myself. And I know you wouldn't either. It can't happen again, Sothea. Do you understand?"

Sothea sat down beside him and nodded silently.

"I wish things could be different," he said, looking off into the distance. "For one, I wish I could take your place and send you far away, where you could live a normal life. Where you could go to school, have friends... have boyfriends, even." He shook his head. "I can't help but think that your mother would handle all this much better. So much better. She always seemed to have the right answers."

Sothea hardened. "She is still around. I can feel her."

Her father's jaw clenched and he nodded. "I hope she knows that I'm doing my best. I'm trying my best, Sothea."

She nodded. "I know."

He looked at her with a frown, then shook his head and turned away. "It's time," he said darkly. "You will have to spend the night in the containment room again."

She nodded.

He looked like he was about to say something else, but he stopped himself and stood up, crossing the room.

"Baba?" Sothea said.

He stopped and craned his neck back to look at her. "Yes?"

"You know you won't be able to protect me forever."

The muscles around her father's face tightened and the veins in his neck throbbed. "I know. But I will do everything I can until I am no longer breathing."

With that solemn promise, he left. And not only did he close the door behind him, but he locked it as well. Sothea cringed as the lock clicked into place. She stared vacantly around the silent room, the curtains closed so that barely any daylight filtered in. The dust swirling in the narrow beams that did make it through suddenly stopped, suspended in stasis, just as Sothea clenched her fists.

She felt something in her palm, and suddenly remembered that Ama had put it there. With some hesitancy she unravelled her fingers. Inside was the head of a white rose. She stared at it, feeling more distant from life than the stars themselves. It was crushed, broken by the force with which she had squeezed. As she stared at the disfigured petals, a single tear dropped loose onto the dusty floorboards.

She was destruction. The crumpled rose was a perfect example of how she felt on the inside. But as she looked at it, she remembered Ama's words. She forced herself to take a deep breath. She forced herself to return to the world around her, no matter how much it hurt. She knelt on the ground and extended two cupped palms outwards, with the crumpled rose still upon them.

She pulled at the strings of her heart, and she forced the warmth to return. Her skin began to glow dimly, like the soft halo encircling the moon. Life rushed from her hands into the flower, and it began to bloom again. The old petals died away and new ones grew. Before she knew it, there were at least a dozen roses in her palms. More tears began to fall, and Sothea managed a smile.

Ama was right. There was more to her than destruction. She did not only bring death. She was also life.

CHAPTER ELEVEN

Gabe stood at the edge of the stone circle, looking up at the sparkling stars of energy that rose in an upward current from its centre. When he had returned to the lookout, perched above the Wizard's Well, and seen nothing but rolling hills, he had started to doubt that the mist and castle ruins had been real at all. But then he remembered. He remembered Sothea. She had seen the mana too. She had looked the way Gabe felt the first time he had witnessed it on a nature walk in the woods with his mother. Whatever was happening here was real.

For the first time in his life, Gabe felt like he was living for something.

It was a strange feeling. He felt confident and imbued with a sense of purpose. In his hand was the old book recounting the exploits of King Arthur; an ancient tale in a mystical land in which Arthur faced creatures not of this earth – a land woven in time when many realms were open all at once, where ghosts could speak, and faerie whispers travelled in the wind.

The book itself was practically falling apart. It was tattered around the corners and spine, and now it was covered in drops of blood from the fight on his birthday. Gabe placed the book atop one of the standing stones and knelt in front of it like a knight before his liege, with one knee up and a forearm resting upon his thigh, his head bowed in humility. It was not humility of the embarrassed kind, but one of humble reverence.

Gabe knew his place. He was nothing more than a lowly peon, but still he asked for courage from the otherworldly column of energy that rose from stone circle. Not knowing if what he asked for had been granted, he stood and stepped away. His eyes turned to the setting sun, dipping low against the horizon. He would need to find his way to Bailey Manor before the light fully vanished.

He felt as if he was going into battle and wished, among many other things, that he had a sword at his hip or a full quiver and bow on his back. It was a ridiculous wish, as he knew he didn't have a clue how to use them or if he actually would, but still, having them might make him feel more confident. He took one last look at his blood-stained book before turning and leaving it behind.

S cudding clouds drifted across the night sky, blocking the starlight, and already Sothea could feel herself fading. Her pupils were wide as she stared from her window, the tiny sliver of the waning crescent moon suddenly appearing and then disappearing behind the thin clouds carried by fast currents of wind. She didn't even hear her father approach, but nor did she jump when his hand came to rest upon her shoulder.

"It's time," he said softly.

So much could change in the span of a day. Emotions could

fall and rise with no control, and entire beliefs or states of mind could switch polarities, like the flicker of flame. Sothea had hidden the white rose blooms beneath her bed earlier in the day, and already forgotten how she had conjured them, and the source from which each rose stemmed. With what little of herself she had left, she let her father pick her up.

He cradled her and steadily made his way down the stairs, past Ama who tried to meet Sothea's eyes. But Sothea stared right through her. Right through this world and into another. She could well have been blind, for she saw nothing around her in the realm of physical things. Ama's words still reached her, though they sounded distant, like the creaking of floorboards or whispers through cracks in the wallpaper.

"My sweet child," Ama muttered. "Do not lose sight of your heart. Remember those who love you. Remember that even in the darkest of nights, there is light to be found in the memories of our life."

As she spoke, Sothea saw behind her distance-glazed eyes the image of a chimney full of climbing white roses.

As she faded in and out of awareness, she caught glimpses of steel sheeting, reinforced with a lattice of scaffolding poles. She was dimly aware of lying on a metal surgical table, twitching as the cold metal of the clasps were closed around her wrists and ankles, and her father's comforting whispers as she fought against the one being clamped around her neck.

"Baba?" she asked. "Baba, why?"

Then she was alone.

Gabe arrived at the clearing in front of the house. The sun had set faster than he anticipated, and he had been forced to trudge slowly through the dim woods, carefully avoiding the brambles that so desperately wished to claw at his skin. The house was in total darkness now, a dark silhouette framed by the indigo-black night sky, all but for the sliver of silver from the waning moon. Had Gabe not known where the house stood, he might not have been able to see it at all. There was a cold wind in the air, and he shivered as it nipped bitterly at his skin, raising the hairs on his arms and on the back of his neck.

He frowned. Something was off. The house not only looked abandoned, but there was not a sound to be heard from inside. As he paused to listen, he realised that there was no sound coming from the forest either. No insects, none of the loud night-time scratching of small land scavengers, nor the nocturnal birds and owls. There was something in the air that made Gabe's skin crawl, and it was not just the strange cold in the heat of summer.

He gritted his teeth. Was he too late? It felt as if all the life had been sapped from the world. His fists clenched. He needed to get to Sothea, and he needed to do it now. Looking at the house, it seemed obvious which way was best. After all, he had successfully entered and exited that way before, including once while he was unconscious. He made a sprint for the only remaining scaffolding tower on the western side of the manor, ducking low and sticking close to the house so that there was no chance of him being spotted through one the many windows.

The corner of the blue tarpaulin over the scaffolding structure had broken loose from the metal poles and was flapping about in the wind. Gabe didn't realise until he had started climbing that he could not hear it. He hopped onto the first level and began to ascend the smooth metal lattice frame. He had done it countless times while working with his dad, and he climbed to the top with ease. Biting his lip, he took one step off the metal frame onto the roof. The tiles shifted slightly under his weight and there was a gritty crunching sound.

He mouthed a quick prayer to whatever gods were listening. He could never be sure with old roofing if it was sturdy or secure, even if he had been on it before. He summoned some courage and took his other foot off the scaffolding, crouching low at first and crawling on his hands and knees towards the closest chimney. Once he could wrap his arms around the brick structure, he let out a small sigh of relief. The space between the stacks was like no man's land. Somehow there was already a deadly layer of moisture on the tiles, which made them slippery, especially with so many covered in carpet of lichen. Besides that, any one of them could come loose at any moment, clattering noisily to the ground and alerting Sothea's dad to his position – not to mention potentially causing him to fall to his death.

He made his way over to the next chimney stack as quickly and securely as he could. He held his breath as he scrambled across the steep roof, all the way feeling as if he could slip at any moment. Any noise he made sounded deafening in the silence, and he expected Mr Bailey to pop out at any moment. He was taking a safer route, involving a little detour to Sothea's room, when something outside of the noise he was making suddenly reached his ears.

He stopped dead and craned his neck to listen. On the wind was a voice, a moan that sounded like pain. A female voice. *Sothea.*

It was not coming from the direction of her room and Gabe followed another moan further east, across the apex of the roof. He eventually came to the gable end of the roof, before it dropped off to one of the lower levels, and then again to the huge greenhouse extension to the manor – the palm house, his dad had called it. There was no light coming from inside, except through a narrow crack that Gabe assumed was a door at one end, but the plant life inside the greenhouse was so dense that he couldn't see clearly. Frowning, he slowly lowered himself down a drainpipe and onto the small roof below. The moaning in the wind grew louder.

How had he not heard that before? Even as he approached it now though, the sound didn't seem to make sense to his ears. It was more like the sound was coming from within him than from an external source. But then how could he hear a direction? Gabe shook his thoughts away and continued towards it. He had stopped trying to answer the questions in his head the second he had found the strange tunnel in the rock. It was easier that way. The mind just didn't have answers to some questions.

He dropped down to a lean-to with a pitched roof to his left and a sheer drop to the ground on his right. Straight ahead was an expanse of glass that made up both the domed roof and ceiling of the palm house, supported by intricate Victorian ironwork. If he was to get to the source of the sound, he would have to get inside... He spotted a small window low down in the wall behind him. It was frosted, so he assumed it had to be a bathroom. Crossing his fingers mentally, Gabe tested it. It budged slightly, resisted, and then with a creak, swung open. He had been pulling hard and the momentum of it opening caused him to lose his footing. He began to slip, but at the last second grabbed hold of the window ledge with the tips of his fingers.

He was sprawled almost flat against the roof tiles, barely hanging on. He cursed and managed to adjust his grip, getting a solid handful of wood in one hand. He used that leverage to readjust his other hand and pull himself up, feet slipping on the tiles beneath him, but getting enough traction to make it the rest of the way.

He sat on the edge of the windowsill breathing heavily. Even a fall from one storey up could be lethal. He was no stranger to construction site horror stories, since they were often repeated to him as cautionary tales when he would inevitably lose his concentration on the job. His uncle had fallen off a low roof and landed badly, cracking the top of his head open.

Gabe tried to gather his wits and turned his attention to the darkness inside the house. It took a moment for his eyes to adjust, but he could just about make out the shape of a bathroom – one that looked like it hadn't been used in a very long time. There was dust on every surface, cobwebs strung across every corner, and dead flies littering the sink and ground. He took a deep breath and swung his legs around, gently easing himself onto the stained tile floor before carefully pulling the window closed behind him.

He paused, listening out for any sign of movement. There was nothing but the creaks of the old house within. They groaned and moaned alongside that other ephemeral voice, as if the house too was in pain. His entire body tensed as he took a step forward. He took another, and there was a crashing slam behind him. His eyes bulged as he swivelled around and saw the window had blown open, caught on a current of wind. Before he could do anything, it slammed shut again.

Gabe cursed to himself, sure that he was done for, but he reached back over to the window and flicked the latch shut. The silence afterwards was gut-wrenching. He stood in the dark, waiting for the inevitable. Holding his breath. Heart thumping in his chest. Expecting a light to turn on, or for Mr Bailey to come rushing up the stairs. But as long second after long second went by, nothing happened.

Once his heart rate had returned to double digits, he crept carefully out of the bathroom into a hallway. To the left was a dead end, the exterior wall of the house. To the right, the hallway branched off at a ninety-degree angle. He only had one option.

He was thankful for the pale-yellow glow of the wall lights. He set off, quickly realising that he couldn't avoid the small creaks when his shoes made contact with the wooden floor. There was nothing to be done about that. And if the banging window hadn't got anyone's attention, he doubted the tiny creaks would alert anyone either.

He followed the landing and found that it stretched on for a good distance, leading eventually to a familiar corridor and a peeling wooden door. It was the entrance to the staircase that led up to Sothea's room. He took in a deep breath, and continued along the landing, taking equal care and measure with every step. He tried to ignore the portraits on the walls. Their oil-painted eyes seemed judgemental, as though their spirits were watching every step he took.

Past the portraits, Gabe let out an exhale and his breath came out foggy. An almost paranormal chill hung in the air, as if it was the height of winter. When he reached the top of the large main staircase, he stood for a moment, observing the way it curved down to the ground floor. He steeled his jaw against the instinct to chatter. The cold was seeping into his bones and his muscles were beginning to quiver.

He slowly descended the stairs, his footsteps padded somewhat by the threadbare red carpet that tracked along the centre of them. It was faded and had been sapped of most of its colour, leaving it peeled and grey in some parts. As he looked down at it, he realised there were dead insects in the corner of many of the steps, some still moving. Wasps dragged their barely functioning bodies along the ground. He frowned and wondered what was going through their heads. Where were they trying to go? Did they have a destination? Or was it simply the will to live that kept them moving, kept them going until they finally drew their last breath and twitched into foetal balls, like the other insects around them?

He stepped down onto the ground floor, and the wails and moans seemed to echo louder in the large open space of the entrance hall. But there was another sound alongside them, something closer. It was guttural, and it sounded like... snoring? Gabe poked his head around one of the banisters and was surprised to see light seeping into the hall from the crack underneath a door. He took a step towards it, then another. The wood of the door had strange markings on it. The paint had peeled, but there were red blotches on the surface, dark, dried, and crusted like rust on iron.

Light shone through the keyhole too, and so instead of opening the door, Gabe crouched down and peered through it. He could make out very little: the back of an armchair, an empty glass tipped on its side on the floor. And then movement. An arm twitched. A male arm. *Mr Bailey.*

He was fast asleep. Gabe pulled away from the door as quick as he could while remaining silent. But he backed up straight into something soft. Almost yelping, he spun around. An old woman stood above him – the same woman who had silently helped him escape from Sothea's room. She raised a finger to her lips, indicating for him to stay quiet. Gabe looked back at the closed door behind him, and then back at her.

"Sothea," he mouthed, without speaking.

At first the woman didn't react, but when Gabe went to speak again, she repeated the gesture of a finger over her lips. Her eyes slowly looked to her right and as he followed her gaze, he knew that direction had to be the source of the moaning that still carried in the space around them. The woman met his eyes then walked away. She went in the direction of the sound, but then turned and seemed to disappear into the shadows that enveloped most of the entrance hall. It was completely dark, save for the crack of light escaping from the door to the room where Mr Bailey was sleeping.

Well, at least Gabe had someone on his side now. He didn't really know what role the woman played in Sothea's life. It seemed like she wanted Gabe to find her, but he couldn't help but feel fear at the fact that he was getting closer to doing just that. If Sothea was the source of that haunting sound, he wasn't sure he would be ready to see what awaited him.

He knew he had to act quickly. There might not be another time to set her free. Pushing away the cold shivers in his body that were now accompanied by the cold sweat of fear and the jitter of anxiety, Gabe made his way towards the door the woman had indicated with her eyes, which was slightly ajar.

It creaked open and when he stepped in, he found himself in a small room with a steel door opposite the wooden one he had just entered. It wasn't really a room at all. It was more like a buffering space, an airlock of sorts. It reminded him of the time he had gone to see the butterfly conservatory with his mum. There had been a space very similar to this with a sign that read: *Keep this door closed at all times.*

He took in a deep breath and opened the steel door ahead of him. It made a loud clunk as he pulled at the handle, which was like those he'd seen on walk-in freezers, and he was immediately met with a rush of humidity and the glare of moonlight. He was in the palm house. Inside were hundreds of plants, and some larger trees, all growing beneath the glass roof that he'd been peering through earlier. Through the middle of them was a central walkway lined with herb bushes and shrubs that ended at another steel door.

He swallowed a giant lump in his throat and continued forwards. The moaning rose and fell like the tides of a banshee in mourning.

"Sothea?" Gabe said out loud.

There was no response, but the wailing continued. So he took another step, the metal grate beneath his feet moving slightly as he did, and the metal clanging softly. The door was soon within reach and Gabe extended his shaking hand out towards it.

"Please don't do this."

The deep voice came from behind him, making his heart nearly jump out of his skin. He turned to see the silhouette of Mr Bailey standing at the other end of the palm house. The lengths of hose lining the floor and walls all twitched and became rigid, releasing a fine mist.

"You have no idea what is really going on."

Gabe stood his ground outside the door, despite struggling to see Sothea's dad well through the spray. Small droplets of water formed on his face and clothes. "I think I do," he said. "I think you are a sick man. A sick man who is abusing his daughter."

Mr Bailey took a step forward, but swayed as he did so. Gabe knew that sway. He had seen it from his father many times. Anger began to boil up in him.

"You're drunk, aren't you?" he said.

"Please. You are an intelligent young man. Just give me time to explain." The man's voice was sluggish as he inched forward.

"Don't come any closer!" Gabe yelled.

But Mr Bailey didn't listen. "Sothea is sick!" he said. "She isn't normal."

"Sothea's absolutely normal. You're the sick one!"

Her dad was getting dangerously close. "Sothea's sick," he said again. "And I won't let you make things worse."

Then he lurched for Gabe. It caught him completely off guard and Gabe's head slammed against the wall, along with the rest of his body, but it wasn't enough to knock him out. The two of them slid to the ground in a struggling heap. Mr Bailey was strong, but he was sluggish from the drink and Gabe managed to grapple his arms around him and toss him off to the side before scrambling to his feet.

But Sothea's dad grabbed hold of Gabe's ankles and pulled. Gabe came crashing down again onto one of the tables of potted plants. Pottery shattered everywhere. Gabe swivelled around and began to kick out at him, the sole of his boot slamming into the other man's face. There was a loud crack and Mr Bailey howled in pain, clutching at his nose.

Gabe pushed himself away and managed to get himself on his feet again. Adrenaline coursed through his body as he watched Sothea's dad writhing on the floor.

"You're a bastard," Gabe spat at him. "You're a bastard just like my father. You never deserved a daughter like Sothea!"

Mr Bailey steadied himself, still holding his bleeding nose, and tried to push himself up onto his hands and knees. His head hung low. "You're right. I never deserved her." He looked up at Gabe. "No one does."

He made another charge for Gabe's legs, but it was sloppy and disoriented. This time Gabe had been expecting it, and he jumped out of the way of the attempted tackle. Sothea's dad went hurtling into a set of shelves that smashed with the impact. Gabe grabbed a still-intact terracotta pot and, without thinking, sent it slamming down into the back of the other man's head. He grunted and went limp on the ground.

Gabe stood breathing heavily, trying to blink away the reality of what he had just done. There were more pressing concerns. He turned quickly to the metal door and yanked it open.

Sothea remembered laughing. There was a time when she used to laugh a lot. She remembered the compliments she got from the villagers about her beautifully braided hair, and the soft pinkish hue of her chubby cheeks. She remembered a time when her mother sung her lullabies and father was at peace. He'd had so much love in his eyes. Sothea used to watch her parents cooking together. They would joke and smile and kiss, even amidst the stirring of hot spices. She remembered playing with other children, and running through temple ruins overrun with thick roots and with trees growing out of the top of them.

She was twelve when she had woken up soaked in blood. The bedclothes had been sticky. She remembered the sight of her quivering hands in front of her face in the dim light of a waning crescent moon. She had run out of bed, run from herself. Deep into the jungle and into the ruins.

She could still hear the whispers in the temple stone as the blood leaking from between her legs dripped onto the carved rock floor. Lightning struck from outside. It tore through the sky, hitting a tree directly outside the rectangular stone entrance, illuminating the intricately carved halls of the ancient temple in a flash of blue light and fire.

"Sothea!" She could still hear her mother screaming her name in the early hours of the morning before sunlight struck. She had tried to scream back a response to her mother's calls, but her voice did not – could not – respond. She yelled only silence, and the more she yelled, the more the lightning struck and the faster the winds picked up.

Voices. Ghostly voices clawed at the air around her. She felt cold. All the warmth drained out of her with the scarlet of her blood. Even though she was encased in stone, she could see the moon as if it were right in front of her, a burning after-image engrained in her vision. And every time she closed her eyes, the shadow grew larger around it, edging its way in to obscure the last of the moon's glow.

She remembered the way that same shadow stretched at the edges of her eyes, crawling like tendrils towards the black of her enlarged pupils. Then nothing. Screams. Flashes of blood, teeth, and nothing.

Her father. Carrying her through the village back to their home in the light of morning. Her nightgown no longer a pearly white, but the burnt brown of dried blood – as was her father's shirt. She remembered the faces of the villagers, aghast and in fear, muttering prayers over mala beads.

Those were the memories that haunted her as the door to her prison was ripped open, before the moon's curse came for her.

CHAPTER TWELVE

G abe pulled the door open and dropped to his knees. The world seemed to move in slow motion.

Sothea was chained across a table in the middle of the room, covered in blood from the waist down. Her arms were outstretched on either side, her face the image of terror. The room must have been no smaller than twelve square feet, but every bit of floor was coated in crimson. It was slowly soaking up into the fabric of his jeans. The smell of iron was so thick in the air that Gabe found himself choking on it.

The floor had been angled, like a wet room, so that everything flowed down to a central drain below the table, but the syrupy plasma still coated what seemed like every inch of the floor. Everything slowed down as Gabe's eyes darted from one place to another. His vision blurred and distorted, leaving afterburn images of the segments of moments that came before.

He could see Sothea screaming at him but could not hear what came out of her mouth. He couldn't hear *anything* other than a high-pitched continuous tone, like a scream turned up to a frequency just on the edge of his range of hearing. He watched dumbly as she thrashed against her restraints, everything in slow motion. He tried to make sense of things but couldn't.

There was so much blood.

Ga-a-ab-e!

A voice stuttered into his awareness like a staccato violin. It had multiple layers, like hundreds of voices all calling out at once. He continued to stare silently at the scene. In the air was magic – like the mana he had seen at the stone circles, except very different. The sparkles of light were crimson instead of star-white and flowing downwards instead of up. No, not flowing. They were being funnelled towards Sothea from every direction, like she was a black hole sucking in all that surrounded it.

Ga-a-ab-e! said the staccato screech again. This time Gabe could make out a familiar voice amidst the hundreds. It was Sothea's. He stumbled to his feet and started to move towards her. He had to get her out. That was why he had come, was it not? To get her out? He slipped and slid across the slick metal floor, almost skating towards the prone Sothea.

She was crying. Her lips and facial features moved as if she were pleading, though for what Gabe didn't know.

"Don't worry…" he said, but it sounded muted and unconvincing even in his own ears. "I'm going to get you out."

He didn't really know what he was saying. Or even if he was actually speaking at all. His blood-stained hands fumbled at the chains around her wrists. They wouldn't budge. He tugged and pulled at the shackles, knowing his efforts were futile. He could see welts like burn marks on her skin where the iron had been in contact with it. It didn't help that she too was fighting against the restraints the entire time. Then something in Gabe's brain clicked. There must be a key.

The restraints on her wrists, ankles, and neck were covered in blood, but each of them had a small keyhole. His eyes helplessly searched the room. Sothea was crying black tears now. They stained her face in dark streaks that dripped to the corners of her lips, covering her teeth in black tar. It was grotesque. Gabe retched, his body buckling with the effort. His mind reeled with disgust as he fought every natural instinct to run as far away as he could. But despite the trauma of it all, he only had one thing on his mind. He had to get Sothea out.

He turned and ran back towards the door. His feet slipped on the slanted floor, and he plunged face-first onto it. Darkness. Then Gabe gasped for air, his clothes soaked in the dark, almost-black viscous plasma. He clambered and crawled across the floor on all fours, barely able to see past the curtain of blood that draped across his eyes. He could hardly breathe.

His hand slapped onto the sill of the door-frame, and he used it to heave himself out of the room. And that's when he saw them. A set of keys on a silver ring. They had fallen out of Sothea's dad's pocket and were lying beside his motionless body among the spilled soil and shards of terracotta plant pots. Gabe dragged himself into the palm house, one ounce of will at a time.

His slippery fingers finally wrapped around the tiny bunch of keys, and he clutched it tightly in his fist. The night was starting to break when he turned around, light from the rising sun beginning to stretch into the sky. It painted the horizon with subtle high-lights, and the darkness of deep morning began to fade.

Sothea stopped writhing and the wails started to subside. Gabe trudged back through the bloody mess on the floor and unlocked the shackles binding her hands, neck, and then ankles. Her body lay limp on the blood-stained metal counter like a rag doll.

He parted the matted hair that was plastered to her face, revealing her soft moonlight skin, and picked her up in his arms.

She was unconscious, her eyes flittering beneath her closed eyelids. He trudged up the slant of the floor and stepped into the palm house with a heavy clank. He stepped over her still-unconscious father and stumbled out of the palm house door into the slow rise of early morning.

There were crows in every tree, cawing madly, murders flying overhead in harsh black brushstrokes. Gabe wasn't strong – he was more bone than muscle – but he didn't even feel Sothea's weight as he walked into the forest. She was like a feather in his arms, light and ethereal. Soon dawn became day, and he and Sothea were covered by the tall canopy of the trees.

He took each step at a time, trudging with a singular determination through the brush and brambles. He walked the dirt road until he came alongside the brook and continued along the bank until he reached the Wizard's Well. Gabe knelt down and lay Sothea against the rock. He cupped the sacred spring water and used it to wash her of her own blood, baptising her in the magic waters and cleansing her body.

Her skin was pure white, without a hint of peach or cream, and her lips were blue, but she did not shiver as the cold water washed across her bare arms. Gabe could not think or speak, he simply set himself to the unconscious motion, one cupped hand of water after another. Again and again and again.

Sothea's eyes stirred as he rinsed her legs and feet, but she did not speak.

He carried her to the hollow beneath the roots of the ancient tree. His task complete, he was overcome with fatigue and barely made it to her side before his exhaustion took over. He reached out a hand and entwined his fingers with Sothea's, feeling a gentle pulse and grip in return from her. Then there was nothing but the emptiness found in the depths of sleep.

He had done it. He had saved her. All was right in the world.

J ames awoke with a pounding head to the pungent scent of incense. He jolted upright and found Ama kneeling before him with a large bundle of smoking herbs in her hand.

"Sothea," was the first word out of his mouth.

Ama muttered something he didn't understand as his eyes darted towards the metal door at the end of the palm house. It was wide open. God... It was bloody open.

He tried to stand and felt his whole body protest. His ribs ached with pain and the pounding in his head only became more defined. "What?"

Ama's eyes met his. "The boy," she said in Khmer. "He took her."

James cursed and positioned himself more upright. "What time is it?" he asked in English. Then he noticed the morning light shining through the glass roof of the palm house.

"Seven hour," she replied.

"We have to get her back." James winced. "We have to get her back before it's too late."

Ama didn't say anything, nor give any indication that she agreed with him.

"I had to do it," James said, although it felt more like he was talking to himself than to Ama. "It was the only way to protect her from herself. I had to..."

He found the will to push himself to his feet, stumbling in the process and leaning against the tables in the palm house. Without regard for Ama's sensibilities or his own modesty, he began to strip off his clothes. He turned his attention to the room where Sothea had been kept. Most of the blood had drained away, but the counter-top and floor were still stained, as was he. He picked up the pressure hose attached to a tap by the door and set to work. He had designed the room specifically for the purpose of an easy clean up.

He fumbled in his pocket and found his phone, dialled, and then raised it to his ear. "Hello. Yes. This is James Bailey," he said quickly. "Police, please. My daughter has been kidnapped."

He hung up immediately. He knew that would be enough for a police car to be sent over.

By the time D.S. Hughes had arrived with two other squad cars, James had already cleaned out the room, hidden the chains, and changed into respectable clothing. There was nothing to be done about the bruising on his face nor the new limp he had. But that would only help his cause. When the officers stepped out and saw the state of him, he was sure they knew who the culprit was before he even opened his mouth.

"Find him." It was all James needed to say.

The morning larks roused Sothea from her sleep. A gentle slant of sunlight touched her skin, and she could feel the gristle of leaf litter and forest soil beneath her feet. Her memory was a dark, unpainted canvas. Her blurred eyes slowly scanned her surroundings. It took a moment for her to realise that her hand was entwined with Gabe's.

She frowned and pulled her hand away, sitting up beneath... She recognised this place. As she turned, she saw the trickle of the spring. This was the Wizard's Well. Sothea drew in a sharp breath. How had she gotten here? She scrambled to her feet, noticing that she was still only dressed in her silk nightgown. She recoiled in horror as she saw the colour of it. It was a dark and dried crimson. Fear filled her and she looked to Gabe's motionless body.

No.

She kneeled at his side and shook his body. "Gabe! Gabe!" she cried out.

He suddenly jerked into consciousness, and the second she saw his eyes open she let out a sobbing breath of relief and staggered backwards, putting a hand over her mouth.

"Sothea..." Gabe mumbled as he rose.

She muttered her thanks to every deity she could think of as she watched him quickly push himself up to a kneeling position and raise his palms.

"It's okay," he said. "You're safe now."

"I-I thought you were dead!" Sothea managed to say through stifled cries.

"Dead? Why would I be?"

She pulled him into a vicious hug. Gabe returned the gesture, nuzzling his face into the nape of her neck.

"What are we doing here, Gabe?" she asked as she pulled away.

His eyes glazed over for a moment. "You don't remember?"

She frowned at him.

"Your dad... He had you chained up. You were bleeding..." He looked up at her and took her hand. "I had to get you out. I couldn't just leave you there."

Sothea's frown deepened even further, and she pulled her hands away. "You shouldn't have done that!"

Her reaction seemed to confuse him. "Did you hear what I said?" he asked. "I risked everything to get you out."

"And who told you to do that, Gabe? I need to go back."

She turned to leave, but Gabe stood up and grabbed her wrist. She froze at his touch and her head snapped furiously in his direction.

"Let. Me. Go," she said slowly and deliberately. Raw. Primal.

The oxygen in the air seemed to thin, and the world darkened and went out of focus as she stared at him. The sound of the birds snuffed out, and thorny arms of bramble bushes began snaking towards his ankles. Sparkling energy appeared around them and was sucked towards her as if she were consuming her surroundings.

He let go.

Sothea released the breath she was holding, and the world was given its colour back. The light returned and the birds resumed their song, but she did not hang around to take too much notice of it. She immediately set off back towards the house at a brisk pace.

"Are you a witch?" Gabe shouted after her.

Sothea stopped. *Witch.* She hated that word. She had heard the village people in Cambodia say their equivalent of the word much too often.

Her teeth gritted together and she spun on him, raising an accusatory finger, but when she saw his face she found that no retorts came to her lips. He wore a look of innocence, a look of curiosity, and what else was there? No, it couldn't be. She frowned again. It was admiration. No one had ever looked at her like that so soon after the word "witch".

"Everyone called me crazy for believing in magic," Gabe said.

He looked at her with a childlike wonder. He didn't know the truth though. If he did, there was no way he would still look at her with those eyes. And yet he had seen her on the night before a new moon. Was it possible?

No. He still hadn't witnessed all of what she was.

"Sothea." His voice was soft and inviting, like the gentle play of fingers across the ivory keys of a muted piano.

He stepped towards her, and it took all her will to look away from him, but he kept coming closer. In the next moment his hands were once again on her wrists. Warm hands. She knew the dangers, and still she couldn't bring herself to pull away.

"You don't have to go back," he said in that beautiful voice of his. "I found something the other night." She could hear the rolling hills of excitement on the peaks of his accent. "We could run away there and leave this world behind."

The words were like an invitation she had been waiting to receive her entire life.

"I can't," she replied, still looking away.

"Why not? We could go together. There is nothing left for me here, and I know you don't want to be trapped in that house for the rest of your life. I may not understand exactly what's going on, but I do understand that there is more to life than this."

She finally looked up and met his eyes. Whatever he had found, there was no running away for her. There was no fancy dream. She stared at him with a life-or-death glare.

"I can never leave with you," she said. "I will hurt you."

"What?" Gabe stared at her in confusion. "No. I know you would never do anything to hurt me."

"You still don't understand, Gabe."

"Then help me to understand."

She pulled away again.

"You're just afraid," Gabe accused her. "You're afraid to see what's really out there in the world."

"You're right! I am afraid. But not for the reasons you think. You don't understand anything."

"There we go again! Stupid Gabe. He doesn't understand. I've heard that so many times before." He shook his head. "The thing is, no one bloody well took the time to help me understand. You keep saying that word over and over again, and you've never even tried to explain. You say you're dangerous, but I know in my gut that you wouldn't hurt a fly if it laid eggs on your skin. You say you can't leave, when all that awaits you at home is that prison. So excuse me for not *understanding*! But you haven't given me anything *to* understand."

"I killed my own mother!"

The words screeched out of Sothea's lips, interrupting Gabe's rant. They tore through the air, straight and true, silencing him.

Gabe froze, but Sothea dropped to her knees, already crying.

"I killed my own mother..." she said again through her tears. "I didn't mean to. I... I..." She couldn't get the rest of the words out.

Gabe was already kneeling with her and pulled her in tightly to his chest. She sobbed into him, her whole body convulsing. Her hands were balled into fists, and she beat them against his arm, but not because she wanted him to let go or because she wanted to hurt him, but because she did not know how to handle the emotions passing through her.

For a while Gabe just held her like that. Then he spoke.

"I killed my mother too."

CHAPTER THIRTEEN

Sothea froze. She pulled back and stared into his eyes. They were mirrors of her own, carrying all the guilt and shame she fought so hard to not let consume her.

"How?" she whispered.

Gabe's features hardened and his eyes narrowed, as if he was trying to hold back a wave of tears of his own.

"We were at a river." His voice was choked. "She warned me not to go in too deep. But I thought I saw something. I thought I saw..." His voice cut off, and Sothea grazed her fingers across his cheek where a tear had streamed loose. "I saw something shiny. I thought it was a sword at the bottom of the riverbed. I tried to get it, but there was a drop I didn't see. The next thing I knew I was under the water."

His eyes glazed over.

"The current took me and by the time I surfaced, I had probably swallowed half of the river. I was never a strong swimmer." He shook his head. "Mum came in after me. I remember she looked so scared..." His voice broke for a moment. "We were both carried along by the current and then we were in white water. Rapids. I remember being thrown all over the place, and there was a crack when my arm broke on some rocks, but then I must have hit my head. Next thing I knew I was on the shore, and there were people all around me."

Sothea stayed silent as he paused. She could tell he was reliving the moment, and that there was still more he wanted to say.

"I fought with the people trying to help me when I realised she was floating in the water. Then my dad came back with ice cream for us and... His face when he saw her too. It's like it happened in slow motion. They all tried to revive her, but..."

"Gabe..." Sothea said softly. "You can't blame yourself for that. It wasn't your fault."

"It was!" he shouted. "I should have listened to her! If I hadn't gone chasing that sword, she would still be alive. I thought that sword would make me into something. But it was probably just a pipe or a piece of metal... She died over a piece of metal!"

"Gabe, you were just a kid."

"How old were you when your mother died?!" he replied.

Sothea paused. "Why does that even mat—"

"How old?" Gabe interrupted, clenching his jaw.

Sothea took in a deep breath. "Twelve."

"See. You were just a child too."

"Yes. But it was different. Your mother's death was an accident. The river took her."

"What are you saying?"

"I killed my mother with my own hands." She shook her head. "My father tried to hide it from me. But the memories started coming back in my dreams."

Gabe seemed genuinely shocked.

She looked at him with venom in her eyes – not directed at him, but at herself. "I am a monster."

Gabe still didn't say anything.

"I can't control it when the transformation happens," she said. "I become something else. Something horrible." Sothea pulled away from him and stood up, turning, her black hair falling over her eyes. "Now you know why I can never leave that prison. I am dangerous."

"The dead cows..." Gabe said slowly, seeming to fumble for words. "That was... That was you?"

Her head snapped towards him. "Yes."

She was expecting Gabe to run, but instead he looked up at her with compassion. It took her completely off guard.

"How often?" He cleared his throat. "How often do you... change?"

She looked up to the sky. She could sense the last slivers of the waning moon fading behind the shadow of the earth.

"Every cycle," she replied. Her pupils narrowed. "Always on the new moon."

"So what was last night?"

"That was just the warm up..."

Sothea saw the realisation dawning on him. He hadn't freed an innocent girl from captivity, he'd let loose a monster! She turned to leave again, but suddenly Gabe shook himself out of his daze.

"You can't control it," he said suddenly.

She shook her head.

"But what if you could?" he asked. "What if there was a way?"

She laughed. "There isn't. You think my father hasn't tried?"

"Arthur," he whispered.

"What?"

"Legend says that any who find and wake the sleeping King will be granted a favour. I had always planned to ask him to make me a knight so that I could leave... all of this. We'll just change the request."

Sothea slowly turned back around. " You would have to find him first."

"You've *seen* the magic," Gabe said. "You've used it. Interacted with it. There's something special about this place and you know it too. I have been here a thousand times trying to figure out how to open the doorway, but I was missing something this entire time. *You*. Don't you see? You're the key. This... this place is like a circuit board."

He picked up a stick and began to draw in the dirt. "Here is the stone circle. It was put there on purpose. It sits on two inter-secting ley lines."

"What are ley lines?"

"They are underground currents of energy. If you look at all the stone circles, they all sit on at least one. The hill was carved into the shape it is today," Gabe continued, drawing more in the sand. "You see this part here? It loops right to the spring, and goes on to the face in the stone before looping back to the circle."

Sothea frowned.

"Can't you see?" he said. "It's a circuit. Like with electricity. The stone circle is a generator. Except the switch has been turned off. It's inactive. It hasn't been used in God knows how long. But there is a reason why myths stick around. There is a reason why some legends don't die."

As Gabe spoke, something arose in Sothea that had never been there before. It was like a single pearl poking out of an infinite bed of sand. It glimmered in its own light. Hope. That was what it was. Hope. Something her father, nor Ama, had ever been able give to her – no matter how hard they tried.

"But how?" she asked.

Gabe paused then turned to his book. He picked it up excitedly. "The answers to the hardest questions are always hidden in plain sight," he said, smiling. "I bet you anything the secret is in here somewhere."

"Gabe, do you really think—"

"Yes," he interrupted, before she even finished the question. "We can enter the sleeping barrow of King Arthur and ask him for the favour to keep you from transforming."

The thought was like an ancient dream. Her father's words echoed in her memory. He had said himself that he wished there was a way for her to lead a normal life, to go to school, and even have a boyfriend.

She thought for a second about going back to the house and telling him about her plan, but quickly stopped that train of thought. Despite what he had said, there was no way he would go along with this. Even though he had seen the impossible become true before his very eyes numerous times, he was stubborn in his belief that *his* solution to her affliction was the only solution.

"Okay," she replied, taking Gabe's hand. "Let's do it."

CHAPTER FOURTEEN

James sat in Sothea's room with his hands desperately pulling at his hair. The day was slowly creeping away from him and still he'd heard no further news from the police. He stared, with eyes unfocused, trying to think of any clues that could lead him to where Gabe might have taken her. Alderley Edge was not a large place, but who was to say they had remained in town.

At first he'd thought of the woods behind the house. They were vast and it would be easy to hide there, but what would they do for food and shelter? If he knew anything about teenagers, especially boys, it was that they were hungry every thirty minutes. Surely Sothea would be smart enough to return of her own accord. Especially if she was feeling cold and hungry. He cursed Gabe, even though he knew that the boy was only trying to help her. Don't children rebel against your wishes just for the fun of it? By forbidding her from seeing him, he'd just made it all the more desirable. Maybe if he had been more open to them seeing each other, and insisted on a clear schedule, none of this would have happened.

Even before he had found out his daughter was... well, different, his wife had told him that he was too strict. He figured he got it from his own father. It was a tale as old as time, passed down from generation to generation. You think you are doing things for your own reasons, only to find out a little later down the line that it was not your will at all. It was most likely not the will of his father or his father's father either. It was an accumulation of many generations of bad parenting. A learned behaviour triggered by wars or famines, droughts or plagues, greed or bad choices. Whatever the origin of the trauma, it changed a man. Whether he knew it or not.

A flicker of movement slowly pulled the focus of his eyes back to the room. He watched as a white petal gently cascaded from the chimney and fell like a feather to the ground. He frowned.

White petal. That was what her mother had called her, albeit in the Khmer tongue. He stood and knelt in front of the fireplace. He was focused solely on the petal, and he picked it up in his fingers, noticing for the first time in his life the thin veins that ran through it. They reminded him so much of when Sothea had been little. She had been born premature and he could see the veins through her papery skin. Even then, she had smelled like a rose. Bloomed like one too – full and boisterous with a piercing cry that belied her apparent fragility.

As he stared at the petal, another fell onto his palm beside it. James caught a whiff of rose, as if Sothea was standing right beside him. Where were these petals falling from? The chimney? He looked up in confused shock and awe at the inside of the structure, overgrown all the way to the top with thorny vines, and moon-white blooms, as if he were staring into the pages of an old fairy tale come to life.

The scent was overwhelming now that he could see it all. He was astonished that he had not smelled it earlier. When did this happen? How did this happen? He thought he already knew part of the answer to the latter.

"Sothea."

There was a creak on the staircase and James instinctively moved his head, hitting it on the mantlepiece and coming out of the chimney rather disoriented. It was Ama. She stood there silently, a leather satchel over one shoulder, watching with those eyes he had never been able to read, though he knew those same eyes saw all of him.

He put a hand to his head, his headache from the previous night made worse by the knock on the mantlepiece.

"You should announce yourself," James said in English. "It's rude to sneak up on people like that."

"I allowed the stair to creak, did I not?" she retorted in Khmer.

That held his tongue. He was still cradling the two petals in his hand and Ama shuffled over to him, slowly tracing a finger over the soft white satin of the rose.

"You know where she is," James said bluntly. "I know you do."

Ama looked up for a moment, before looking away and walking to the large circular window. "She does not want to be found," she said.

"I don't care if she wants to be found! The night is almost upon us. A new moon and a full transformation. If we don't get her away from that boy, his death will be on my hands. And yours."

She *tsked* her disapproval and it set James's teeth on edge.

"Do you not have faith in her?" she asked.

He was getting angry now. "I have full faith in her, and none in the demon that possesses her."

Ama turned to him sharply, moving quickly towards him, far quicker than any old woman should have been able to move. "Sothea, and what she becomes, are one and the same!" she chastised him. "You have kept her sheltered from herself for too long. You have destroyed any confidence that she can overcome what haunts her. You may be weak, but Sothea is not."

"You would leave her to kill an entire town?!" James yelled back at her.

She *tsked* again. "Fine. I will take you to her. But I will not be here when you get back."

He hardened. "That's okay with me. You've done nothing but give her false hope and encourage her to follow roads that only end badly!"

Ama snatched the petals out of his hands and turned her back on him. She took a stone mortar out of her satchel, threw in the petals, pinched in a few herbs, and ground them all down with a pestle. She poured the sticky mixture carefully into a small leather pouch and proceeded down the stairs. James followed her, but when he reached the bottom, she was nowhere to be seen on the landing. He ran down the main staircase and out the door and found her standing at the edge of the clearing.

He didn't have time to question how it was she had gotten there so quickly, because she was already walking into the forest. He had to shift into a full sprint to catch up with her, leaving the front door to the manor wide open. A moment later, he too disappeared into the foliage.

***

There was something different in the air as Gabe walked towards the stone circle. He couldn't quite place it, but he knew *something* was happening. It was as if everything in his life had been a dream, and this was the most real moment of his whole existence. It was strange because he was attempting to try something that most would call him insane for even thinking about. He had never crossed over the boundary of the stone circle. He had never felt worthy even to try. It would be like trailing a pair of dirty shoes through a newly carpeted living room.

The stones were large, and they had a strong presence – as if they emanated a sound so deep that it couldn't be heard, yet the vibrations could still be felt on the surface. Gabe watched with fascination as Sothea focused on the sparkling column of energy that lay within. She reached out her hand and her fingers met the light as if it were solid. She could feel something. He didn't know what, but he could see it in her expression, closed eyes, and brows in the furrow of focus. Suddenly, she turned to Gabe with a surprising urgency.

"We have to release the current," she said.

Gabe frowned.

"The current," she said again. "Underneath the ground. It's like the flow is blocked somewhere, and only a trickle is getting through."

Gabe's heart missed a beat. Was she talking about the ley lines? She understood! He had searched for them many times, even tried dowsing them out with a pair of sticks. The lines had to be connected to the stone circle and the entrance to the Wizard's Well – but where exactly?

"How?" he asked.

In response, Sothea began to walk away from the circle. Gabe followed. She burst into a sprint towards a rock and began pushing to no avail.

"Help me move this," she told him.

Gabe had so many questions, but he didn't bother asking them. He grabbed a large fallen branch and propped it underneath the rock, using it as a lever to lift it off the ground. Sothea got underneath it with her hands and pushed. It rolled over.

"Yes," she said, her eyes darting around to look at things that Gabe could not see. "There are more."

She went back to work like a hound sniffing out a scent. Gabe helped her roll away a fallen log, then a couple more stones and small boulders. The more they moved, the more Gabe felt a shift in the environment. It was subtle. An increase in the pitch of the birdsong in the trees, a different hue to the sunlight as though the exposure was increasing, and a blooming of the smells coming from the foliage – no longer a generic forest aroma but the discernible, individual scents of pine, birch, and oak.

Gabe knew time was passing but he could no longer tell how much. It seemed like a dream, Sothea walking gracefully and barefoot along the ley line, adjusting all the objects she could and requesting Gabe's help with the heavier ones. He followed a slant of sunlight shining through the trees and noticed the familiar yellow-orange tinge. The golden hour was upon them. The most beautiful time of day in Gabe's opinion. A time that seemed to make everything glow and stand out in beautiful definition.

In a moment, he realised what it meant. They were already in the last fragment of daylight. After this, the sun would set, and the shadows of night would be upon them. A new moon would appear, barely visible in the night sky, and the delicate girl before him would transform into something terrible – although quite what, he did not know.

"Sothea. We have to hurry." His voice sounded strange even in his own ears, as if it were coming from outside of himself.

"Almost there," she whispered, in a trance of movement.

Gabe looked up at the sky again. "This has to be enough," he said, impatiently.

She shot him a glance. "It isn't!"

Gabe was beginning to get nervous. It wasn't that he feared Sothea, it was more that he was worried for her. If her transformation was anything like what he saw last night, then he would rather she not go through it again if that was possible. If they could make it to that ancient place, make it to the tunnel... He had been thinking about it more and more. He didn't think that reappearing in Sothea's room had been random.

He had wanted to see Sothea the night he ran away. He had wanted more than anything to be in her room, feel her arms around him. That was what his heart had desired and that's where the tunnel had led. He didn't know how or why it had appeared to him that night on the fringe of dreaming, somewhere between wakefulness and sleep. But the reality was that it had. Gabe had known that world. He had imagined that rock and architecture when he read the stories of King Arthur. He had wandered that world a thousand times in his own mind. And that night he had walked it for real.

The only thing different from the version in his head was that time seemed to have taken its toll on it. The castle and structures he had imagined were not crumbling, nor were the streets full of mist. But Arthur had lived thousands of years ago, maybe more. Some of the stories called him the King of many realms. Gabe had always assumed that the word "realms" was in reference to different kingdoms or cities. But now that he had seen that misty world, he thought it might mean more.

The sky was darkening. The night was creeping ever closer. He clenched his jaw as he helped Sothea tip another heavy stone out of the ley lines' current. He followed her through an archway formed by two trees, past some brush, until she stopped suddenly. He frowned and peered over her shoulder at what she was looking at. Right in front of them was an enormous bush of roses.

She looked at them with a pale expression. Gabe took her hand.

"This is the last thing we need to remove." Her voice was sullen.

He didn't understand why she was acting so sombre. She should be excited, shouldn't she? He stepped closer, squinting to make out the bush in the low light. It took him a moment, then suddenly he realised that what he thought were trees and other foliage around it were in fact more parts of the same bush. He let out a breath in awe. It was giant! It was like a monster rolling up from dark depths, overtaking and snuffing out the life of everything around it, strangling old trees that had died long ago as a result of its thorny grip. It was sharp and wild and beautiful. Full, boisterous, scarlet blossoms protruded from the tangle of hooked vines. They had a sweet aroma, but that sweetness was only part of the smell. It hovered on the surface, gentle and tempting. The other part lingered deeper. It was a wet, musty smell, the smell of rot.

Those very same petals had fallen and decomposed alongside whatever poor living creatures had gotten tangled up in the chaos of thorns. As Gabe's eyes adjusted to take it all in, he could see the remainder of a rabbit's foot among the brambles, mostly decomposed but still recognisable by the white tufts of fur that barely clung to it.

This was not a rosebush. This was a predator. A snare of false pretence. A siren of its own terrain.

Sothea began to back away. Gabe looked wordlessly from her to the bush.

"Wait," he said. "There is still time."

But there wasn't.

Sothea shook her head.

"We can pull it up!" Gabe shouted, as Sothea continued to back away.

Frantic, he attacked the rosebush with his bare hands. He

began to pull at the roots. Large, hooked thorns pierced his skin, poking deep, scratching at his arms like a harpy's fury. He fell backwards with an agonising howl, holding his hands up in front of him only to see them sticky with his own blood.

The sky was getting very dark now.

A howl of wind shuddered through the trees and Gabe knew that it was not any ordinary sound. Every hair on his body stood on end. A cold shiver rattled the insides of his bones. When he exhaled, his breath released a mist of its own. Still on the ground, he turned to Sothea. She wasn't moving anymore. There was an expression of terror on her face as she stared dead ahead at the roses.

At once he knew that it was no coincidence that the roses were there. A whisper in a strange tongue began to snicker through the wind and Gabe felt everything that was good in the world drain from within him.

"Sothea!" he shouted.

But he could see from her haunted expression and the size of her pupils that she was no longer in the same world he was in. She was somewhere else. Here and at the same time far away. The trees groaned and their burly branches clacked. The wind moaned and whispered, the layers of it wrapping over one another like folds in a fabric. Then suddenly he heard his name.

"Gabe!"

Gabe turned. "Dad?"

It was not his dad.

Mr Bailey appeared behind Sothea as if he had stepped out of some distant realm himself. His face was bruised and swollen.

"Gabe, you have to leave!" He knelt before Sothea and began to shine a light from a small torch into each of her eyes. Her pupils did not dilate. But they did begin to pulse. Gabe watched in shock as they flickered between reptilian slits and wide circular voids. Then a red stain spread over her nightdress.

"Get out of here now!" her father shouted again.

But Gabe could not. Would not. They had been so close.

He got to his feet and took one step towards Sothea's dad before a shriek screeched through the air, sharp as a knife tip scraping glass. In the next moment Sothea's face changed. She was a terrifying ghoul of her former self, her wide eyes full of malice and her suddenly sharp teeth bared. Her dad tried to move her, but it was too late. She threw him off her with a shrug, like he weighed nothing. There was a horrible crunch as he crashed into the sturdy trunk of a tree and crumpled to the ground.

Gabe was in shock as he stared at Sothea, and then her eyes flickered over to him. There was nothing of her in those eyes. No recognition. Something had taken over her body.

Her fingernails were like glistening talons, suddenly sharp and claw-like, curled into malicious weapons. Everything around them, including the air itself was pulled towards her. Streams of mana broke through the surface of the ground from the ley line below and careened directly towards her. The air in Gabe's lungs was siphoned out of him, and he found himself gasping like a fish out of water, unable to draw a breath. It was like he had been winded. His brain fought to breathe, but he could do nothing but gasp helplessly. Branches, twigs, and leaves ripped from the trees and raced past his head in a maelstrom.

Sothea.

He tried to say her name, but with no air in his lungs it was impossible to form the word. He watched through fogged eyes, suffocating, face turning purple as Sothea began to rise from the ground in the eye of the storm. She was the very centre of the chaos. Dark shadows twisted around her body. At least he thought they were shadows. If it wasn't for the small beam of light coming from her father's fallen torch, Gabe may never have seen the shadows for what they truly were. Blood.

The shadows writhed and twisted around her body like a cocoon, moving up towards her neck. Parts of her began to disappear. The skin and bones of her feet dissolved. The energy surged inside her, and as Gabe's vision began to darken, the rest of her disappeared before his very eyes. It did not so much vanish as it did liquify, first into a collagen-like jelly, before flowing away.

Her intestines hung loose, trailing to the ground, and the rest of her organs were exposed as her skin and bones became liquid. Gabe held a hand to his throat, the other reaching to her, his mind persistently trying to call her name to no avail. She wailed when her transformation was completed. All that was left of her was her head and neck, and the organs that hung from her spinal column.

In a sudden and very sober moment, Gabe realised he was going to die. There was nothing of Sothea in those vicious fangs and serpentine eyes, black as the absence of the moon. He didn't know how long he had gone since the last breath he took, but he knew that if Sothea – or rather the monster she had become – didn't get to him first then he would die from asphyxiation.

So close. They had been so close. A language spoke in his head, dark and rumbling, like a snake sliding through his ear canal and into his brain. It was not a recognisable language, and Gabe felt the last of himself slipping. He saw the surface of water. Felt his mother's arms around him. Then from nowhere, the smell of incense smoke. And two brass cymbals clanging richly together in a high-pitched note, followed by a horrific wail.

Gabe's lungs heaved in a breath. Something washed through his body, though he couldn't tell if it was the water he had seen a moment ago or if it was air. It was cold and sudden. He rolled over onto his side and saw someone standing between him and Sothea. His lungs heaved another breath.

The brass cymbals chimed again. There was a mist creeping along the ground. Or was it incense smoke? He was so disoriented he could hardly tell up from down.

"Go," he heard a voice say.

A pure voice. A voice that was warm, full of compassion and love. It animated his muscles and seemed to ward off the chill that bit at his marrow. He stumbled to his feet and saw who the stranger was. The older woman from Sothea's house. Did Sothea say her name was Ama? She was dressed in a colourful robe with string tassels, feathers, and wide-cuffed sleeves.

Ama paced back and forth, an incense bundle in one hand and the two brass cymbals in the other. They were tied to one another and with a flicking movement of the string that held them, she chimed them again. Sothea roared in pain. It was a terrible sound, because Gabe could hear her voice in there somewhere, beneath the venom and hatred and growls.

The mist was thick now, and it was only them that weren't shrouded by it. Like an invisible circle had been cast around them, warding the mist away.

"Take him," Ama said.

And even without her pointing, Gabe knew she meant Sothea's dad. Gabe's limbs kicked into action as if the demand was not something he could ignore. He heaved the barely conscious man up onto his feet. He was muttering something, but Gabe couldn't make out the words. There was a thick gash in the back of his head, probably from a gnarled branch of the tree he hit when Sothea had thrown him.

Her dad resisted. He didn't want to leave her.

Another chime of the cymbals. Each one seemed to infuriate the monstrous Sothea even more.

"Burn the roses," Ama said. She turned her back suddenly to

Sothea and spread her arms out parallel to the ground, dropping the bundle of herbs and the chimes.

"Go now!" she told Gabe. "And burn the roses. All of them!"

Then Sothea broke free of the enchantment Ama seemed to have put on her. She moved faster than Gabe's eyes could see, and her razor-sharp fangs were in Ama's neck a moment later. There was a moment that seemed to move in slow motion, where he saw the light in Ama's eyes. Initially, they did not flicker or show a hint of pain. Then the light vanished, and Gabe knew the woman was dead.

He turned and he ran. He ran into the mist with Sothea's dad limping by his side, still muttering incomprehensibly. He could hear the sickening sound of flesh being rent from bone. He could hear guts being spilled and the squelch of organs being consumed. He didn't know where he was running, but his heart was in tatters. He felt cowardly and at the same time knew that he did not possess the power to help or subdue Sothea. The last words Ama spoke rung over and over in his head as he ducked through the trees, and avoided the ruin of rock. *Burn the roses.*

He stumbled over a chunk of stone, almost letting go of Mr Bailey in the process. Ancient ruins began to appear in the mist all around him, and Gabe recognised the shapes. He had been down these phantom streets before. Sure enough, a towering arched bridge came into view, with a tunnel at its centre. It seemed the work they had done on the ley line had shifted enough energy to open the doorway to this realm once again.

Or perhaps this place had nothing to do with the ley line. Gabe had accessed it a couple of nights before. He did not know how this place worked but he did not question it, as a wail tore through the fabric of mist. It seemed to come from all directions, far and close at the same time. He crossed the threshold into the tunnel and when he turned around Sothea was hovering in the open clearing before it. Her limbs were missing. She was just a floating terror of fangs and a spinal column dragging behind loose organs.

She stopped at the threshold of shadows and growled. Something about the tunnel didn't permit her entry. *Magic.* There must have been something preventing her from accessing the tunnel beneath the bridge. He turned to her, face mere inches away from the threshold, and met her eyes – her black reptilian eyes.

"I will come back for you, Sothea," he whispered. "I will come back for you, and we will leave this world together. I promise."

Her growling stopped as he spoke and something about her seemed to shift. Her eyes seemed for a moment a little less alien, and a little more like her own. But he may have imagined it, because in the next moment she charged at the tunnel. She was repelled violently by an unseen force and unleashed a fury of screams.

Gabe didn't look away. "I promise."

At last, he turned and dragged Sothea's barely conscious father the rest of the way into the darkness. Unsure where the portal would take them, Gabe surrendered to the twist and turn of space around him, let the shadows seize his senses and become undone. The weight of his promise was the only thing he felt as a nothingness enveloped all that he was.

———

CHAPTER FIFTEEN

Gabe awoke face down in the mud. There was a strange sensation along the surface of his body, a feeling like the earth was not solid, like it wavered beneath him. Pulsating. Breathing. Waiting. He took a disoriented breath and felt once again as he had the morning he'd woken in Sothea's room – lost and foggy headed.

He groaned and his eyes opened enough for him to take in his surroundings. He was back in the grounds of Bailey Manor.

Ama was dead.

Gabe barely knew her, but it didn't stop it hurting. She was kind and that meant a lot to him. He still remembered the gentleness in his mother. It was a gentleness he had not felt since. Not until he met Sothea at least. Gentleness was an underrated thing. So many he knew tried their best to be the opposite, as if it were a trend. Was gentleness something that had to be taught? Or was it something that everyone was born with, and the teaching really was how *not* to be gentle? Regardless, his mother had escaped that education. And it was not because she herself had come from a place that didn't teach that sort of curriculum. Her parents, bitter and cold, surely hadn't encouraged her gentleness. She must have fought to keep it. And it was her that Gabe had to thank for his own gentle nature. To his father it was a flaw – an unforgivable weakness – but to Gabe, it was the greatest gift of all.

Groggy and disorientated, he scanned the darkness for Sothea's dad. He'd been right with him, unable to walk unaided. Gabe had had one arm wrapped around his waist, encouraging him forward towards the portal, but now he couldn't see him anywhere. Something touched Gabe's index finger. Then the fingers on his other hand. The ground was moving.

He felt a strange revulsion rise in his stomach and up to his throat. *Worms.* Crawling across his arms and legs and neck. There were thousands of them. Tens of thousands. Gabe sat dumbfounded as he stared at the surface of the earth, at countless worms wriggling and writhing as far as his eyes could see. He was not typically put off by worms, but he had only ever come across one or two at a time. This was something else entirely.

He retched violently at the wrongness of it all. They were usually the earth's unseen caretakers, buried until dug up. To see so many of them, inches thick, slipping and noodling over one another, put things into a different perspective.

There could only be one reason for this. *Sothea.* As soon as she popped into his head, he was made suddenly very aware of the memory of Ama being brutally killed. He threw up again until there was nothing left. He had to get off the ground, had to get away from the infinite ocean of interlocking segmented bodies. When he stood up, he felt a worm or multiple worms squish beneath his shoe. He closed his eyes in dread. The door of Bailey Manor was open before him, as if to beckon him inside, but there was at least fifty feet between him and the entrance.

There was no getting around the mass of writhing bodies. He

took another step forward, wincing as he slowly lowered his foot down through inches of thick, juicy annelids. There was only one solution. Gabe sprinted for the door, ignoring the worms beneath his feet. Sweet relief washed over him as he stepped onto the stone porch at the front of the house. He grasped at the railing with one hand and hunched over.

What was happening? How had everything in his life flipped on its head so quickly? Then he realised that it hadn't really been quick at all. It had been building up for most of his life. It had started the second he woke up to the absence of his mother. The second he saw the grief strike his father, and the ice cream he had gotten them – three identical cones – drop to the floor. It was in the way his father blamed him. Never outright. He never said the words, but the way he treated Gabe had changed on that day. A passive, and sometimes overt aggression became embedded into everything his father said and did. He hadn't just lost his mother, he had lost his father too. Exchanged him for a bitter man who drowned his grief in drink and masked his frustration in a barrage of insults and shame.

Gabe forced himself to stand up. This wasn't about him. This was about Sothea. And he had no idea how long it had been since he left her on her own in the woods. She could have been anywhere by now. And her dad... They had walked through the portal together, but now he was nowhere to be seen. Had the tunnel transported them to two different places? He couldn't pretend they were friends. Only last night they'd tried to hurt each other, but given what had happened – and what he'd learned since – he was the nearest thing to an ally Gabe had. He gritted his teeth. He couldn't control what he didn't understand, but there was something he could control. Resolution set into his features and he strode into the house.

He still had something to do before the night was over. He

had to burn the roses in the forest. Burn the roses, then find Sothea. They would activate the ley line, open the door in the face of the rock, and awaken King Arthur. Ask him for his favour and then leave this world behind.

The plan he set out gave him the agency he needed not to crumple into non-action and despair.

It was asking the impossible, but Gabe was now used to the idea of the impossible. Sothea, for example, was an impossibility. A terrifying, ferocious impossibility. One that he still found his heart yearning for. None of it was her fault. He may not have known what made her that way, but he knew that it was not her fault. Just like a child raised in a family of assholes would most likely become an asshole themselves. It was not the child's fault. They were subject to the age-old battle of nature versus nurture, with both forces determined to carve the path into the future.

Gabe had read many tales of curses. He knew the gist. Ancestral mistakes, dark magic, generational trauma. Her case was one of them. Because there was no way in *all* the worlds that he could believe Sothea had done anything to deserve this fate. She had been a child as well. A gentle and innocent child. The pain she must have to go through every day, and yet she had found a way to still put on a smile.

It drove him to move faster. He began rummaging through the cabinets and drawers in the kitchen, tossing things about, looking for the items he needed. He found petrol, not in the kitchen, but in a small storage area in the utility room above the washing machine. Matches he found in a drawer with spare batteries, lightbulbs, and what looked like a lifetime supply of elastic bands. He packed a bag, tossing in cleaning rags, and then rushed to Mr Bailey's study to scoop up the empty bottles of whisky. The rosebush had been endless. A dark twisting lattice of overgrown beauty and malice. It would take a lot more than a gentle dowsing to destroy such a large and deeply rooted plant.

Eventually, he zipped up the pack and returned to the front porch, ready for his mission. A knight tasked with his sacred duty. This time he did not hesitate as he stepped back onto the earth, treading over the worms without remorse. He had a fire to start.

James awoke at his wife's grave. He thought he was dreaming, or dead, as his eyes opened to the familiar steeple-topped temple of the traditional Khmer tombstone. It was, of course, an impossibility, as he had been in the woods between Alderley Edge and Bailey Manor not a moment ago.

He was already kneeling. He did not remember arriving nor positioning himself in this way, but he supposed that was how death went.

"I failed," he said to the bones of his wife, buried six feet beneath the earth. "I failed you, and I failed her." He paused, tears starting to form in his eyes. "I thought that taking her away from here would change things. I thought that her curse might be tied to the land it came from."

Oh, James.

His wife's voice.

James closed his eyes as a tear fell loose. Yup. He was definitely dead.

"I just wish I had allowed her to live more. To be a child. I shouldn't have kept her locked inside. In the end, that didn't make a damn bit of difference. It just caused her to hate me." He drew in a ragged, guilt-stricken breath. "I thought I was protecting her..." He shook his head. "But now I know I was only protecting myself."

A soft wind caressed the side of his face, and as James leaned into it, he felt the cool touch of a palm on his cheek.

"Chantrea..." James whispered. "I've missed you so much." More tears fell.

The wind shifted across the back of his neck, around to the front of his body, and then away. He followed the feeling with his eyes and there she was. She stood, half visible, half not, at the foot of her own grave. She was not facing him, but stood in profile, a hand over her heart looking up to the sky. His emotions choked in his throat. It was an impossibility. He thought he would never see his wife again.

"She needs you," Chantrea said softly.

James shook his head. "I've already failed her."

The mist drew closer.

"She is lost," Chantrea continued. "The boy hasn't given up yet, so why have you?"

"The boy?"

Gabe. Memories started to filter back. Gabe had carried him away. Carried him through a tunnel.

"But... I'm..."

"You're not dead, my love." Her voice was distant and ethereal. She turned to him in that moment, and James stared upon the eyes that he had fallen in love with an entire lifetime ago.

"Then how?" he asked.

Chantrea laughed. It was a precious and incredible laugh, just the same as when she had been alive. "We do not see much of the world when we are living. We choose to live our lives in darkness and ignorance," she said. "There are roads. Invisible roads connecting many things. One brought you here. To me. I walked another to..."

Her voice grew more distant. James suddenly realised that her form was more *not* now, than *was*. She was disappearing.

"No. Wait. Please don't go! It's not me she needs. Sothea needs *you*!" James looked up at her, pleading. "*I* need you…"

She laughed again, not mocking but full of love. James felt it ring through his entire body, filling the chambers of his heart.

"I have chosen to stay," she said. "You do not see but I am always with you both."

James suddenly remembered how Sothea would not allow anyone to sit in the front passenger seat of their car. The seat where her mother had always sat. Sothea knew. She had always known. It was he who lived in a world of his own, he who had pushed Chantrea away even when she had been there all along.

She smiled. "I will be here until the end. At one moment or another you will have done enough. Then all three of us will walk the invisible road home together."

James started to reply, but she was no longer there.

A wind touched the back of his neck again, and he understood. Even though he could not see her, he understood. As he clambered back to his feet, the mist swallowed his wife's grave. Before it could disappear completely, however, James picked a white rose from the flowers that lay on it. He slipped it into his inner jacket pocket, feeling the thorns catch on the lining, and then turned to walk the narrow path that led from her grave to their old house.

He didn't think he would ever return. Staring at it now, he was filled both with the joy of peaceful memories and the haunted feeling of what came after. It was a pain he had forced himself to ignore, but now he was here – by some miracle – he had no choice but to look. He saw the window where it happened, that night when his entire life took a twisting turn into the darkness.

The wind brushed at his neck again. Things were different this time. He had been uncertain of death up until this point. Now he saw it was not the dead who should be pitied, but the living.

Chantrea had been radiant. She had been a phantom angel, aglow without the chains of grief or the prison of form. She looked upon the world with knowing eyes, eyes that knew truths the living were not permitted to behold.

As the mist slowly obscured the whole house from view, he felt his desperate need to find his daughter. He had to help her, even if it was the last thing he ever did. And he had an idea. He just needed to collect some tools from their new home first.

When he took his next step forward, a stone bridge and an arching tunnel appeared before him. It was both strange and familiar. His mind recalled fragments of memories appearing like flashes – Gabe supporting him, trying to keep him upright, forcing him forward one impossible step after another. He'd seen and felt the soft earth of the forest become solid rock as Gabe pulled him through an in-between place, a realm on the border of two worlds. The shadows reached out as he walked over that same border now, wrapping around his limbs and whisking him through time and space.

CHAPTER SIXTEEN

Sothea craved blood. Her vision was red-tinted with sharp edges, and she could see scent trails through the woods, moving at a speed that did not make sense in the normal framing of time. She was a seething fire of hatred and malice. And yet a part of her knew that all this was wrong. It was the same dissonance she felt from extreme anger, the dual nature of being a slave to the tides of emotion and knowing that whatever arises from it will only cause harm. Riddling guilt and shame sat within her, and yet she was powerless to change the course of action. All her emotions were somehow justified, no matter how illogical or cruel she knew they were.

She screeched as she reached the clearing in the forest and stared out from atop the hill onto the sleeping farmland below, the faint outline of houses sparse and far between for a while before the lights of the distant town accumulated. In a flickering blink of red, Sothea was at a farmhouse. She was a shadow outside, a movement that made the cat inside hiss, and a chill wind scrape at the wood beams. She was the phantom that set the copper weathervane in the shape of a rooster at the top of the house spinning wildly in all directions.

She was seeking a way in, through an open window, a door slightly ajar, or a wide chimney stack. And she soon found it. The window above the sink had been left slightly open. Through it, she could see a woman rocking gently on her rocking chair, knitting needles clipping expertly together, and a hot cup of tea still wafting the scent of chamomile and honey. Her only company was a cat and a small television that was on at full volume, large letter subtitles covering the faces of the presenters.

As Sothea watched for a moment with red-tinted eyes, the cat came closer. She blinked into the kitchen. Then the cat's innards were smeared across every inch of the wall and floor. A putrid smell was in the air, and the little creature's face was a petrified, wide-mouthed look of horror.

"Tigger?" asked the old woman, rising slowly from her seat. Seeing the carnage, she gasped and reached for the landline phone beside her, but only got so far as pressing the third number before Sothea was upon her. She only had air enough to let out one blood-curdling scream before her throat was torn out and the receiver fell to hang limply from the wall. Sothea fed on the old woman's stomach, tearing up her intestines and shaking them out of the sanctity of her body.

Sothea revelled in the fulfilment of desire, ravishing the juicy organs, feeding, drinking the pints of blood that swelled from the old woman's severed arteries.

A voice came from the other side of the phone. "Which service please?"

Sothea barely heard it as she continued feasting, chewing greedily on the old woman's remains.

"Hello?" another voice said, after a while. "Is that Mrs Dowsett...? Elsie?"

Sothea screeched as her feast came to an end and already, she desired more. She sniffed the air and caught the trails of a scent before disappearing through the open window like liquid smoke.

———

D.S. Hughes frowned as she put down the phone. The dispatcher had played her a recording, hoping for a second opinion on the strange call. The experienced detective felt uneasy and couldn't explain the horrible feeling that was sinking in her gut. She stood up suddenly and grabbed her hat.

A stormy wind almost took it from atop her head, but she caught it before it flew away. She clenched her jaw against the cold, a cold that was much too bitter for summer, and made as quickly as she could for her car. There was a foul stench in the air. Like fertilizer, thick composting manure, and something else. She wrinkled her nose in disgust.

She jumped into her car and slammed the door shut, starting the ignition, and switching on her blue lights. They bounced off the walls as she sped out of the police station car park, fuelled by a gut-churning anxiety.

Elsie's front door was ajar when she arrived, and she almost threw up from the smell as she stepped into the simple, cosy cottage. She had been there a few times as a girl, when she had been friends with Mrs Dowsett's granddaughter Caroline. They had brushed one another's hair, played with dolls, and even ridden horses together. Caroline had moved to London after college, and they had lost touch. But the memories felt like yesterday when she saw her friend's grandmother torn to bloody pieces on the ground.

This pile of loose flesh had once been the woman who made

sponge cake with strawberries and a double serving of cream, bringing it out to her and Caroline on the porch with cups of warm tea. It had been the woman who had occasionally picked her up from school when her parents had been too busy fighting to remember her. And now she was dead.

A second wave of nausea hit her, but Hughes forced it down. She would not contaminate the crime scene and tarnish this sight with her own weakness. She swallowed some bile and stepped around the wide-open carcass, the entrails spilled in a spiral around it. Then she had a moment of recognition.

It was the same pattern as the cattle on Crowley's farm.

She swallowed a hard pang of dread. The consistency of the spiral indicated that whatever was doing this had an intellect. It wasn't a wolf or rabid animal. It had to be a human committing these crimes. A sadistic murderer. In Alderley Edge. The thought struck her hard, and she had to turn away from the sight.

On the kitchen wall, hanging from a spiralling rubber cord, she saw the sage-coloured house phone stained with blood. Mrs Dowsett had died at the phone, that much was obvious. Then she was dragged six feet. There were blood smears on the wooden floor to suggest that. Hughes took another couple of steps forward and had to fight another rush of bile when she saw Tigger. The cat had seemed to be immune to death. Nineteen years this cat had lived, with no sign of illness. And yet there it was, torn to bloody ribbons, its mouth open in a perpetual scream.

Hughes knew she would have to call this in. Knew she would have to report it. But she couldn't bring herself to do it just yet. She could only think about why someone would have done this. Why Mrs Dowsett? She kept to herself, didn't bother anyone. And all of her belongings seemed to be in place. Her handbag was sitting where it always did on the kitchen table, the purse inside untouched. It clearly wasn't a burglary. Though the window was open. She walked slowly over to it, but it offered no reprieve from the stifling atmosphere inside. It was as if the air had been stolen from this place.

Hughes had to get out. She needed to breathe. Needed to clear her mind. She left through the front door and her boot squelched on the earth. It was the right sort of sound but the wrong sort of feeling. She looked down and was disgusted to see thousands of worms, stretching all the way back to where her car was parked.

———

Gabe was lost. The night was pitch black without the light of the moon to guide him, and he struggled through the thick undergrowth of the forest. He had found his way to the stone circle with relative ease, but while trying to trace the ley line back to the rosebush, he had somehow lost his bearings. He did not have any dowsing rods on him and had to make do with a two-pronged stick, but his dowsing abilities were limited at best. He was not like Sothea. Sothea seemed to feel the ley line inside her; she knew without a doubt where it ran beneath the ground.

Gabe was full of doubt. He was filled with urgency to get to the roses, but his mind was wild and foggy. He cursed as a bramble caught the skin of his forearm and yanked him backwards. It took several long moments of impatient detangling to free himself from the thorns. He was sore and bruised from his fights with both his dad and Sothea's. His face ached, his legs ached, his ankles itched, and his arms were covered in scratches. He needed to calm himself. He *needed* to find the roses. Ama's last words replayed constantly in his head. *Burn the roses. Burn them all.* She had died for that message. She had died right in front of him. Gabe was not a stranger to death, but he had never seen it happen right before his eyes in such a brutal manner.

He shook away the image of Sothea's teeth ripping into the old woman's neck. The fierce demonic look in her blackened eyes. Gabe had read plenty about magic in his books – even stories of witches gone dark and restless spirits. But the reality was very different. Is this what Arthur had to deal with in the ancient days? Was this the dark magic he had spoken of?

Gabe had read other myths from Greece, much more detailed and descriptive accounts of the beings that roamed their underworld and all the other places in between. Harpies, gorgons, and many-headed hydras. All of them paled in comparison to the gruesome brutality of what Sothea had become. Or perhaps their true forms had dulled over time like fairy tales, which were once dark and bloody stories, given happy endings by softer generations.

Gabe tripped over an exposed root and fell, his pack of supplies tumbling off to the side. He cursed and slammed his fists into the soil. He didn't pick himself up immediately, and for a while he lay face down in the dirt, breathing heavily in and out. As he took in deep breaths through his nostrils, he felt a hint of clarity in his mind for the first time since he set out from the stone circle.

The fall had cleared his head of the fuzzy confusion. His steady, considered breathing – along with the pain in his body – had forced him to focus, quieting the white noise of his thoughts. He closed his eyes and willed his mind deeper into that silent meditative focus. At first there was nothing, then a crack of light pulsed about ten meters to his right. He recognised it instantly as the energy of the ley line. He set his mind on it, clamped down on it with a vice-like grip. This time he would not lose the path. He would not stray from the road through the dark forest.

He slowly pushed himself to his feet and grabbed his pack, his eyes still closed. A new sense was taking over, a new brain. It was not the overthinking analytical brain that sat whirring thoughts through his skull. It was a brain of instinct, of guided intuition that resided deeper down in his gut. He kept his eyes closed and instead followed his instinct like a compass, and when he aligned with the ley line's energy, he felt a surging swell in his heart. It guided him, rushes of mana connecting with his chest as he stepped directly onto the tightrope of energy. If he lost focus even a little, he knew he would tip over the edge and into the darkness of uncertainty once more.

One step at a time he edged forward. It took all his resolve not to open his eyes a touch. Trust was the key to this sense, and every step he took affirmed that. He had to trust that his instinct would not lead him the wrong way. There was no room to question whether he was making it all up in his head. He needed to listen to his own voice. For the first time, it was his voice that was truly guiding him. Not the voice of his father, or the teachers at school, or the boys who bullied him. The path he followed now was entirely his own – a path drawn in the magical veins of the earth and walked many times before him, an ancient whisper in the folds of time and space.

The line abruptly stopped. And this time Gabe could feel what Sothea must have felt. He could sense something blocking the flow of the ley line's energy, like a tumour or clogged artery. Knowing it was time, he opened his eyes. He almost cried at the sight of the main trunk of the giant rosebush before him, but despite it, he laughed. He had done it. He had found his way to the source. And it had only taken trusting himself to do so.

In his moment of relief, he felt his entire body swell with bright tingles of energy, as if the ley line was rewarding him. He felt a warmth and an embrace around him, and in that moment he knew that the ghost of his mother was with him, congratulating him, telling him how proud she was.

When Gabe finally stopped smiling there were tears in his eyes. He didn't know when they had started or when they had ended. But he could feel the warm wetness of them against his cheeks. His mood shifted in an instant, and he was suddenly set with resolve. He knew what came next. For once in his life, there was no hesitation.

He unscrewed the cap of the petrol can and started drenching the thorns.

Months after Sothea's mother had died, when the tears had finally abated, her father had sat her down to have "the chat" with her. For most girls of a similar age it was an awkward conversation covering the mechanics of making babies and how a girl's period marked her transformation into a woman. It was both a celebration and a rite of passage. Access to a new club. In Sothea's case, that transformation was something else entirely.

She realised that her mother had been trying to tell her since she was a toddler. The stories she had recounted, the appointment of Ama as her nanny, and the hours of instruction she'd received regarding the healing and protective qualities of the herbs, plants, and flowers that surrounded their villa. Flora and fauna that could help limit the number of nights she transformed. Her mother had been training her. But Sothea had never felt more underprepared. Not once had her mother told her what she was. What she would become. Not once had she whispered what resided within her. Thanks to her father, she now finally had a name for what she was.

An arb.

A malevolent figure from Khmer folklore, arbs were cursed to roam the night to feed on any and all living beings. For most children growing up in Cambodia, it was a story their parents threatened them with if they didn't finish their dinner or brush their teeth before bed. A fairy tale. But what was myth to millions was Sothea's harsh new reality.

Unfortunately it was not as her father thought it, or how others wrote about it in books. It was not possession or complete lack of control. Being an arb was a splitting of one's mind, where one part sought only to kill and feed, whilst the other fought to hold back. Each part was equally Sothea, each part was equally her own will. Except one will was louder – the one that promised power and beat the drum of an endless insatiable desire. It was this will that Sothea now followed with a dark pleasure.

Oh, how it felt to kill. How it felt to sink her teeth into soft and supple flesh, to tear organs from tissue, and to savour the life force of another being as their souls were untethered. To feel their spirits cast aside, and to revel in their pain and horror.

Stop! yelled the other part of her, the weaker of the two wills – weaker but no less determined. This was the part of her that had grown a chimney full of white roses from a single dying petal. The part of her that had set her soft lips against Gabe's mouth. The part whose heart was softer than honeysuckle velvet, and loved and cared and danced to the moon when she shone.

This was the truth of her curse. She was both women. She knew that both had power. Except the part she was now was confident and ancient. She knew how to harness her power and magic as if it were the same as breathing air. The arb version of Sothea waited on the fringes of shadow for the entirety of the moon's cycle, waited for that one night when she could come to the surface and lay her will on the world of men and mortal things.

The power of the Sothea who kissed boys and danced and

liked the smell of flowers was a subtler thing. It was grace – not taking, never stealing, and always a little uncertain. She was light, yes. She was creation. But her power flowed in small and gentle ways, like the nuzzle of a baby against its mother. It was nothing compared to the destructive shadow that lay in wait for the final sliver of its prison to shy into nothing.

Sothea saw and felt everything, enjoyed it in the part of her that did it, and hated it in the other. She winced and rejoiced at every tear of muscle and sinew, every crunch of bone. But when she came to the end of her rampage the memories were someone else's, taken back to that dark place where the other half of her resided. She had just devoured her second person. She could have done much more, had the houses not been so few and far between. She was wandering chaos, and her will – while relentless – followed the pattern of a tornado more than the calculating mind of a human.

She didn't travel in straight lines or always take the quickest path. As an arb she was a force of nature, and she did not just take pleasure in killing, but also in making things wrong. Wrong like a bitter cold in the peak of summer. Wrong like the mass of worms that rose to the surface in her wake. Wrong like the whispers in the wind, and the lack of oxygen in the air, and the plants that withered and died because of it.

But Sothea's chaotic path came to a sudden stop when a searing pain started in her abdomen. It was not yet time for her to be done. She knew that by the threads that connected her to the moon's shadow. This pain was something else. Her head snapped up and her mind stretched out tendrils of shadows as her vision writhed towards the source of the pain.

Fire. A great and roaring fire.

It was mesmerising and yet she knew it was her that burned. A part of her, at least. A part she had planted the first time she had transformed in this strange and foreign place. She had spilled her blood over the energy line to draw from it – a dark magic spell that would ensure, once the rosebush grew just a little more, her complete dominion over the other half of her. Permanently. With her blood drawing mana directly from the ley line, the arb's will would at last become dominant, no longer forced back to the periphery with the changing phases of the moon.

She had wished to taste these strange new humans on that first night, but the weak Sothea had redirected her towards the tasteless cattle. It was that boy! That stupid teenager was burning her connection to her power, and already she could hear the voice of the weak Sothea getting louder. Stop! it said. There was a flicker of guilt in her bones. She snarled. The scent of guilt was a rotten thing, and it took away from the true sweetness of blood.

Her own blood curdled with rage. That stupid boy. This Sothea despised them all. Especially despised the one who kept her trapped. The one who called himself her father. The one the weaker version of Sothea loved so dearly.

Her rage built into fury, and she unleashed a terrible screech like the grinding of sharp metal. Her force took over, and the tendrils of shadow were soon taking her back to the forest she had come from. She tore at the earth with phantom talons, raising the worms and leaving deep gashes in the earth. She would savour killing that boy, savour in the grief that the other Sothea would feel as she did it.

Gabe had to hold a hand up to protect his face from the flames that burst forth when he threw the whisky bottles. He had filled them with petrol and stuffed them with rags, lighting them they erupted when they hit the mass of thorns. It singed the hair on his arms and bellowed thick clouds of black smoke. Almost as soon as the fire had started, he heard a deafening screech tear across the land, making the very marrow in his bones quake. His heartbeat quickened and there was a sudden howl of wind. It bashed through the trees and hit him straight in the stomach, sending him hurtling backwards.

He got up immediately, wincing as he did so. This was it. Sothea was coming. It terrified him to his core, but he did not run. Arthur did not become King by running from his dragons.

Gabe's suspicions had been confirmed. Somehow Sothea and these roses were connected. It was not a big leap to make considering what he had found growing in the chimney back in her room. Those had been white and these were red, but he had made the connection the second he saw them. He didn't know how quickly that other Sothea could travel, but at the rate the roses were burning he hoped that enough damage would have been done by the time she arrived. They were directly on the ley line, a parasite soaking up its power.

If Sothea was harnessing that power, then it was possible that destroying it could weaken her. Not only that, but it was the last blockage in the ley line. If he could remove it, the entrance to King Arthur's resting place might open.

Might. It was a massive leap of faith.

Gabe assumed the phantom wind that sent him flying would start fanning the flames to even greater heights. But the opposite seemed to happen. The wind began to choke the flames, suffocating them of oxygen and making them waver. No. Gabe poured more petrol onto the fire and there was a giant burst of flame for an instant before it began to die down again.

"Damn it!"

Gabe ran and tore off a branch of ferns by the trickle of a stream and began to fan the flames himself to no avail. How was he meant to combat the power streaming from a magical being? He was just a human. He didn't have any magical powers.

There was another screech and this time it was much closer. The wind started to pick up even more and the air was now thinning to the point where he was having trouble breathing again. He looked at the dying flames with a helpless pit growing in his stomach. They were going to fizzle out. The fire had burned through roughly half of the roses' bulk, which was a lot considering how dense they were, but it was not enough. Not nearly enough. He snatched a glance up at the sky. It was useless though; he couldn't tell if daylight was an hour away or five. He certainly couldn't wait around here, defenceless, with the flames subsiding and a terrifying predator on the loose.

So, Gabe turned and ran.

CHAPTER SEVENTEEN

B*efore Arthur was King, he was just a boy. He grew up in the dirt and grime, born the son of a whore. At least that was what the townspeople called her, as well as the other street urchins who chased him through the streets throwing small rocks and pebbles at the back of his head. Arthur lived in the shadow of the castle and in all the moments he could snatch, he would look up at the stone towers and intricately carved architecture.*

He wore a perpetual frown on his face that made him look rather angry, but any that knew him – which was truly a small sum – would say that it was simply the face he made when he was concentrating.

His mother was not a whore. In fact, she was worse.

Arthur would sneak out of bed in the middle of the night to watch as she cast spells with her coven sisters. They chanted in a strange tongue and drew the blood of animals over complex symbols cast onto the floor in ash and black salt. Arthur watched as the sky would change through the window, and thunder would rumble over the town.

They always cast their spells in darkness, and as if the new moon night wasn't dark enough, they veiled their eyes with heavy cloth whilst the rest of their bodies were exposed and naked. It was something Arthur knew he was not supposed to witness, and yet he could not help himself as his mother and her coven sisters plucked at the very threads of fate, tying certain possibilities off for good, and widening the stream of some others.

After they were done, they would laugh and roll on the floor, breaking the spell in wild cackles and making love until the sun rose. One night his mother caught him watching and she broke away from her sisters to anoint him with a press of blood to his forehead.

"A king, Arthur. A king one day you will be," she whispered in his ear, before returning to the tangle of limbs below.

The blood on his forehead burned like wildfire, and Arthur did all he could not to cry out. There were none he could go to, none except for the young baker's daughter – his friend and, he hoped, perhaps one day, much more. She took Arthur to the river to help wash the blood from him and for a moment, with her cool hands against his head, he felt a gentle reprieve.

Enide smiled as she looked into Arthur's eyes. "When you become King, will you take me with you?" Her gaze flickered towards the castle. "I want to smell the honeysuckle in the castle grounds."

Arthur did not know why she said it, but she had. And instead of objecting to the notion, he frowned and nodded. Arthur didn't speak much. Perhaps he spent too much time in his own head. But that night as they lay together, he couldn't shake a foreboding feeling of grief.

Sure enough, the next morning when he woke, Enide was not there by his side. He snuck to the bakery and peered through the window, but she was not there either. At the sound of armour clanging, Arthur hid behind a barrel, peering out with one cautious eye. It was then that he saw her, chained and tied to four other young women, being led from the town by a foreign lord's knight.

She met his eyes with no sadness or fear. She smiled at him with the weight of her last dream being left behind. Arthur wished he had done something. Wished that he had tried, at least. But all he did was sit and hide, frozen, as she was thrown in the back of a cart and trailed off. Her eyes never left his. Even years later, when Arthur had become something more, Enide's eyes were still watching him, waiting for him to fulfil his promise and take her to the castle.

Promises were a binding thing once upon a time, back before language became a lie and promises could be thrown out left, right, and centre with no intention of fulfilling them. They were a spell in themselves, not to be broken lightly. They set forces in motion, held weight in the world like a stone dropped onto stretched-out fabric. Promises were not given lightly, and one way or another they would be forced to come true, lest death be the scissors that snipped the thread of the contract.

Knights did not die at the hand of their king or queen for betraying their oaths. That was a later custom. Instead, the words would thread themselves into a garrotte, and an oath-breaker would run from their broken promise until it caught up with them and slit their throat, like an assassin in the night.

Arthur had not known this then. But even if he had, he still would have made the vow. Even with the knowledge that his promise would haunt his every step, whispering in his ear until the contract ended.

CHAPTER EIGHTEEN

It was such an abhorrent act that word of murder usually spread very quickly. But something about tonight was different. There were no locals in the street in their pyjamas, no lights being switched on in bedrooms as news spread from neighbour to neighbour. Not yet anyway. And when D.S. Hughes radioed the police station for the fifth time, the only response she got was the crackle of static.

She was about to press the call button again when she spotted something in the periphery of her vision. Fog crept along the ground towards her. A wind blew, but the chimes outside Elsie's house were deathly still. The door that she had unintentionally left open rocked on its hinges and the swinging chair on the porch nudged silently back and forth, but the chimes did not move.

Frost crept across the dashboard and windshield of her car, making a slow cracking sound. Hughes swallowed a lump in her throat, but the action did nothing to dislodge the discomfort she felt there. It remained, and when she coughed, a black glob of something ejected from her mouth and oozed in her hand. Then she heard it. The screech.

All at once the windows of her car shattered, and sharp blades of glass flew in an infinitude of directions. Instinctively she scrunched her eyes shut and raised her arms to cover her face, and it was lucky too, because she felt the hot cut of razor-sharp glass slicing into her forearms. There was a howl and a moan, and even though her eyes were closed Hughes saw something – a flash of a monstrous creature, quick and terrifying like it had invaded her very mind.

She forced her eyes open, but the creature was still there. It moved like a phantom, floating effortlessly and with terrifying speed across the surface of the mist. The colour drained from her face, and she ducked low. It was only then that she noticed how much she was bleeding. Her arms, chest, and lap were pockmarked with small lacerations.

The creature was almost upon her. It was gruesome, bodiless with entrails hanging from the fibres that clung to a blood-coated spine. Its hair floated as well, matted in part by blood, and seeming to search of its own accord, as if it was made up of shadowy snakes sniffing out a scent.

The creature suddenly stopped, turning away from her, its eyes fixed on a single point and its focus unwavering. Hughes followed its gaze and saw smoke billowing high above the forest. A fire. Her eyes darted back and forth between the creature and the smoke. Something about it was drawing its attention. And then a thought suddenly occurred to her, and she couldn't see how she hadn't come up with it before.

This was what had killed Elsie Dowsett. This was what had slaughtered Crowley's cattle.

A whole library of the Alderley Edge myths suddenly rushed to her mind. Myths of mist and other worlds. Myths of witches and soothsayers. Myths of sleeping kings and fae creatures. Almost every child who'd grown up in and around Cheshire had heard these stories. Of course, Hughes had never taken them for anything other than that. Just something to recount to tourists to keep the tea shops and pubs in business. But here in front of her was a direct contradiction of that belief. Her mind went to Mark's son, Gabe, who constantly went on about the myths to anyone that would listen and clung to his books like they were treasure and fact.

The pieces of a puzzle started to fit together. Gabe's obsession with the stories, his draw to the Bailey girl, and now this impossible creature that was heading straight for a fire in the woods in the direction of Bailey Manor. Hughes may have been born and bred in a small town, but that didn't take away from the fact that she had the mind of a detective. And the facts were all pointing her to an unlikely but evidently real scenario.

Or perhaps she was simply in shock and hallucinating a bodiless monster with the head of a girl floating in the night, because her mind wanted to give her something more frightening to ponder than her childhood best friend's grandmother slaughtered so brutally.

Whatever it was, she knew she could not just sit back and wait in her car until it decided to attack her. And since the radio appeared to be down, and her phone had no signal, she didn't have much of a choice. She pulled the first aid kit from the glove compartment and quickly set to bandaging the cuts on her arms. Then she went to her boot, lifted the false bed where a spare tyre should have been stored, and pulled out another box.

Inside was a licensed hunting gun. Officers in Alderley Edge were not issued firearms – the nearest Armed Response Unit was in Stockport – but Hughes carried this gun with her anyway. It was something she could not explain, nor had she ever told anyone about it. Absently she loaded the rounds into the magazine and turned off the safety. She cocked the weapon and then, like a lion tracking its prey, she padded quietly into the mist, following the monster into the dark.

Gabe stumbled as he ran through the forest. He could feel shadowy fingers reaching towards his neck, but every time he turned his head there was nothing there. The wind and world were playing tricks on him, whispering false things into his ears, and brushing phantom limbs across his nervous system.

He ran towards the only sacred thing he knew. He ran to the Wizard's Well and the stone circle nearby it. There was a howl, and this time he knew that it was no trick of his mind. It reverberated through the air around him. God, Sothea could move fast. He cursed to himself. It had barely been any time at all and already she had closed the distance at a speed that shouldn't have been possible.

Gabe found his way back to the spring of water, which now seemed to be more of a surge compared with its previous trickle. The water called to him like life itself, and he realised his mouth was like sandpaper. He didn't know how long it would be exactly, but he knew there wasn't much time before Sothea found him. Whatever she was now had clearly not liked that he had tried to burn the roses.

He had a target painted on his back, and this might be the last drink he ever took. He plunged his entire face into the surge of water pouring from the crack in the rock. The cold shock of it hitting his nervous system gave him a crystalline clarity, waking up his dulled and frayed senses. He drank thirstily from it.

Suddenly his vision was filled with colour. Time unravelled and Gabe was no longer drinking water but breathing the cool air of a world that was not his own. He was in a familiar landscape; he recognised the rolling hills of East Cheshire. They were almost unchanged in their appearance, but everything else was different. There were no houses, no electricity pylons, no roads. The world had a different hue. There was a large body of water in the basin where the town of Alderley Edge should have been. A giant lake. Birds called to each other in ways that he had never heard before, and the sky was filled with the sparkles that he had only ever seen come from the ley line and the stone circle. Mana was potent in the air, like every breath was an act of magic. And by the lake was a man.

His dirty-blond hair was parted down the middle and hung to his shoulders. He stood staring out over the water with a distant gaze, his eyes bright pools of emerald. On the grass by his feet was a sword in its sheath. Even after only a second's glance, Gabe knew the sword to be Excalibur.

"Arthur?" he asked, but the man did not reply.

Instead, the man knelt and touched the water with his palm. It rippled slightly and where there was nothing before, a chain appeared in his hand. One that trailed deeper into the lake. He turned and met Gabe's eyes. Or at least that was what Gabe thought until a young woman walked through him, as though he were a wraith. She wore cloth made of leaves that clung to her body without string or fastenings. She seemed to glide across the floor, the soles of her feet barely touching the ground, and on her back were small gossamer wings.

"You will only find ghosts at the end of that chain," she told Arthur. Her voice tinkled like chimes and the patter of butterflies, and there was a deep sadness in her song.

"I made a promise," Arthur replied.

His voice was not what Gabe had expected at all. Gabe had always pictured a deep sounding gruff, like a hero in the movies. Arthur's voice was... Well, normal. Soft, even. They spoke in a language that must have been Old English, but somehow Gabe understood it all.

She offered him her hand. "Not all promises have to be kept. You do not have to spend your life atoning."

He shook his head. "I cannot go with you. My duty is to my people. I made a vow, which I intend to see through till its end."

"And how many will die because of your promises?" the fae asked.

That seemed to bother Arthur, because he cast his eyes away. "I would not expect your people to understand the meaning of death, nor the sacrifice we make to ensure the ideals of our hearts are upheld. There is a sickness in the land of men, and I do not intend to abandon them."

Her wings flared. Clearly, it was not the response the fae had wanted to hear.

"Then the fae will help you no longer," she said. "Your *kin* have harmed the natural way. It is no longer possible for men and fae to live with one another."

Arthur nodded, his jaw clenched. "What will you do?"

"We draw a veil. It is so, even as we speak." Her words were already fading into the wind. "Farewell, King of Men."

With that she was gone, and Gabe was suddenly spluttering by the spring again. He pulled away from the water and forced a breath in. The air here was thick and wrong compared to the light beauty it once was. What had just happened? What had he seen? And why? He tried to piece the memories together. Something about promises, about sickness and a veil.

His body surged with adrenaline when he felt the wind change direction. And suddenly, there she was. In the small clearing ahead of the stone spring, Sothea hovered in place, motionless, her unblinking reptilian eyes staring straight into Gabe's skull.

"Sothea," he said, standing.

Surprisingly he felt no fear as he stared at the shadow of her form. What he saw was a mask, a strange façade. But what he felt beneath was the true Sothea. He could feel her gentle touch against his skin, feel the bloom of a white rose, sweet and velvet. Gabe had made a promise to her. He had promised that they would leave this world together. And he didn't make promises lightly. Whatever happened, he would follow the thread of this path until its end.

He could feel the other possibilities starting to close in. This was the only one left. He stepped forward and almost immediately felt the suffocating choke of her aura. Saw how the plants withered around her, how a sea of worms surfaced from the earth in her shadow and how the air twisted and screamed.

Sothea.

Gabe said her name, but the sound only echoed in his head and not the air. A wild maelstrom of emotions battered his mind. He didn't recoil. So, this was how it felt to be her. It was so much worse than he could have ever imagined, so much worse than anything he had ever felt within him before.

Sothea. He said it only in his head this time, knowing she could hear it anyway. *You don't have to hide this side of yourself from me. We can leave this world behind. We can go where no one will hurt you for what you are.*

He was met with two conflicting waves of emotion. One was brutal and thought his words were childish and petty, whilst the other warmed and rejoiced in them.

"You are right," Sothea said. The one he knew. "Let's go. You and me together."

Gabe couldn't hold back the relief that filled him. He stepped forward.

"No! Gabe, stop!"

Both Sothea and Gabe's heads snapped in the direction of the voice. It was her father. He was at least ten feet outside of Sothea's dark aura, holding something in his hands.

"That isn't Sothea talking!" he shouted again. "She is trying to trick you!"

Sothea screeched in fury, and immediately Gabe realised that her dad had been right. Some sort of spell had been cast over him, like a lure or a glamour. Now that he played it back, the sweet voice was tinged with darker undertones. It had used Sothea's voice to trick him. And he had fallen for it.

Suddenly Sothea's razor teeth flashed, and she was skimming over the earth towards her dad at an incredible pace, shadows tearing the fabric of the space around her. But he seemed to be ready for her. He clutched something in his hands, keeping them remarkably still as the shadow sped towards him. At the very last moment, just before Sothea's bared teeth tore into the exposed flesh of his neck, a metal net hurtled through the air, catching Sothea unawares.

She screeched as solid weights on the end wrapped the latticed prison around her. She went crashing to the ground, skidding along it, and her father stepped out of the way like a matador – just in time to avoid the bite to his neck, but not quickly enough to prevent her razor-sharp teeth from raking down his forearm, tearing out large chunks of flesh and skin.

Sothea writhed and squirmed, and Gabe couldn't help but run towards her. As he got close, he saw that the net her father used had been fashioned from steel wire. He remembered the steel-plated door to the containment room next to the palm house, and the iron shackles around Sothea's wrists and ankles. He remembered the old myths about how the fae and creatures from other planes hated iron. His knowledge of chemistry was basic to say the least, but he had paid attention enough to remember that steel was a type of iron alloy. And it was clearly working. He watched as Sothea screeched and struggled, the stifling feeling in the air diminishing. Once again, myth was proving to be reality.

"Quick," her father said. "Hold this while I attach the other end to the net." He spoke with a calculated calm, despite the pain from his mutilated arm, and thrust the metal net into Gabe's hand.

"But..." Gabe started, but Sothea's dad was already scrambling in his bag for something else.

Sothea was trying to gnaw her way out of her metal prison. Her teeth had already shredded some of the steel wire, but she recoiled every time she bit down onto it.

"Gabe, please," Sothea pleaded in that voice that was hers and not, all at once. "Save me! It hurts!"

"Don't listen to her," her dad said, avoiding a snapping bite as he tried to drive a wedge into the earth with a hammer to keep the net tight around his daughter.

It was harder than it looked. She was writhing and flailing, making it almost impossible for him to hit the wedge each time. The smell of cooking flesh filled the air as the steel wire dug into Sothea's organs.

"Please, Gabe. You promised me. You promised!"

Her voice rang in his head, guilt gnawing at him. Then it happened. Suddenly, Sothea lifted from the ground, net and all, dislodging the partially buried wedge. She threw herself at her father, mustering what little power she had left. It seemed to happen in slow motion. Gabe saw every moment – her dad raising his hands in self-defence, Sothea's jaw clamping down on his forearm, biting deep and twisting as if she was trying to tear it off.

Then there was a deafening bang.

Sothea screeched and let go of her dad's arm, rolling away like an animal on fire. Another bang rang out, and Gabe turned in the direction of it to see D.S. Hughes walk out of the mist, staring down the sights of her rifle.

"No!" Gabe shouted.

But it was too late.

Hughes fired again. And again. And again.

Gabe's eardrums were ringing. Sothea was motionless now. Her dad was clambering to his feet, the tattered remains of his left arm hanging limply by his side and the other waving at Hughes as he screamed at her to stop. He put himself between the officer and his daughter.

Everything went silent except for the high-pitched ringing in Gabe's ears. His focus was torn between the three of them. Hughes was already loading her gun again. Sothea's dad was now running towards her. And Sothea...

She lay coughing blood into the dirt, the net still digging into her, as the first glimmer of light began to rise over the horizon. Her face was the face he had always known. Her fang-like teeth were gone, and the flesh and skin of a single shoulder and arm had grown back. Her eyes were no longer black. And she reached for him.

Gabe didn't think about the gun or about her father. He ran for her, thinking only of the promise he had made. He removed the tangle of the net and picked Sothea up in his arms. Her entrails were scalding hot against his skin. He could feel them burning him, but he did not care. The smell of smoke and gunpowder stung his nostrils.

He prayed as he ran up the hill towards the well. He prayed that he had burned enough of the roses. He prayed that Mr Bailey and D.S. Hughes would not catch up with him. He prayed that Mr Bailey would understand, and forgive him.

And when he risked a glance backward, he saw that his prayers had been answered in part. Sothea's father and the officer still stood at the bottom of the hill, staring after him. Mr Bailey seemed to be struggling to decide whether to chase Gabe or stop D.S. Hughes from trying to shoot them, but when she raised her gun again, the decision was made.

He charged her, taking her entirely by surprise, and tackled her to the ground. Gabe ran.

The gun fired one last time.

CHAPTER NINETEEN

Arthur carried the bones of Enide to the castle. His beard was grey, and it had been almost sixty years since he had made his promise to her. The bones were still small. They had never gotten the chance to grow. She had lived as a child and died as one – a spent concubine disposed of by a foreign lord when she could entertain him no more. Arthur had waged bloody war on the principality and been victorious. But it brought no joy or solace. Each step was a reminder of all of his failures. His kingdom revered him, but Arthur knew that he was not worthy of their praise. Not worthy of the title "King". He had made so many mistakes, so many bad choices, all in a quest to bring honour back to the world.

He saw now that the world was beyond saving. The great turning of the cosmic calendar had plunged the minds of men into obfuscation. They were slaves to greed and corruption and there was nothing Arthur could do to change that. He was just a man, after all. A man with a mortal life that would run out.

There was a patch of honeysuckle growing on the castle grounds and Arthur dug a grave amidst the blooming petals. He lay Enide's bones out on the blanket he had slept with for most of his childhood. There were no words to say. He shovelled the earth atop the bones and could feel her ghost finally coming to rest.

The promise had been kept. Arthur had brought her to the castle. Of course, she was dead now, and he only wished he could have fulfilled his promise sooner.

"A king." His mother's words rang in his head. "A king one day you will be." It was not a blessing, and it was not a curse, even though Arthur had believed in the latter for most of his life. It was prophecy.

Then it was Enide's voice that he heard. "When you become King, will you take me with you? I want to smell the honeysuckle in the castle grounds."

He knew now that this was always how fate had meant it. A cruel and unjust thing. Enide, while she had not known it then, was speaking from the future. Or perhaps she had known. It did not change the feelings in Arthur's heart to know that the promise he made had been with a ghost.

He stood over the grave for countless days, as the world he tried to rebuild already began to crumble. No matter how many weeds he picked, they always grew back. Would there ever be a day when men would find their honour again? Would there ever be a time where the world was right and just?

The fae had been right to hide themselves. To split the worlds that once were one. The great ocean of magic that had touched every speck of air was slowly seeping away. He could feel it in the withering of his bones and the crack of his lips. Magic was dying, and he had been a fool to think he could change that.

Even now, many of the great bodies of water had been reduced to trickling streams. There had been too much blood shed on sacred land. The world would feel the loss of it for countless generations to come. But maybe someday there would come a man, maybe someday *there would come a time when the world no longer slept in darkness and the dream that he fought to uphold would come dancing back. Maybe.*

It was as good a hope as any. So, with the last whispers of magic in the air, Arthur made his final promise. He ordered that a chamber be carved in the rock, and that the last men of honest word rally by his side. He vowed that for eternity he would slumber and endure. Endure the madness of the world above. Endure, so that one day, if such a time came where the minds of men were willing to listen, if enough fought for the sanctity of the heart, then he would rise from his slumber and fight once more.

He would fight for the dream he had lost, that men could return to what they once were. That, even despite the evil that lay before them, they could turn their gaze back to their hearts and find light amidst the darkness of their own ignorance.

CHAPTER TWENTY

James's ears rang as his vision swirled in and out of consciousness. He remembered seeing Gabe running off with his daughter, but Hughes had been in the heat of the hunt. She would not stop until Sothea was dead. She did not know. She did not know that the monster she hunted was the only thing that mattered in his life. She had arrived to see it attacking him, had thought she was protecting him.

Tears came to his eyes. In that moment, the words of his wife had echoed in his head, and he had felt the faint strands of her ghost. *At one moment or another you will have done enough.* And so he had bitten down hard on his instinct to go after his only daughter and turned back towards Hughes. He had to let Sothea go. He had to let his daughter go.

His hand went to his stomach and found that it was covered in blood. But there was no wound there, no pain. His eyes widened as he saw the detective lying motionless on the ground beside him. There was a gun next to her.

Oh God.

He remembered the feel of metal against his hand, and the sound of the trigger being pulled. A wave of nausea hit him, and he forced himself to move closer. She was face down in the earth. The sun was low in the sky and the mist that had veiled everything was no longer present. James clenched his jaw and, using his one good hand, tipped Hughes's body over. He almost choked on the bile that rose in his throat.

Her eyes stared wide and open into nothingness. Her face was pale, drained of all colour, and there was a bloody mess in the centre of her body, right below her sternum. In the chaos of redirecting her shot, he had shifted the gun so that it pointed at her. He knew he hadn't pulled the trigger; she must have done it out of instinct. But although she had died by her own hand, he had been the one to point the gun in her direction.

He cursed. Soon the town would wake up and the events of last night would catch up to him. Not just to him, but to Sothea as well. His eyes darted suddenly in the direction he had last seen her. Gabe running up the hill with her on his shoulder. Where had they gone?

There were too many questions. His head throbbed and his arm... God, his arm hurt like hell. He winced as he pulled his jacket off and ripped off the sleeve from his shirt. Sothea's attack had been ferocious and chaotic, and she had managed to savage him with her teeth, even if she hadn't been able to bite his throat. There was a good chunk of flesh missing, starting from his wrist and ending about halfway up his forearm. It was barely recognisable as an arm now.

James used the sleeve he had ripped off as a bandage, tying it around the wound to stop the blood still seeping from it. He whimpered from the pain, his eyes searching frantically again through the woods for any sign of Sothea and Gabe.

He let out a string of curses. They would have cleared the area a long time ago. But Sothea had been shot. He did not know the ins and outs of Sothea's curse, did not know if her wounds would have healed in time. He scrabbled over to the gun. His hands shook with panic as he ejected the magazine and took out a bullet. Relief washed over him when he confirmed that the bullets were not made of iron or silver, just lead alloy and a copper-plated casing.

He knew how resistant Sothea's arb form was. It was a dark and powerful force that animated her. He had seen her do incredible things. Terrible, but incredible nonetheless. James knew he had no right, but he prayed to all the gods, prayed to the very air itself, that she was okay. His attention wavered as the act of sitting up suddenly became dizzying. He had lost a lot of blood.

James tossed the gun and magazine to the ground. Gritting his teeth together, he forced himself to stand. It was an act that almost sent him stumbling right back into Hughes's lifeless body. As he looked at her again, the moment replayed itself in his mind.

It should have been him. He had been ready to die. He had thrown himself at her, knowing full well that it might have been his last act in the mortal world. But fate seemed to have spared him. It was cruel. That split-second decision had filled him with peace. He had seen Chantrea in the space behind Hughes. His charge had been a death march, and his heart had been more than ready to finally leave the world behind.

But fate had taken the police officer instead. Why?

Sothea.

It was the only explanation for why he was still here. Sothea still needed him.

The day was dawning now. Soon families would rise, and word of Sothea's frenzy would spread quickly. James didn't know what she had done before her rampage had ceased. But James knew small towns – he had grown up in Alderley Edge after all, before moving to university and eventually abroad – and he knew that when all else failed, when a certain line was crossed, the citizens would take matters into their own hands.

No doubt the police would be investigating Hughes's disappearance already.

***

Gabe watched in both horror and fascination as Sothea's body grew from nothing. It first formed bone, then wrapped sinew and tissue around it, weaving fascia and muscles over veins. She was convulsing, twitching, and seizing up, her eyes flickering back and forth between void black and the circle of her iris. The bullets that had embedded in her organs were sent hurtling out of her body. The first one nearly hit him as it did so.

Blood magic wove her form into physicality, her torso growing full and bare, before the length of her legs followed. He knew he should look away from her naked form, but the miracle he saw in front of him glued his gaze to the spot. Sunlight seeped through the cracks in the trees, making her newly formed skin glow like the light of the moon reflected on the surface of a shimmering lake.

The blood that pooled all around her, that twisted like strands of DNA around her body, now began to float up into the air. Droplets and globs all converged into a large swelling orb. Her lungs suddenly seemed to kick in and she filled her body with a sharp inhale. In that single breath, the blood was all drawn into her body through her mouth. Her back arched, then all at once she fell still and silent.

Gabe sat there in dumb awe, just staring at Sothea's perfect body suddenly manifest and pure, where once was a gruesome vision. Then, almost as if realising that he was ogling, he shot to his feet, running for the cave and pulling out the blanket he had owned since he was a child.

He helped her to sit up, wrapping her in the blanket to cover her body. He hugged her close to him, rubbing his hands up and down her back in an attempt to bring her some warmth. Her eyelids fluttered. Gabe suddenly knew what to do, and he picked her up in his arms.

She weighed nothing, as if her bones were hollow like a bird's and her flesh was made of air itself. He slowly carried her towards the trickle of spring water that ran from the rocks, sitting her down in front of it like he had done the other night and laying her head by the stream. In the light of a new morning, he baptised her in the sacred spring.

S othea stood in the echo chamber of her own mind. She stared into a mirror at the other version of herself. The arb stared back at her with deep sunken eyes, no longer fuelled by the power of the new moon. She looked weak and vulnerable, as she always did after her release.

Sothea, the version of herself that was human, stared at her horrible reflection with tears in her eyes. She could feel the ragged breath of her arb, weakened by the transition into the new phase of the moon. She was an ancient and weathered soul, splintered and fragmented in so many ways, a curse to so many before her.

"Why?" Sothea asked, letting her tears stream freely down her cheeks.

Her arb reflection looked back at her with ancient black eyes.

"Why does the sun set or rise? Why do stars live and then die? Why is there up and down? We are two poles that cannot separate." The arb spoke in Khmer, in English, and in other languages that Sothea did not recognise but understood, all at once. "I am only your opposition. There is no why."

Sothea frowned at the version of herself that she hated so much. The monster that had killed her mother and so many others. The gruesome shadow that lived inside of her. But as she stared at her now, weak and frail, she could not help but feel pity.

"You speak of polarity," Sothea said, "and yet you fail to mention balance."

At first, the arb showed no acknowledgement that she had heard Sothea's words. She just hovered, her head and organs drooping like a withering plant exposed to too much sun. Sothea was surprised when the arb finally replied.

"There is no balance when you try to contain your shadow, little princess." Her voice slithered through the mirror and into Sothea's skin, accompanied by the phantom toll of funeral bells. "You fear the other end of the scale and weigh the feather too heavy at its tip. If the pendulum is swung, so too must it drop."

Sothea had never spoken with her arb for so long. She did not know what courage possessed her now that had not been there before. Somewhere in the distance she could hear the trickle of water. Somewhere in another world she could hear the hum of a gentle voice, feel the stroke of fingers on her skin.

Her frown deepened. "You kill for sport. I know your thoughts." Tears fell down her cheeks despite herself. "You killed Mama..." Her voice wavered. "And Ama."

Anger raged inside her now.

"You mistake yourself again," the arb said. "We are different sides of the same coin. I am your unspoken desires."

"You lie!" Sothea yelled. "I loved my mama! I loved Ama! I would never hurt them."

"It is not what you want, nor who fell at your hand. It is what you deny, and who happened to stand in the way of your fight. We are a force, little princess. As unruly and wild as the winds of time. As vicious and defensive as the serpent's bite. As fierce and destructive as the tornado's blight. We could work together, but you wish to keep us separate. It is your fault that we strike in blindness, as enemies rather than allies."

Sothea had enough of the arb's venomous words. She screamed and the mirror inside herself shattered. Her eyes shot open, and her body was plunged into frigid cold. She coughed and spluttered, crying, choking on her tears. Then there were arms around her. Invisible arms. Soft hands against her back, and light – blinding light – pouring through an endless sky.

Someone was saying her name.

"Sothea."

The voice came again, and she followed it to find herself staring into Gabe's ocean-blue eyes.

Elsie Dowsett's body had been found and word had spread about how she'd been killed. The people of Alderley Edge were in open revolt outside the police station, despite the officers' best attempts at quelling the mob.

"We assure you, we are using every means at our disposal to find the culprit responsible!" P.C. Taylor shouted, barely able to make himself heard above the uproar.

He was only twenty-six and new to the Alderley Edge police force, but somehow he was the second highest-ranking officer here after the desk sergeant, who couldn't leave the custody suite.

"Where's D.S. Hughes?" someone from the crowd shouted.

Taylor swallowed nervously. They had found her car outside Elsie Dowsett's cottage, windows shattered, doors unlocked, and the boot left open. There had been blood on the steering wheel and front seat, and no sign of the detective.

"D.S. Hughes is making inquiries," he managed to reply.

"Or she's dead too!" someone else shouted out.

Another uproar broke out, and Taylor tried shouting over it. "Please! We need your cooperation if we have any chance of catching the man or woman who did this!"

He looked out hopelessly at the crowd, and noticed the shape of it moving around someone who was pushing forward. When the man emerged, he shot a dangerous glare at Taylor before turning to face the crowd, raising his hands, and waiting patiently for the mob to simmer down.

Taylor watched in surprise as they all stopped and hushed one another, waiting for the man to speak. Of course, he knew who this man was too. Mark Francis. Gabe's father. His eyes were haunted pools of rage with deep shadows underneath. He'd been the one to find the body that morning when he'd arrived first thing to fix Elsie's kitchen window.

Mark's voice cracked when he spoke. "Elsie Dowsett was not just murdered last night... She was violated."

People started exchanging whispers.

"She was desecrated!" he continued. "She was mutilated and her body destroyed."

His thick accent twisted in the air, capturing the attention of everyone present, including P.C. Taylor himself.

"Whatever did this," he continued, "was not just a killer. Whatever did this took sick pleasure in tearing a defenceless old woman apart. This was evil. A demon or the spawn of the Devil himself."

Shocked murmurs rippled through the crowd.

"The police are looking for a murderer. At one point they suspected it was my lad, Gabe. My own flesh and blood!" He pointed straight at Taylor without turning to look at him. "But they will find no such man. What we should be looking for is a monster! We all know the tales of Alderley Edge! I used to laugh at Gabe when he went off on one, talking about faeries and unicorns and such like. But we all know the stories of this place. An evil has been awakened and set loose on our town. Is it truly a coincidence that a load of Crowley's cattle were slaughtered just days after Bailey returned to his manor? Is it not common knowledge that Bailey's family is tainted with the occult and pagan worship?"

People started frowning and looking at one another with puzzled expressions. In response, Mark pulled a photocopy of a newspaper clipping from his jacket pocket and held it in the air. Taylor squinted at it. There was a picture of the Bailey family, dating back to October 31st, 1923. It had been taken by a journalist, and the picture depicted the Bailey family standing in a circle wearing dark cloaks, hands joined around a fire. It was odd, he'd give him that, but really it proved nothing except that the Baileys celebrated Halloween. Mark, however, seemed to be way too far down the rabbit hole to require irreputable proof.

"He returned, and the killings started again. After a hundred years! This is no coincidence!"

Taylor shook his head. "Alright, Mark. That's enough now..."

"No! You refuse to face the facts!" Mark turned on him. "Where is Bailey now? When the entire town is here, he continues to hide away! Elsie Dowsett and Crowley's herd of cattle were both within a mile of Bailey Manor!"

This seemed to get people's attention again.

"Have the police even questioned him?" Mark said. "Why haven't you got him locked up? It was only yesterday you were knocking down my door accusing my son of assault and trespass. Like Bailey was the victim in all of this. People are dead, and you're harassing innocent teenagers when you should be arresting a murderer."

Taylor was acutely aware now that the crowd seemed to see Mark's point, and people were beginning to murmur their agreement. He didn't make eye contact when he responded, trying to calm them all down again. "Look, I can assure you we are investigating every person of interest—"

Mark scoffed. "Listen to me now!" He faced the other people in the crowd. "Will you stand around and wait for the incompetence of the police? It could be you next! It could be your children! The police would have you believe that they have everything under control, but I call bullshit!" He spat the final words. "They are not in control. I say we take matters into our own hands. I say we march up to Bailey Manor and demand answers. If they won't do it, we should!"

"Damn right!" someone in the crowd shouted. "If he's innocent, let him prove it."

Taylor was shaking his head when the crowd roared in agreement. Surely the people of Alderley Edge were not buying this? He had been warned about small-town mentality when he left Manchester, but this was madness. The occult? Pagan worshippers? Monsters? All of it sounded like something from another age.

"We'll police our own streets!" Mark shouted, then he pointed with a shaking hand to the road. The road that led to Bailey Manor.

Taylor protested, but the crowd was already moving. He tried to fight the flow, but people were suddenly moving all around him and eventually he tripped and fell to the floor. In the rush, he caught a few kicks as boots and shoes stomped past all around him. He held his arms over his face to protect himself from being trampled.

A hand grabbed him by the collar and pulled him out of the stampede. He turned to face the person who had helped him and was shocked to see Mark's red face staring back at him again. They held each other's gaze for a moment before Mark let go of his shirt.

"We both know there's only one reason D.S. Hughes isn't here," Mark said in a low voice. "She's dead. You know it. And I know it."

Taylor shook his head.

Mark raised his eyebrows. "Am I mistaken?"

He didn't reply. Couldn't bring himself to say "yes". Because that's what he thought too. That's what everyone thought.

"Call for some back-up and meet us at the manor," Mark told him. "I hope to God that I'm wrong."

With that he disappeared into the current of the crowd, leaving P.C. Taylor beaten and bruised with dread sinking into the pit of his stomach.

***

"Where are we?" Sothea asked.

But Gabe didn't need to answer, as she soon heard the familiar trickle of the spring behind her and turned to look at it. This wasn't the question he'd been dreading. But it didn't take long for that one to come. When she realised for the first time that she was naked beneath the blanket, her eyes went wide with horror.

"Oh God. Gabe. What happened last night?"

He couldn't hide the grief that flickered across his eyes.

Sothea started looking around frantically. "Where's my dad? Where's Ama?"

Gabe's jaw clenched and he had to look away from her.

"Gabe!" She pulled away from him, her eyes searching desperately around them. "Tell me what happened!"

Gabe wanted to tell her everything, wanted to tell her it was not her fault, to reassure her that he knew she had been fighting the arb within the entire time. But he knew that none of that would matter to her. Just like it hadn't mattered when the school counsellor told Gabe it wasn't his fault that his mother had died. It didn't change anything. It didn't bring her back and it didn't make him feel any better.

"Ama is dead." It was better to be straight to the point.

Sothea silently screamed and grabbed her hair as tears started to flow down her cheeks. Gabe looked away again, this time to the carved face in the stone. They shouldn't even be here anymore. No doorway had appeared and no magical gateway had opened, despite all their efforts. He had burned a large part of the rose-bush, but obviously he hadn't done enough.

He could hear Sothea trying to get her breath under control again. She was breathing in and out as if sucking air through a straw. When he looked up at her, she was already looking back at him, on the verge of saying something but not quite making it. Her eyes asked the question without her having to say it out loud.

"I don't know what happened to your dad," Gabe replied.

"What?" Sothea said, looking distraught and barely holding herself together. "What do you mean, you don't know?"

Gabe shrugged. "I mean I don't know." He paused to pick at some grass. "When I saw that you were changing back, I grabbed you and ran. Your dad was still in the clearing when I left."

He purposefully omitted the fact that Detective Sergeant Hughes had been there too and had attempted to shoot Sothea down. And he definitely wasn't going to mention the gunshot he heard as he ran.

Hope flickered through Sothea's eyes. "We have to go back," she said urgently. "We must find him. He will know what to do."

Gabe shook his head.

"Have you lost your mind?" she said. "We have to make sure he is okay. I need to know."

"No," Gabe replied. "We need to get out of here. We need to burn the rest of the roses and open the gateway in the stone."

He'd been thinking about this before she woke. Hughes came to the clearing for a reason. Something must have drawn her there. It could just have been the smoke from his attempt at burning the roses, but would that really have spooked her enough to be carrying a gun? No. She must have seen something much scarier, and there was no doubt in his mind that that something must have been Sothea as an arb. He also knew Alderley Edge; word spread fast. News of what happened in the forest would have gotten back to the town by now. Really, it was nothing short of a miracle that no one had found them yet.

"Enough about your stupid gateway!" Sothea shouted. "You haven't figured out a way to open it. You don't even know for sure what's beyond it. We're out of time. My dad is out there somewhere and he might be hurt. None of this would have happened if you had just kept me locked up!"

Tears forced their way from her eyes, and she had to fall to her knees as sobs hit her. She let out an exasperated cry.

"Ama is dead..." She buried her face in her hands.

Gabe felt her pain hit him with the force of a tidal wave and in it he felt all the grief and horror he had worked so hard to bury following his mother's death. He numbed himself against it. Numbed himself against her words, telling himself she didn't mean them, even though he knew very well that she meant all of it. Every word.

Sothea stood up again and began to storm away, still wearing only his blanket. Gabe wanted to call out to her, but he could only watch as she got farther and farther away from him. His voice was empty. The words wouldn't come out. They were smothered by memories of cold water. The current of a phantom river dragged his body under, and the screams of his mother rooted him to the spot.

CHAPTER TWENTY-ONE

Sothea tore through the forest with no clear direction in mind. She could not face the consequences of her actions. Not yet. The branches whipped at her face as she ran through the trees with only the thin blanket wrapped around her body like a sarong.

The woods around Bailey Manor were large, stretching across the entire hillside. She hadn't had the time to properly explore them, except in her few encounters with Gabe, her short strolls through the trees with Ama, and the time she had got lost chasing the fox. Each time she had been following someone or something else, placing her trust in her guides rather than preoccupying herself with navigation. And as she moved through the trees now, she once again felt like something was guiding her. No. Not something. Someone.

She could feel the whispers of ghosts in the leaves. The nape of her neck tingled as distant voices spoke. *Turn here,* they said. And she did, taking a sharp right and following the pathway carved by the wind through the fluttering leaves.

She knew in her gut that her baba was in trouble. But the tremendous amount of pain that she felt only fuelled her limbs to move faster. She was faint and dizzy, but the hope that her father might still be alive kept her going. The branches high above clacked loudly against one another. The wood groaned and the songbirds had gone still, leaving only the caw of crows to add to the hush of ghostly voices in the air.

She stopped when she reached a copse of trees and saw her father hunched over in the centre of it. There was a pool of blood around him, staining the leaves and soil red. Her joy at seeing her father alive sent a spark of gratitude rushing through her body. She almost burst out crying right on the spot.

"Baba..." She didn't move from where she stood, wanting to run to him, but she saw the way his arm hung limply from the elbow and she knew that it had been her that caused him harm. And when he stood and turned, she saw that below him was the dead body of a woman. The scene was altogether too familiar, casting haunting memories of the night when everything had changed. As she stared at the body, little white daisies sprouted from the ground around it, blossoming instantly and shimmering in an ethereal sparkle.

Her father didn't even notice. He sounded weak. "Sothea. You're okay."

"I'm sorry," she said. Tears formed in her eyes again, and she cursed herself. She had cried too much in recent days. "I should have listened to you. I should have stayed inside."

Her father began walking towards her slowly.

"I should never have talked to Gabe," she continued. "I should never have left with him or run away. I just... I just thought that—"

She was cut off as her father wrapped his arms around her.

Both arms. He didn't even seem to feel any pain from the injury she'd given him.

His palm cupped the back of her head, and he pulled her close to his chest. She shivered, only now feeling the cold in the air. Her hands gripped him back. She never wanted to let go.

"Ama…" Sothea found herself crying as she said the old woman's name.

"Shh…" her father soothed her. "Ama knew what she was doing. She is in a better place now." Before Sothea had the chance to argue, he continued, "I saw your mother."

This caused Sothea to pull back and stare into her father's eyes. How could that be?

"Your friend. Gabe. He took me through a doorway." The way her father spoke made it seem like he was trying to remember exactly what happened. "More like a tunnel actually… Your mother wanted you to know that she is always with us. She is waiting for us patiently, and she wanted you to know how proud of you she is."

Again, Sothea went to open her mouth, but her father cut her off before she could speak.

"She was there, Sothea." Her father's eyes became rippled pools, staring off at the traces of a ghostly memory. "She helped me to see the truth." He brushed her hair back behind her ear. "You remind me so much of her."

A gentle wind moved through the space between them, twirling around their bodies like the wrap of a hug. Sothea watched the wind as it continued through the trees.

"You need to find Gabe," her father told her. "He's a good kid. Strong. He can help you."

Sothea's attention snapped back to her father and she frowned. "What about you?"

He smiled. "There are some things I need to take care of."

In the distance she could now hear the low wail of sirens, and they seemed to be drawing nearer. Her heart began to beat quickly.

"Baba?"

"Go," he said. "Find Gabe. We will see each other soon."

Sothea knew that the last words that came out of her father's mouth were both a lie and a truth, all at once. "Soon" was a relative word – a word that was bound to no particular time at all.

The sirens drew nearer. She could hear cars on the road approaching the house.

"Let me deal with this," her father said. "I have made many wrong decisions as your father. Let me make the right one for once."

"No." Sothea's voice quivered. "I won't leave you."

The sirens were loud now.

"This is your chance to be free," he told her. "I have kept you trapped for far too long. I will never forgive myself if I hold you back any longer. Gabe will help you. He'll know what to do. You must go. I will be fine."

He smiled and kissed her on the cheek, then made the choice for her. He heaved up the woman's body with a surprising show of strength and rested her on his shoulder. Then he turned and walked toward the noise, leaving Sothea alone in the woods.

She felt like a young fawn left to fend for herself. She looked around her, but this time there was no wind whispering to her, no guiding voice offering her a way through the trees. Her father had told her to find Gabe; she had to hope he was still at the Wizard's Well and that he'd accept her back. They'd hardly parted on good terms before she had run away. The only problem was that she had no idea which direction to go to get there. As she scanned her surroundings, her eyes landed back on the small patch of daisies that had appeared as she approached. They formed the outline of the body that had been there on the blood-soaked earth.

But the flowers didn't remind her of death. Instead, strangely, they conjured up the memory of Gabe's face when he saw Sothea use her magic for the first time. She closed her eyes and focused on the image. The moment was palpable. She could sense the essence of what Gabe was. The truth of him behind his pain, behind the idea of him, behind his body. The essence of him that lived beyond space and time. And as she reached out to it with her mind, she felt a thrum in her veins and a golden cord extended out from her chest, winding into the world before her.

She opened her eyes and watched the floating cord weave like a snake into the forest. She almost ran in the direction it was leading, but in that moment, she felt another tug at her chest. It whisked her in the opposite direction, and she knew that the second cord that extended from her heart belonged to her father.

Two paths, both leading in different directions. One to freedom, the other to capture. And yet neither of these paths were her own. She clenched her fists and closed her eyes again. She hated that she had to choose between them. She began to breathe deeply, working with the force inside herself to carve a way that was entirely hers. The cords belonging to Gabe and her father collapsed and, as they vanished, a new path appeared.

It did not appear as a cord. When Sothea opened her eyes this time, the world was as it should have been, except that on the ground was a path that was slightly brighter than the ground around it. It curved into the forest and the leaves seemed to shimmer where it passed through them. There was a rustle and disturbance in the undergrowth as a fox ran out into the path. It paused for a moment then turned to face her before it ran on. Sothea's heart felt the yearning to move, and so she stepped onto her own path for the first time in her life and began to follow it barefoot through the woods.

G abe stared down at the dense rosebush that blocked the flow of the ley line. Last night his fire had only managed to burn about half of it. This time, in the light of day and without the arb to suffocate the flames, he knew there would be nothing to stop the spread of the flames. The roses were already tinder-dry. They did not look anywhere near as intimidating as they had in the darkness of the new moon. The remaining flowers were already beginning to wilt from the petrol. There was a sadness to them, a defeated droop.

But he could hear sirens nearby. If he waited any longer then he might not get the chance to clear them again. If the police weren't coming for him, then they were coming for Sothea.

He knew she blamed him for what happened last night, knew that she did not believe he would find a way to the sleeping King. But she had not seen what he had. She had not stepped through a portal in the mists. It was up to him to prove it to her. Up to him to offer her a place where she could be herself, where she could be free. He hated to think what would happen if the authorities got hold of her instead. When she eventually shifted, there was no doubt that she would be killed or locked away in prison – or, even worse, experimented on. They would call her a monster. A witch.

The world claimed to have moved on from the burning and drowning of witches, and yet it had not moved on at all. There was no place in this world for a girl like her. Gabe had made a promise, and he had never in all his life broken one. He would not start today.

He struck a match, which quickly caught, and set the roses ablaze all over again.

James's throat was thick with the choke of grief. With every step he took, he heard the bells of fate chiming. The world moved in slow motion, the leaves on the trees moved as if through molasses, and the pollen practically hung in the air. He had lain Detective Sergeant Hughes outside the manor, gently closed her eyes and rested her hands over her heart, and sprinkled white rose petals over her corpse. He stayed kneeling over her body, eyes closed in thought. He knew the police and the rest of the town would be arriving soon, and he had only a few precious moments before he willingly turned himself over.

He would claim the killings as his own and give Sothea some sort of chance at life. Maybe Gabe could succeed in protecting her where he had failed. These were not his daughter's crimes. Not solely anyway. She had never wanted to come to England. It had been him who had forced her to come. He was the one who thought it would be good for her to get away from the place where her mother was murdered. Only now did he realise it was *him* that needed to escape.

He had lost sight of himself, lost sight of his own daughter, all in his stubborn refusal to face reality. Now, in the face of whatever came next, he saw more clearly than he had since the night of Chantrea's death – perhaps in all his life. He had known the risks in bringing Sothea here and now he would pay for it with his own sacrifice.

The sound of a gun cocking behind him snapped the world out of slow motion and back into speed. He hadn't heard the police cars driving up the gravel-lined approach to the manor.

Whoever this was had come to find him on their own. James didn't dare turn his head to see who the gun belonged to. He simply raised his arms in surrender.

"Where is it, you bastard?" It was Mark who spoke, slowly drawing out the moment. He seemed to be enjoying this.

James cleared his throat. "Now, why don't you put down the gun? We can talk about this." He went to turn his head, but Mark pressed the tip of the rifle into the back of his skull.

"Where is it?" he repeated.

James still didn't know what *it* was. "I... I don't know what you're talking about." He decided he too would take his time, squeezing every second out of the interaction so that Sothea would have as much time to get away as possible. "Is this about your son breaking into my house?"

Mark let out a dark laugh. "He did no such thing. And you know it. You're not going to pin murder on my boy. I'll tell you that for nothin'!"

Oh.

There was a sinking feeling in his chest, and he attempted to turn his head again. This time, Mark let him.

"I am truly sorry," James said. "I never meant for—"

"Never meant for what?!" Mark yelled at him, spit flying every which way. He shook his head and seemed to rein in his anger again, speaking more calmly and slowly. "Now, I don't know about this one here..." He flicked the gun at D.S. Hughes's body. "But I know it wasn't your hands that killed Elsie. So, I'll ask you again. Where is it?"

James frowned.

"Don't look so taken aback," Mark said. "I've seen my fair share. Lived on the streets for a time, even. I know how evil men can be. But whatever did that to old Mrs Dowsett was no man. Probably not even something that belongs to this world."

James felt fear spike in his gut. Not for himself, but for Sothea. There was no way Mark would suspect her, would he?

His mind went to his study. There were several ancient Khmer texts referencing what Sothea was. If this man searched the house, he would also find the shackles and chains barely hidden in the filing cabinet in his study, and would see the ritual sands, incense, and chicken bones in Sothea's room that Ama had used to find her last night.

It might not paint an incriminating picture in the eyes of the law. But the law was no longer what James feared. Mark was a father who felt his son was being framed. There was probably nothing more dangerous in the entire world.

"I killed Mrs Dowsett," James lied. "The fact that you would mistake my work for that of something supernatural is insulting." He tried to put as much hatred into his voice as possible.

"Aye. I bet you've been planning that alibi between you," Mark scoffed. "But it doesn't quite cut it."

Mark kicked him in the chest. He felt a few ribs crack and a sharp pain through his sternum as he was sent hurtling to the ground.

"You see," Mark continued, "I found some of her hair. Jet black, a great tuft of it, caught on the old woman's splintered door-frame when she went about murdering and defiling."

"You're mistaken," James panted from the floor, struggling to fill his lungs through the pain in his chest.

"The other thing is…" Mark looked down at him. "I've had my eye on you. All the time we've been working up here on the house. The way you prance around this place like butter wouldn't melt. The way you keep your own daughter a prisoner in her own home. Truth is, me and the lads had you down as a nonce. We all thought you kept her locked up for your own perverted pleasure.

But that's not it. Is it, Bailey? You know what she is. What she does to people—"

He was interrupted by the scratch of tyres tearing at the gravel driveway.

Mark put a heavy booted foot onto James's cracked ribs, and James let out a cry of pain. He was now staring down the barrel of Mark's gun, which was positioned directly in the centre of his forehead, between his eyes. Mark looked furious at having been interrupted. Whatever calm he had been trying to hold up broke away into untamed fury, like the walls of a dam collapsing.

"You bastard!" he raged. "You endangered us all!"

"Drop it, Mark!" shouted a voice James recognised as P.C. Taylor. "Don't do anything you'll regret!"

James risked a sideways glance to see Taylor and Quinn approaching, along with three other officers, their tasers all pointing at Mark's chest. When he looked back at Mark, he too was looking over at the police, and James took the split-second opportunity to get his feet around Mark's ankle, twisting and pulling it out from under him. Mark came crashing to the ground and the deafening crack of a gunshot echoed through the air.

Sothea heard a bang, but gritted her teeth and continued jogging. Her dad had known they were coming for him. He had welcomed it, even, to give her a chance to escape. To turn around now would be to undo all of that and jeopardise her own chance of a future... But she hadn't expected to hear a gunshot.

"Baba..." She clenched her fists in frustration.

She was used to fighting a constant internal monologue commanding her to do things that she didn't always want to do.

Things that weren't always in her best interest. But this was different. The voice speaking to her now was truly her own voice. She had only just begun to take her first steps on her own path, but she couldn't just abandon her father when he could be in danger.

She broke into a sprint and found herself back at the clearing by Bailey Manor much sooner that she had anticipated. Her own path must have taken her close without her even knowing. She hid behind a tree and took in the scene unfolding before her. Her dad and another man were wrestling on the ground together. The man still had a rifle in his hand. Her eyes darted to the right and she saw the police cars. The police officers had their tasers drawn but seemed hesitant to approach, presumably because there was a gun involved.

She ran to the trunk of an old oak and ducked down behind it. She had tried her best to escape their notice, but even in the heat of the brawl, the man with the gun turned to look at her. Their eyes connected and Sothea saw who it was – Gabe's dad. Without taking his eyes off her, he swung his elbow back and hit her father square in the temple. Sothea watched as her father went down, his body going limp like a rag doll.

"I see you, devil!" Gabe's father announced. "You're an abomination. A temptress. I'll put you down like a rabid dog." He pointed his gun at her.

She barely ducked out of the way when the first shot fired. It splintered through the side of the tree that she was now hiding behind, mere centimetres from her head. She stayed hidden as she heard a couple of heavy footsteps in the gravel.

"Stay down if you know what's good for you!" Gabe's dad spat.

"Mark!" cried out one of the police officers. "Drop the weapon! Now! No one needs to get hurt."

The footsteps stopped.

"People have already been hurt, sunshine," Gabe's dad shouted back. "It's a bit too late for that now."

Sothea risked a glance over the tree trunk. Gabe's dad was standing still again, facing away from her now, as most of the officers held their tasers up at him. One officer though, who she recognised as P.C. Taylor – she'd seen her father talking to him after Gabe appeared in her room – was rushing over to the house. He seemed to be completely distracted. When he reached the front steps, he skidded down on his knees. It was only then that Sothea realised there was another body lying next to her father. The woman from the woods.

"No..." P.C. Taylor cradled her in his arms.

Gabe's dad was still facing away for now, but the other officers had started to lose their focus on him. A large group of people had started to arrive behind them, jeering and shouting, and the officers had to reorganise themselves to block their access to the house. The feral crowd gathered behind the police cars, cheering Gabe's dad on.

She knew he could turn again at any moment, but she couldn't look away as one of the more junior officers rushed to administer first aid to her father. He was trying to crawl towards them, but he was clearly struggling. And then her attention was torn away by another shot, which sent a spray of wood chips up into the air as it hit the tree again. In all the chaos, Gabe's dad had resumed his march towards her.

She ducked down and froze as the thundering crash of recent memories swarmed her waking mind. She saw an old woman wandering into a kitchen. She saw the terror in her face. All that followed was the shred of flesh and the haunting tear of screams in the air. She caught a last glimpse of a telephone receiver on a long cord as she had turned to chase the burning of roses. These memories were not her own, and at the same time they were hers entirely.

She had killed someone – the other her had – and now Gabe's father was seeking revenge.

She deserved this, then. She deserved death.

Sothea opened her eyes and forced herself to be present. She got to her feet, still protected by the thick trunk she had chosen to hide behind. Then she stepped out into the open to face Gabe's father. Tears streamed down her cheeks as he took aim, but she squeezed her eyes shut instinctively as he squeezed the trigger, ready to accept whatever fate had in store for her.

The gun fired.

In that same moment, something grabbed her arm and pulled her down. She felt a hot sear over her right cheek as the bullet whizzed past, and then opened her eyes to find herself on the ground with Gabe hunched protectively over her. Everything seemed to move at a fraction of real time. Her fingers rose to the burning feeling on her cheek and when she pulled them away, they were coated with blood. The bullet had only grazed her, slicing a thin line that seeped blood slowly and thickly down her face.

Her eyes flicked up to Gabe, who met her gaze with a wide-eyed intensity. He pulled her to her feet as the world turned into a thick blur of motion. She could hardly hear anything over the sound of the blood pumping in her body. Then she was running. Gabe was pulling her through the trees.

Another bullet whistled past her face, and right over Gabe's head.

"Run, Sothea!" she heard her father yell.

She glanced back, still being yanked along by Gabe, and saw Gabe's dad scrambling up off the ground. Her father was on the floor beside him, hands still wrapped around one of the other man's ankles. She watched in horror as Gabe's dad stomped on her father's arms with his free foot. A scream began to swell in her throat as she realised what was coming, but it didn't have time to escape before Gabe's dad pointed the gun downwards and fired it point-blank into her father's chest.

Her scream was swallowed in the vacuum clench of her shock. Everything went silent as she watched the man who had just shot her father turn to her with blood splattered across his distorted features.

Sothea's world broke.

It cracked like pressure building on the surface of a mirror. Then all at once it shattered, and her scream finally broke to the surface. Her voice hit a shrill note of grief-stricken terror, and the force of it threw Gabe away from her, sending him hurtling through the air. His dad fired another bullet but just as it was about to hit her, it splintered into a thousand pieces, swirling into geometric shapes around the aura of Sothea's horror.

Her hands clawed at her face as she saw her father's body go limp. But not before he tried to reach out for her one last time, his arm straightening just before it fell and his eyes became vacant. The earth began to rumble, and as Sothea tore her hands away from her face she felt the magic welling inside her, ready to explode.

She thrust her hand in a clawed frenzy at Gabe's dad and thorns erupted from the earth, rolling towards him like an ancient wyrm writhing through the earth. His eyes went wide with the brilliant terror of witnessing the impossible. Before he could even blink, the razor-sharp thorns were on him. The vines twisted and wrapped around his legs, clawing up his body and pulling him to the ground.

He was forced to his knees as the hooked barbs dug deep into his skin, drawing blood almost instantly. His hands clawed at them as he tried to tear himself free, but the vines were thick and the thorns only cut deeper gashes into his fingers and palms as they worked their way to his throat.

Sothea felt the force of a thousand suns as the energy so close to the ley line fuelled her power. Hatred and anger writhed in her body as hot tears flew from her face, cast into the air by a phantom wind of her own conjuring. Then something broke her focus. The touch of skin against her hand. Suddenly Gabe was in front of her. His face blocked her view of his father. His left palm gently grazed her cheek, and even though he spoke without sound, she could read the words on his lips.

Let go.

All her pain, all her anguish, was swallowed up in the compassion of Gabe's deep-blue eyes. She felt her fear soaked up by their depths and the silent world became suddenly saturated in sound once more. Reality returned in a rush as she let go of her grip on the magic. It fell away, and she almost collapsed as a result. But Gabe caught her.

Gabe knew how he was supposed to act. Despite everything, somewhere – deep down – a small part of him wanted to run back to his father. He wanted a hug, some reassurance that everything was going to be alright. After all, he was the only family he had left. But a much larger part of him wanted to flee as far away as possible.

Gabe knew he had a choice to make. His dad or Sothea.

It should have been a difficult decision, but it wasn't. If there was any doubt in his mind, it was quickly quelled by a barrage of memories. All the times his dad had chosen the pub over spending time with his only son. All the forgotten birthdays and nights without dinner. The jibes and the insults and the constant mockery. All the times he had lashed out at him, leaving him battered and bruised. And now, besides all of that,

Gabe had rushed back to Bailey Manor to find him aiming a gun at Sothea.

Sothea had released her magic, but his dad was still his dad.

Gabe made his decision.

He took one last glance at his father – struggling to free himself of the now-limp vines as two burly police officers ran over to him – before forcing his gaze away and heaving up a barely conscious Sothea onto his shoulders. He was determined to put as much distance between himself and his dad as he could. As he ran off into the woods, he could still hear his cries through the trees.

"I'll get you, witch! I'll burn you and flay you alive! Mark my words! I *will* get you!"

CHAPTER TWENTY-TWO

The forest surrounding Alderley Edge was ablaze. Gabe could see it from the vantage point he had on the hill known as Castle Rock. He had only meant to burn the roses, but the dry summer heat and an easterly wind had stoked the flames, and they had spread quickly to the surrounding brush and trees.

Something was in the air. Gabe could feel it. And it wasn't just the thick smoke. Magic had returned. He had witnessed it with his own eyes, seen Sothea cast a spell and seen the energy of the ley line rush to her aid like a river being diverted from its main flow.

Magic has returned.

He said it in his own head, still struggling with the idea even though he had wished for it his entire life. Magic *had* returned, but it had come at a price. Sothea's father was dead. Ama too. And D.S. Hughes, from what he had seen. He couldn't be sure there weren't more.

Sothea was awake now. Well, her eyes were open at least. But she could barely stand on her own feet, and her arm was draped around him as he held most of her weight. He forced himself to keep moving. He doubted the handful of officers would be able to hold his dad or the rest of the baying crowd back for very long. He had to get Sothea to the circle and he had to find a way to open the wall of stone, because if he didn't, then all their deaths would have been for nothing.

A promise had been cast in the air and Gabe was bound by it.

Sothea was now muttering things to herself in a language that he didn't understand. A quick glance down and he could see that her eyes were glazed and distant. He may have been holding Sothea's body, but her mind was far away. There were more sirens in the distance. No doubt this was the fire brigade on their way, and he was sure additional police resources would be drafted in from Stockport, Macclesfield, and Manchester to help find him and Sothea – all more than likely armed.

This had to happen now. Even if these were not the circumstances that Gabe had always imagined. He had envisioned the opening of the rock countless times, dreamed of meeting King Arthur and his men. None of his imaginings had involved so much blood. Or so much fear. Or so much death.

He saw the familiar crest of a ridge and, clambering over it, he spotted the stone circle that stood on the other side.

Many men, even in our time, will forget the purpose of our circles.

Gabe heard Arthur speak, memories told through old myth.

As shadow falls over the mind of men, they will lose knowledge that was once commonplace, become lesser, forget the truth of things, and lose the language of the world. The stones will stand the test of time. I have seen the last one close. As the druids disperse, so does the magic of their altars. There was a time when the four corners of the earth were joined as one. Even the stars were not far from reach for the man who stood within the stone. Wood may rot, and iron rust, but stone will stand till the world collapses.

There were crows gathering in great numbers around the stone circle, cawing like the frenzy of a storm. The wind gusted through the trees, stoking the flames and casting smoke across the land in thick plumes. Gabe helped Sothea down to her knees. The stone circle was alive, thrumming with energy. Vast currents of sparkling mana surged in spirals within it.

He was entranced by it. His heart beat frantically with awe and heavy with grief all at once. In the swirl of energy within the circle he could hear voices singing, drums beating, layers of voices from different times overlapping one another. Almost unconsciously, his hand reached out towards it. Then, as if from a distant world, he heard a voice behind him.

"Gabe."

It stopped his hand in its tracks. Eyes still wide from the sight of the mana, he turned to see Sothea looking at him.

"My father?" she asked.

Gabe reached out a hand to touch hers. It seemed that was all that was needed to confirm what she already knew. She nodded.

"Are you sure you want to do this?" she asked, looking at him with a solemn severity. "You see what follows me. You will probably end up dead."

Gabe didn't break eye contact. "My entire life, the world always seemed to be an arm's length away. I knew there were rules, and I could see other people abiding by them, but they never seemed to come into focus. When I'm with you, the world comes into focus. My world is connected to you." He smiled, squeezing her hand. "Besides, there is nothing left for me here. There has been nothing here for me since my mother died."

Sothea nodded. "Me neither."

"Then let's go."

Gabe stood and helped Sothea up. Together they stared at the swirling column of mana that shot straight up into the sky. For a moment, he thought he heard a voice somewhere in the forest, but the roar of flames in the trees and the rush of magic were so overwhelming that it was impossible to tell. Anyway, they'd be gone soon.

"I'm scared," Sothea said in barely more than a whisper, as the crows cawed loudly above.

"What is there to be scared of?" Gabe asked.

"What if the world on the other side is worse than this one?"

"It isn't. I'm sure of it."

"How do you know?" she asked.

"Because I've had one foot in it my entire life."

Sothea didn't seem convinced.

"I'll go first," Gabe assured her. And he took the first step.

As he did, something flashed in his peripheral vision. He shuddered as if someone had walked over his grave. He lost sensation in his body as he passed into the column of energy. Instantly, he became liquid, incorporeal, as his consciousness floated through the veil between worlds. He could see nothing other than an infinite ocean of sparkling energy, and then his foot touched down onto solid ground.

Suddenly he was physical again, but the world around him was entirely different. He didn't have time to gawk or wonder at it because his hand was still joined to Sothea's, and he needed his wits about him to guide her through. From this side, her arm stretched out of a shimmering portal, encased in an archway of blue twisted branches. There was a ripple in the surface of the gateway and Sothea appeared through it.

He was struck by her beauty as she stepped into the otherworldly light. Hues of pink and lavender fell on her porcelain skin, dyeing it like the petals of a flower. Her eyes opened in the new world and Gabe had a front row seat to the expression of awe that filled them. He was smiling and about to walk on, when suddenly the portal rippled again.

Sothea's body was almost completely through when she started to shift. Her face jolted like the static of a television, shifting back and forth, and her face split in two. One was the beautiful Sothea he knew well, and the other was the vicious fragment of her arb. But before Gabe could even react, there was a tug from the other side. Sothea was yanked back through the portal and her hand came loose from his grip.

"No!" he shouted.

He ran for the portal threshold but crashed into it like it was a solid wall. He cursed, his adrenaline spiking as he banged his fists against the shimmering surface. Each hit sent pulses and ripples through the fabric of the portal, and it gave way slightly each time, but didn't let Gabe back through. He could see the dim outline of Sothea being carried away by a larger figure, like a sepia projection into a distant world. He was powerless to prevent it.

He screamed, digging his nails into the fabric of the portal and trying to tear it open. But nothing worked. No matter how much he kicked. No matter how much he punched. Each and every attack was repelled. Sweat beaded on Gabe's forehead, but frustration at the injustice kept him going long after he was physically unable to continue. When he could no longer lift his arms, he finally stopped. Head bowed in defeat, he collapsed to his knees, pointlessly pounding his head against the shimmering wall in vain. They had been so close. So bloody close. He felt the tether of his promise unravelling within him. He had failed.

No.

He gritted his teeth and stood up. He would have to find a way. He didn't know the rules of this world, or why it was that he couldn't get back out, but he would fight to keep his promise until he drew his last breath.

Gabe stood and turned away from the portal. Despite his anger, he could not help but have his breath stolen. He had been expecting ancient collapsed ruins but the realm before him was the twinkling shimmer of an eternal dusk. A canopy of trees domed over a lavender meadow of dancing flowers. Specks of golden light drifted on a wind that smelled of sandalwood and honeysuckle, and pinkish-purple slants of light beamed through the gaps in the blue and green leaves.

It was a world greater than Gabe's imagination. It was a world of myths and stories. It was an enchanted forest full of strange trilling sounds and little chirps that were familiar and alien all at once. It was a land spoken of in fairy tales and children's stories, in ancient manuscripts, and by Arthur himself. Gabe recognised it at once. This was the realm of the fae.

It struck him straight in the heart, like an arrow through his chest. He reached out with his hand and the air seemed to meet his fingertips, twining around them like vines, grazing his palms and trickling down his wrist and forearm. This was where the magic had gone. Gabe knew at once that he was still on earth; it was not so foreign that his body struggled with the harmonics of the world. It was familiar, like an ancient chord being struck in the very recesses of his genetics. It felt as though once upon a time his ancestors had known this feeling.

He had read that the fae and humans had once lived side by side, sharing one world. Magic spells had been cast with simple words, and fabled creatures stole the tides and travelled stories. He had witnessed the memory of the unravelling of that arrangement, when the fae turned their back on Arthur and on man. He had seen the grand bridge that linked both worlds reduced to rubble, a poor facsimile of what once was. Now he had traversed into Faery, the realm of the fae, and it was magnificent.

He took a step forward and something in the world withdrew.

He frowned and looked down at his boots, and all in one moment felt how wrong it was that he was wearing them. Sothea had always been barefoot. He'd wrongly assumed it was because of her Khmer heritage, not because of her magical ancestry. Of all the priorities in his head, it suddenly became the most important thing to be rid of them.

He laughed as he pulled them off along with his socks, and as he set them down, the ground stole them. Gabe could only watch as they sunk into the earth as though it was quicksand, and in their place rose a wrap of clothes. A navy-blue cloak sat atop the bundle. *A trade for a trade.* This was a place where the currency was not money or gold, but the value and worth of what an item represented. Gabe found his mind was already slipping out of rationality, and into something more natural. He did not question what happened, for there was nothing to question. All was as it was, simply and truly.

This world could not be defined by rules. It was a dreamscape, and to set rules and parameters on it was to limit what this new reality was able to offer. Gabe put on the clothes in the soft bundle of fabric. They had no seams or stitching, each piece seemingly woven into a single piece of weightless light fabric, and they fit perfectly. The cloak seemed to hug him as it nestled onto his shoulders. His old clothes disappeared as well, and with his next step he found a long wooden staff in his hand. Its bottom hit the ground with a soft thud, and the brown wood brushed softly against his palm.

Gabe suddenly felt at one with his surroundings, as if this world had been waiting, and now welcomed him home. A song began to emerge through the texture of sound in the air. It filled him with an otherworldly feeling, hollowed out his bones, turned them into crystal, and enriched his veins with silver light.

His heart yearned for that song, yearned to find the source of the sound, to lay his eyes upon the being who was singing it. The soft female voice tugged at the strings in his heart, fluttering like the wings of butterflies. The edges of his vision began to blur and swirl like a kaleidoscope, and only a tunnel of pink light was clear before him.

He moved forward, swaying like a drunken sailor on a rocking tide. Floral scents filled his nostrils – the scent of love itself! Oh, how his body yearned as the song pulled him deeper into the fae woods, and farther away from the portal. Away from Sothea.

He began to hear laughter, like chimes in the wind. Lots of voices and tiny giggles, some from his right, and others behind him. All around, in little bursts of joy. The laughter made him feel even lighter, made him feel like he was floating above the ground. He could just make out a flicker of movement on the periphery of his kaleidoscopic vision, blurry shapes made of light that glowed a bright leaf green.

He followed the sound until the forest trees parted and in front of him was a crystal-blue lake. It was not flat as most lakes would be. Perhaps it was not actually a lake at all. There were several rock pools, all surrounding a larger one. The pools on the outer edges each flowed into the next, and the water cascaded gently downwards. There were several tiers in fact, with some of the pools more raised than others, and each of them was home to a number of seals, which swam gracefully through the blue water.

And in the centre of the largest pool, seated on a rock, was a naked woman. Her long silver hair was pulled back to expose pointed ears, and her face was not quite human. Her skin was a mix of grey and aquamarine and her eyes were like dark, round pools. The parts which would blush red on a human instead had a hint of sea-moss green. There were amphibian whiskers of sorts above her eyes, vibrating along with the melody she was humming.

She glanced at Gabe flirtatiously from the side of her eyes. He took another step towards her and his bare feet touched the edges of the water. It rippled, and the woman too seemed to shudder. Her humming did not stop, but she began to speak.

"It has been a long while since a human has set foot in my waters." Her voice sounded like a full choir singing in a cathedral building, bouncing off invisible walls so that it sounded like more than one person.

In the next moment she was no longer on the rock but gliding gracefully through the pool. As she got closer, Gabe noticed something strange about her hands. There was skin between each of the fingers, a webbing of sorts. She laughed and kicked forward. It was only then that Gabe realised she did not have legs, but a large silver-grey lower body that tapered into two tail fins. Like a seal.

A part of him, hidden deep away, was terrified. *Silkie!* his inner voice warned. *Run!* But his legs would not move. He had read about her kind. A half woman, half seal, who inhabited the water within the fae realm. Some navigated through deep ocean tunnels on the new moon to find their way to the human world, and lure men back to their domain. This part of him was screaming to get away, and yet he was helplessly attracted to her, lusting for her in a vicious and primal way.

"Do not be afraid, boy," her soothing voice told him. "I am merely curious. Come out a little deeper, so we can swim together. I promise I won't bite."

She grinned and a flash of sharp canines cut over her perfectly plump lips. She twirled in the water, rolling onto her back so that Gabe could see the fullness of her torso. If it were not for the braided knot of a promise in his chest, he might have forgotten about the realm of humans altogether. He might have followed her commands without question. But the promise he found inside him allowed Gabe to resist the pull.

She seemed to grow impatient. "A man with a vow, hmm? A man who has yet to break a promise. What a rare thing indeed."

She was moving closer. Gabe noticed he was nearly submerged up to his hips now. Were the waters rising or had he wandered in farther than he thought? She glided gently on the surface of the water, her face half-submerged so that only the bridge of her nose and the dark orbs of her eyes were visible. And yet when she spoke, it was still clear as day.

"I can see that you have not yet tasted of the fruit. You call yourself a man, but you are still a boy at heart. Let me show you what lays on the other side of boyhood. I promise my nectar will be sweet."

She giggled, and it took everything Gabe had not to sink into the water completely. It was up to his chest now. He shut his eyes and managed to clasp his hands over his ears, but her song was not in the air. It was in his bones, in his flesh, in his very soul. He could feel her circling him. Circling, but not touching. He had read the horror stories about men who fell prey to a silkie's song.

A silkie preys on a man's desire. And yet her lips may only touch when a man at last doth surrender.

That was it. In the small portion of his mind that was still his, Gabe remembered the old Gaelic verse that said she could not touch him unless he gave himself over to her. All he had to do was hold out. All he had to do was turn around and walk back to the shores.

Then he realised that the water was already up to his chin.

He could barely stand up anymore, his toes straining to find purchase on the bottom of the lake. He wanted her with every molecule of his being. She twirled around him and stopped with her face right in front of his. Every detail of her was perfect. She had soft blushed cheeks, and her movements were not just seductive, they were the very definition of desire – as if she had authored the book on the subject herself. Her eyes were black as night. Just like Sothea's had been when she had transformed into an arb.

The silkie saw his memory of Sothea in his eyes and her song turned into a shriek. Suddenly Gabe felt a loosening in his limbs. He didn't hesitate. He looked back to the shore and willed himself there. The world shifted. He felt the ground change beneath him, and suddenly he was no longer in the water. He blinked. There was no song anymore, no enchanting melody.

With a glance over his shoulder, he found that the pools were no longer there either. He was alone again, surrounded by a dusk-lit wood. The silkie was gone. Gabe gasped in a ragged breath of air, like he had been submerged in water and his lungs were about to give in. He could feel the heavy pulse of his blood in his neck and at the side of his head. He buckled over, hands pressing into the ground to hold himself up. He had promised Sothea this world would be better. That she would be safe here. Whilst that might still be true, the encounter with the silkie reminded him that danger lurked everywhere.

Despite the strange euphoria that came with still being alive after escaping the lure of a mythical creature, he was aware how much time was being wasted. The longer he spent here, the longer Sothea would go without help. He figured the person who had grabbed her was his own father. There was no one else that it could be. Why hadn't the police arrested him? What would he do to her? Had he killed her already, or was he taking her someplace else?

He hoped by some miracle that the police would intervene, that someone would notice. But it was a small hope. There was no one left in that town that was on Sothea's side. All her allies were dead. She needed him. He pounded his fists against the earth. He needed to find a way back.

Just as he pushed himself to his feet there was a noise like twigs cracking underfoot. He turned just in time to see a figure walking out of the woods. He couldn't see who or what it was, as the light here cast strange shadows, but he could hear something like a rattle or a child's rainmaker – a sound like hundreds of seeds slowly cascading together. He caught a whiff of something familiar too. Incense.

He could hardly contain his shock when the figure stepped into the light. It was Ama. She was smiling, ancient wrinkles grooved into her skin like folds in bark. She wore colourful clothing, and smoke moved in an aura around her, taking the shapes of different animals. The sound of brass cymbals tinkling together seemed to accompany her every move, though Gabe could see no instrument in sight.

She clasped her hands together and bowed slightly.

"Ama? Is that really you?" He couldn't help but smile. He had never really gotten to know the woman, but she had saved his life, after all. "But I saw you die…"

"Are you still so shocked after everything you have seen so far?" she teased. "Death is just another cycle." She spoke in her native language, but somehow in this realm he understood what she was saying. "To many in your world it is a final thing. That is why so many cry and mourn. But death is a new beginning, and those who know how to navigate the afterlife have some sovereignty over where we choose to go."

"I…"

"You don't need to say anything more, Gabe. I know what you mean to accomplish. I know you want to help Sothea. I have been watching closely."

He nodded, and then suddenly a thought came to his mind. "Does that mean Sothea's father is here somewhere too?"

Ama's lips pursed, and she shook her head. "James has other places to be, other cords that tie him to certain paths. It is very unlikely that you will see him again." She paused. "In this life, at least."

"But how? How did you come to this world?"

"When the body perishes, the soul is freed from its form. If it is bound by contracts of the spirit, or bound by desires, then the soul is ushered unconsciously to a new cycle. It is the practice of my people to free ourselves from these causes that bind us. If successful, we are liberated from the cycle of unconsciousness, from the cycle of rebirth, and may choose to navigate the realms unbound by any worldly tethers."

Gabe didn't quite understand what she was saying, but a small part of him understood a semblance of her meaning.

"You did well to resist your desires this day," she told him. "As you know, that creature may only claim power by feeding on your weakness, may only claim your life if you surrender it over. In death it is similar. If we harbour any weakness, we may be driven into realms not of our choosing. We may fall into a seeking of desires or unfulfilled needs, causing us to be surrendered once again into the cycle of unconsciousness, devoid of true understanding."

Gabe nodded. That made more sense. "So, Mr Bailey has gone where his unconscious desires have taken him?"

Ama nodded. "In this case, it took him to a place he desired most deeply. You should not worry about him. He has been reunited with Sothea's mother. They will continue to guide her until it is her time to pass on as well. There are those within your sphere that seek to guide you as well."

Gabe immediately thought of his mother.

Ama smiled and took his hand. "You may let go of the guilt you hold, young knight. As my people say, do not pity the dead. It is the living who need your help."

"I need to find a way out of here," he said suddenly. "Sothea…
She was taken."

There was a glint in Ama's eye. "Sothea must first face a fate of
her own. She walks her own road, as do you. She has not yet come
to peace with her shadow. There is a war within her. Until she
finds balance, then she will be a danger to herself and others, no
matter what world she is in. You yourself saw the fracturing of her
selves as she stepped into this realm."

Gabe understood, but he could not help but worry. "What do
I have to do?"

"I do not have an answer for that. Nor is it my question to
answer. You have seen some of how this realm works already. It is a
place as much a dream as it is a reality. And dreams have a way of
responding to us, if we are aware enough to know that we are
dreaming." She winked at him.

Gabe started to grow a little impatient. He turned and
gestured to the woods behind him. "I have no idea where I am or
which way to go. Sothea needs me, and—" But when he turned
back, Ama was gone.

In her place was just the sparkle of energy and the faint
lingering smell of incense. Gabe blinked, wondering if he had even
been talking to her at all. The energy in front of him began to
coalesce and sink into the soil. He watched as from nothing, a
seedling grew, then from the stem blossomed a rose with two
heads. One was white, and the other scarlet.

CHAPTER TWENTY-THREE

James knelt at his wife's grave. He looked upon the ornate, steepled tomb and instinctively reached out to brush away some dirt and dust that had gathered on the stone. A gunshot fired in his mind, but he actively ignored it. There was a thick mist veiling everything other than the small space that his wife's grave occupied, leaving a spotlight of clarity amidst the fog.

"I walk your path now," he whispered. "I am yours once more."

The mists wavered and Chantrea stepped from the frosty swirls. "My love," she said, coming to kneel beside her husband. "I was torn for so long. At times I admit I was selfish. I wanted you here by my side. But I knew Sothea needed you by hers."

"I did what I could, for as long as I could..."

"You say it with such sadness and regret."

"I confused her," he said. "She thought me strict and uncompromising. It must have been difficult—"

Chantrea put a finger to his lips. "She couldn't have had a better teacher."

James leaned his forehead against his wife's, his hand reaching up to her neck, fingers interlacing in her hair. "How can you know? How can you be so sure?"

"I cannot know for certain, my love. I can only say what it is I feel."

James swallowed, even though his throat was dry. "She must choose her own path now." He pulled away, meeting Chantrea's translucent eyes.

"She already has." She smiled. "Now it is our time."

James now heard the trilling of birds, and felt a warmth like no other. He turned his head to see that a doorway had formed in the mist. Through the open door he could see a field of green, with strange floating orbs. There were people on the other side. Strange people, with the lower half of their bodies formed of bird legs and feathers. There were lions with the heads of elephants. And there were people who sat in lotus position, floating on clouds and picking fruit from large trees.

Chantrea smiled at the puzzlement on his face. "You didn't think I was waiting at my grave this entire time, did you? I appreciate the time you spent making my tomb look nice, but I have always found graveyards to be quite depressing." She giggled softly.

James was still in awe of what he saw.

"These are the after-fields of my ancestors," Chantrea said proudly. "We may go there if you like. For a time." She smiled, grazing her fingers through James's hair.

He nodded. Chantrea floated to her feet and extended out her hand. James took it and let her guide him through the doorway into the world of paradise, leaving the grave and a life lived in dread behind.

CHAPTER TWENTY-FOUR

Gabe knew there must be a message in the rose that Ama had left behind. That much was obvious. What she meant it to say was another thing entirely. She had spoken about the fae realm like it was conscious, like it was a dream that could be manipulated. But believing in magic and actually performing it were different things entirely.

There were many levels to belief. There was belief in the hope that something could be true, and there was belief in something because that was all one knew. Gabe knew that what he needed was a true belief. An unshakeable belief so strong that it could not be yanked or swayed by the tides of doubt.

But as he stared at the magic before his eyes, he realised that he did not possess that sort of belief. Not yet. He had been told his entire life that he wasn't right in the head, that his obsession with fantasy worlds was all delusion and magic was not real. He'd been told that there was something wrong with him and the sooner he "snapped out of it" and behaved like everyone else, the better. Now he stood in the very proof of its existence, it was easier to quell any lingering doubts. He took some comfort from the fact that he'd held on to his conviction when all around him were trying to beat it out him – both literally and figuratively. And he tried to keep that feeling in mind.

He went down onto his knees, so that he could inspect the rose blooms at eye level. They were perfectly created, like shimmering flakes of stardust. Their smell reminded him of the forest, and his stomach churned slightly at the memory of the smell of ash and fire mixed with a sickly sweetness. When the roses had burned, they had started hissing as the water inside their stalks boiled and then evaporated. And as cracks began to appear in the stems, the hissing turned into high-pitched whistles that sounded more like screams.

He shut his eyes, trying to cut off the memory, but the smell still lingered. He brought a hand to his nose and when he opened his eyes, he was astonished to see that the red rose in front of him was burning. Gabe stumbled backwards and watched as the red rose singed and wilted away, falling to the ground in flakes of ash. Had he done that?

He suddenly remembered Ama's words. *The fae realm is a place as much a dream as it is a reality. And dreams have a way of responding to us, if we are aware enough to know that we are dreaming.* He frowned, looking to where the ash had fallen on the ground. Already there was no trace of it, as though it had simply vanished. His eyes wandered to the other head of the rose. The white one. He ran his fingers over the petals, and in this he remembered Sothea's kiss, remembered the touch of her lips and the gentlest stroke of her fingers against his skin.

As he thought it, there was a shaking in his bones. The flower began to pulse, humming with the exact energy that mirrored his emotions. His mind started to draw connections. Was this place linked to his thoughts and feelings? *Just like a dream.* He held the white rose, closed his eyes, and began to fall into his memories, letting them conjure visions in his mind's eye like they were on a silver screen.

He could hear her laughing, see her hair moving in the wind. *How can I find you?* he asked in his mind, and when he opened his eyes, Faery shuddered, yearning to answer his question. The petals of the white rose spiralled loose from their stem and began to weave through the air at an alarming rate. Gabe held on to the stem as he chased after them.

The world began to blur at the edges again, the dream of the fae realm narrowing so he could only now see the path the roses were leading him down. It was as if the fae realm and his mind were not separate places. It inhabited him as much as he inhabited it.

Then suddenly, he was somewhere he recognised. The petals that fluttered to the ground dissolved as soon as they touched it. He was in front of the Wizard's Well. But it was grander than the Wizard's Well he knew from his countless visits to the woods. Where the trickle of a stream had been, there was now a gush of water. It fell into a beautifully ornate basin carved of stone, with images of faerie creatures, humans with swords, and winged dragons etched into the rock. The basin was overflowing, and the water fell into another basin below it, continuing that way until it cascaded into a large stone wishing pool.

He didn't know why he had called it a wishing pool, but he just had. There were small trinkets and items at the bottom of it, like the fountain his mother had once told him to toss a coin into. To his right, carved in granite, was the stone face. Except this version was not faded with time. The features were so clear it looked like it had been chiselled that morning. But what astonished him most about the place was the clear outline of a doorway that was now visible in the rock. It was not a door made of stone or wood, just the outline of one in a trace of golden light. In the centre of the space was a runic symbol that glowed in a similar fashion.

"The entrance to King Arthur's tomb," Gabe whispered out loud.

He reached a hand out towards the seam of light. There was a tingle of feedback on the tips of his fingers, and he felt the wind begin to pick up at his back, tossing the sandy blond curls of his hair. His palm grazed over the rough stone, moving to the runic symbol in the centre of the doorway. It seemed to react to him and him to it, a ripple wavering through his body.

This was it. He had dreamt his whole life of finding the entrance. But it hadn't been in the world of humans. The true way to enter had been in Faery. So, King Arthur had walked these woods himself, had touched this stone... Maybe he too had made a wish in the pool below.

What did this all mean? Why had the rose led him here? He had asked it to help him find Sothea. Was King Arthur the key to finding her? He took a step back. It began to dawn on him that, yes, he had found the entrance, but how was he supposed to open it?

A sharp pain in his left hand drew his attention. He was still holding the stalk of the rose, gripping it rather hard. So much so that the thorns had pierced his skin. He raised the rose up, slowly uncurling his hand, which was coated in a thin layer of wet blood.

He looked at the stalk, then back to the stone doorway. Gabe needed a way to harness and direct the magic. Something to focus his energy. He needed a tool to open the door. What better a tool than a wand? He closed his hand back around the stiff stalk and pointed it directly at the door, willing the magic to manifest as it had for him before.

Gabe felt the wind, but this time it was rising upwards. He felt a surge of energy in his gut, like the stoking of a flame that rose upwards into his chest and surged through the network of meridian lines in his arm. He watched as the stalk absorbed his blood, the sparkle of mana twirling around it, and in mere seconds the sap-filled stem had transformed into a smooth wand made of hard, dry wood.

It was a light-brown colour, stained slightly darker by the crimson of his blood, and it thrummed and vibrated with energy. In some strange way, Gabe recognised it. The wand was him, as much as a piece of wood could be him. It was perfect, fitting seamlessly into his palm, the shape matching the exact folds of his skin with a single groove further up the handle for his index finger to rest on.

This was a wand crafted out of his own blood, will, and intention. Gabe didn't hesitate. He pointed it directly at one side of the rune, where a line swirled outward, and began to trace the shape, ensuring that his focus was primed and that he felt the flow of energy moving through his body. As he traced the symbol it began to glow brighter, ringing and resonating back to echo in the chambers of his chest.

He followed the swirling rune through a spiral, before finishing in a downward flourish. There was a click, then from behind the stone came a rumble. In fact, it wasn't just behind the stone, it was all around him, making the ground tremble where he stood. He stumbled backwards, catching himself on a nearby stone wall, which was also quivering and shuddering.

He steadied himself and watched as the light from the rune began to leak down the stone and into the ground, forming swirling patterns that zipped past his feet. He turned to watch as it not only ran along the ground, but also up the stone wall that led to the spring. The light illuminated the carvings, bringing them to life. Stone mermaids swam, fairies fluttered, and the water of the spring itself was illuminated in the same golden light as the rune. It rushed down into each of the pools, and around the stone that surrounded them, then raced off into the distance where the stone circle stood. The light highlighted each of the stones at once, swirling in intricate geometric patterns and ancient Celtic braids, and then burst upwards in a column of mana. Then, Gabe felt the earth tremble.

He watched as the stone door began to open. And when it was still, he took a tentative step forward into the darkness of the unknown.

The door slid shut immediately behind him, and the wand turned to ash in his hand. The weight suddenly lifted off Gabe's body and he let out a breath of relief as he drew in air. The stars receded in his vision and his body now felt ten times lighter.

It was cold and clammy within the cave, and pitch black. He could see nothing, and all he could hear was the quiet drip of water from the ceiling onto the stone floor. The shaking and rumbling had ceased entirely, and everything was completely still. Fumbling forward blindly, Gabe began to make his way through the cave. He patted at the walls, using them as a guide until his foot came down on empty air and he almost fell. A stairway.

The dark tunnel grew narrower as he descended the steps. He could tell the path was spiralling downwards by the way the wall curved under each of his hands. The stairway continued down for longer than Gabe thought possible. In the darkness, the passage of time was hard to judge. It could have been hours or minutes, seconds or years, but eventually the ground evened out. Again, Gabe almost fell. It was not just the solid stone beneath his feet that took him by surprise. As soon as he touched the floor, flames burst up in braziers that lined the walls of a circular domed chamber. His heart froze. It was just as he had imagined it. Almost every detail was an exact replica of the dreams he'd had as a child. He had just stepped foot in King Arthur's tomb.

There were hundreds of men standing motionless in the flicker of the shadows, armoured and equipped with weapons of various kinds, each bearing the insignia of a lion on their chest. It was something out of a legend. They all stood in a circle around the object in the centre of the room, facing outwards to protect it.

Gabe could hardly breathe. The thing they were protecting was a beautifully crafted stone sarcophagus. The resting place of the sleeping Barrow King of legends old. Arthur's tomb. His heart swelled with emotion. He approached the first row of knights slowly, his bare footsteps echoing off the cavern walls. Now that he was close, he could see more detail. And almost as quickly as his heart had swelled, it twisted into an uncomfortable knot. He frowned. What he previously thought were armoured headplates were not so at all. The knights wore nothing on their heads, but their faces were cast in stone, not flesh, with their eyes all closed.

He hadn't known what to expect, but he had imagined something else. He had imagined them in a form of stasis, not made completely of stone. He held his breath as he reached out with his hand. He wasn't sure he wanted to do it, but he couldn't hold himself back. His fingers met one of the stone soldiers.

Nothing happened.

Gabe blinked and let out his breath, then drew his hand away. That was when the soldier crumbled into dust. One minute they were there, standing tall. The next they were a heap of dust on the ground, the gold of their lion insignia the only thing poking out of the pile of ashen grey.

"No..."

Gabe stepped backwards as the soldiers on either side of the first fell to dust, setting off a chain reaction. He watched in horror all of them crumbled around him, one by one, until there were none left standing. Their ash filled the air, making the firelight flicker.

No. This couldn't be happening.

Gabe dropped to his knees and ran his hands through the soft dry silt that had once been a soldier. This was not how it was supposed to go. There was supposed to be a ceremony, a fabled rising from slumber, an awakening after millennia in meditative hibernation.

The dust sifted through his fingers like the slow running sands of an hourglass, and in it he could see all his dreams falling to pieces and passing into detritus before his very eyes. What had happened here? Had the magic run out? Did spells have expiration dates? All these men... They had sacrificed their lives for nothing. Gabe's eyes darted up to the sarcophagus in the middle. His heart rejoiced when he saw that it was still intact. If he could still wake Arthur, the King would grant him a favour. And he needed that favour to save Sothea.

He clambered to his feet and ran to it, careful to avoid the piles of ash that were once people. There was an inscription on the tomb, flowering flourishes of script that looked like the Celtic knots he had seen on the cover of his favourite book. They had aged. Unlike the outside of the tomb, they were worn down and faded, dull memories of what they had once been.

Gabe's jaw clenched. Was it possible that his King still slept? Had his promise carried through the ages? There was only one way to find out, and even though Gabe was not ready to face whatever lay on the other side of the stone lid, he knew that his time was limited. His own promise still wrung tight. He had to get back to Sothea before it was too late. He wished she could be here with him. Wished that she could help him tip the lid. It was only because of her that the world made sense – even though his world had been turned upside down ever since he met her. Or perhaps the world he had been in before had been the upside-down one. Full of lies and spiteful people propagating those lies. Sothea had brought him back to the real world. The world of magic and possibility, despite the shape it had taken so far.

He drew in a deep breath and pushed. He put all his weight into it, but the lid did not budge. He found one of the knights' fallen swords. It was only half a sword really, a fragment of metal bolted to a hilt. He rushed back to the sarcophagus and wedged the metal shard into the gap between the stone, putting pressure down on it to try and get some leverage to pry it open.

The blade snapped.

Gabe let out a grunt of frustration and cast his eyes around the rest of the room, trying to find something – anything – to help him move the heavy lid off the base. That was when he noticed the entrance to another chamber in the far corner of the room. It was almost completely invisible, hidden in shadows despite the flicker of flames in the braziers.

He dropped the sword hilt and wove between the piles of dust to reach it. The room was not lit from the inside, so Gabe took one of the braziers off its hinge on the wall and carried it in with him. His breath caught in his throat as he ducked inside.

Treasure. Endless amounts of treasure filled a large chamber, glittering in the light of his flame. There were stacks of trinkets and gold that stretched far above his head – so high it was a shock that it had not yet toppled over. It took Gabe's breath away, but it did not help him. Gold was not what he needed. He needed to discover a way out of this strange realm and find a way back to save Sothea.

He knew that some men would have been compelled to take some of it, even in his situation. But it was of no interest to him. He had read countless stories about men becoming obsessed with wealth and treasure and becoming evil because of it. He had read of dwarven kings who grew sick from their vast amounts of gold, turning on their own friends and family and hoarding their riches for none other than themselves to behold. He didn't want that. Right now, he just wanted something that would aid him in his quest to open the tomb.

His heart lurched in his chest when he saw a figure amidst the gold, and he almost turned and ran before he realised it was his own reflection staring back at him. Tucked away in the corner was a mirror. It was made of a black reflective stone, a shining obsidian of sorts, with an ornate frame. Something about it drew him in. The mirror was not like the ones he was used to back home. It had a strange sort of focus, reflecting his own image clearly, whilst blurring all that was around him.

He stretched out his hand to touch the surface. It was cool and solid under his fingers. He was fixated on it, hyperfocused like the black mirror itself demanded his attention. He felt it inside him, searching, asking a question: *What is it you want to see?*

Gabe wanted to know how to open the tomb.

The blurred edges began to swirl like smoke and the surface of the mirror rippled. He felt a pull in his body, and the world inverted. He had the nauseating feeling of switching perspectives. Whilst he had just been on the outside peering in, he was now within the mirror peering out of it.

He saw himself staring back, then smoke obscured the treasure-filled room and Gabe was looking at a figure not his own. A man stood over his own grave. He was from another time, adorned in odd shimmering armour, and on his hip was a sword in its sheath. Gabe could hear a whisper being sifted through the gaps between the sheath and metal, and the whisper said, *"Excalibur"*.

"Arthur..." Gabe reached his hand out to touch him but came up against the invisible glass of the mirror. He was in the world, or at least his senses thought so. He was no longer surrounded by smoke or darkness, but stood in the shadow of a tall hill by the ocean. In the distance were rolling green fields, slightly veiled in a thin mist. It was obvious that Gabe was just a spectator here, an uninvited observer watching an event unfolding in the past. Arthur could not hear him.

Gabe turned to see a woman walking towards Arthur. Her hair was as black as the obsidian mirror, and she wore a dark hooded cloak made with raven feathers, talismans of bones, and obscure trinkets draped all over it.

Her ravens circled in the sky above her, cawing her name. Morrigan.

"What brings you to the Isle of Avalon, Oathbreaker?" the woman said. Her voice was full of power, laced with magic and subtlety. And bitterness.

Arthur spared her nothing more than a glance.

"Lady Morrigan," he said, eyes still fixed on his tomb. "The ley lines of Avalon have faltered. The druids have already left, the seas are receding, and soon all memory of magic will trickle into memory."

"As it was foretold." She came to stand by his side, and one of the ravens landed on her shoulder. "You should never have made a vow to the world of men. They are beyond saving. Saturn's shadow falls upon our land. It will be millennia before the common folk see truth once more."

"I had to try, Morgana."

"You *tried* to change the tides of fate, dear Arthur. It was a fool's errand from the start."

Gabe stepped forwards. From his position all he could see was Arthur's back, but the confines of the mirror would not let him move any further. The Lady Morrigan, whom Arthur had called by her familiar name, Morgana, rested a hand on Arthur's shoulder.

"You have lost yourself in the swell of your cause," she said. "You have forgotten that you are only mortal. No man can change the tides of the world in a single lifetime."

Her eyes darted to the side and Gabe's breath drew in as her eyes met with his. Her lips quirked upwards in a thin, sly smile. Surely, she could not see him? But she continued to look at him as she spoke her next words.

"There will be others who will seek to further your cause. There comes a time when a man must surrender his oaths and pass them on to the future."

"I would not wish the weight of these oaths on any other," Arthur said.

"Then surely you know the cycles will draw you back. If you do not let go of your promise, you will be forever caught in the churning of this realm."

Arthur didn't acknowledge what she had said. "I came here seeking the last remnants of magic. I see I am too late for that. Unless you know of another way, then I would rather my final moments be spent in solace." He looked weathered and tired, his hair grey, and shoulders slightly slumped over.

"Always so serious, Arthur. I guess I should expect no less from the last true King." She sighed, taking her hand off Arthur's shoulder and interlacing it with her own over her belly. "I can see that your mind is made up, and because of that I wish to help you."

Arthur turned suddenly, and Gabe saw his hero's face clearly for the first time. It was nothing like he expected: grief-stricken, creased with age and worry, and scattered with scars.

"There is another ley line," Morrigan continued. "Far north of here, near the hamlet of Nether Alderley. Its magic still flows. I can take you there. But, Arthur, you must know that what you aim to do is dangerous. Should the magic cease, your soul will be trapped. Your name will go to history, then to legend, and – if you're lucky – myth. Should your memory fade all together, there will be no hope of escape. You will be caught in the fever of dream until the world crumbles. I have spent eternities watching time, and the chaos and bloodshed you see now is nothing compared to what will come. You will become ensnared in it. Feel every cry of pain. You may even lose your mind and will altogether."

Arthur nodded. "It is a risk I am willing to accept."

The lady drew back her hood, and Gabe saw the moonlight glow of her skin. She pulled Arthur's face to hers, grazing her palms against his cheeks. "You are a fool," she said, and Gabe could feel the knot of emotions in Morgana's voice. "But if someday a mortal should find your tomb, I pray his heart and intentions are true." Her eyes flickered over to Gabe's. "Only in the will of your cause will another be able to set you free."

Smoke suddenly swirled around Arthur and Morgana, and a storm of ravens' caws groaned through the air. Gabe felt himself being pulled away from the hilltop, and away from the vision.

"No! Arthur!" Gabe pleaded, reaching out as the vision turned into smoke. "Arthur!"

All at once, he was back on the other side of the mirror and on his knees, weeping. He didn't know when the tears had started. Maybe they had been pouring all his life. He stood, and walked back through the cavern of treasure to close the distance between himself and the tomb. Even as he cried, he knew why the sarcophagus had not opened for him before.

This time he approached it with a different sort of resolve and determination, but also a profound sadness for what he knew he would find inside. With the grief and the sadness flowing in his chest, with the will for the world to be a better, fairer, and more just place ruled by honesty and integrity, Gabe pushed on the stone lid.

It slid forward, stone grinding over stone, before toppling off the other end and landing on the floor with a crack through the centre. Gabe's tears were flowing harder than ever. He stared down at the skeletal remains of his hero. Arthur was gone. There would be no favour. There would be no ceremonious return, no rise of the sleeping Barrow King. Gabe would never stand by his side.

Excalibur lay between interlacing bone fingers, the crown of wood and thorns loose upon his skull.

"We were too late," Gabe said through muffled tears. "I am sorry. I am sorry you were forgotten. I am sorry we lost our way."

There was no whisper in the air, no trickle of hope through the magic, only the vacant sockets of Arthur's eyes staring blankly back at him.

"Don't worry," Gabe said, gritting his teeth and willing his tears to stop. "You will not have died in vain." He reached in the tomb and seized the hilt of Excalibur. "I will find a way to carry out your promises. I will bear your oaths."

He pulled at the sword and bones cracked as he tore it free.

"Forgive us."

He could not bear to look at Arthur's remains any longer. He turned and strode through the piles of fallen soldiers who had also given their lives to the cause and ascended the spiralling stairway from whence he came.

CHAPTER TWENTY-FIVE

The stone doors parted for Gabe before he even reached the top of the steps. Light seeped in, but he did not squint against it. He strode through the doors with Excalibur on his hip, stepping into the familiar light of the mortal world. It took him a moment to get his bearings. So much had changed within him since he had been here last.

He had been unsure of himself, lost and confused, desperately clinging to the dream of a sleeping king who he now knew was dead. He had faced a creature of the fae, communed with the spirit of Ama, traded his shoes and clothes for a cloak, and peered through an obsidian mirror into the distant past. But, most of all, he had opened King Arthur's tomb and seized Excalibur as his own. In so doing, he had also taken hold of the weight of its oaths and the blood it had shed.

He was at the top of the hill, where he had previously failed to open the stone door beneath the carving of Arthur's face. He could see the lower hill where the stone circle stood through a gap in the trees. There were figures there, and he knew at once who they were.

He stared at the back of himself, – his former self who had pulled Sothea towards the stone circle. Had it been merely minutes or aeons since he had lived through that? Gabe barely recognised that version of who he was. And yet at any moment he would be crossing the threshold into Faery and becoming what he was now. It was a paradox in time that would have wrestled with Gabe's reason had he not undergone the trials leading up to this very moment. Someone was going to pull Sothea back from the portal, and he would be there to stop them this time.

A wind lifted the back of his cloak and he sensed that the world was warning him of danger. He drew Excalibur and the sword hissed its own name as it bridged two worlds after thousands of years. As his eyes scanned the scene, he spotted another shape moving in the trees.

His father.

He was rushing forward without a weapon, limping heavily on one of his legs. There was blood splattered across his face and torso. Gabe's brows furrowed into aggression, and he called out.

"Dad!"

His father stopped dead in his tracks, head slowly turning to face Gabe at the stone entrance, sword by his side. The man did a double take, glancing back in the direction of the Gabe he had been following, who was still some distance away, seemingly completely unaware of what was happening. Gabe used this moment of confusion to charge. He rushed down the hill, expecting his dad to run or seek cover, but instead he squared himself and held his ground – as he had done so many times before – baring his teeth like an animal. His right arm was primed, ready to lash out.

Gabe felt a battle instinct rush into him through the hilt of the sword, a knowledge of war and combat. He charged at his father with full force, but at the last second, the other man side-stepped out of the way. Gabe instinctively swivelled on his foot, turning just in time to block an overhead blow with his arm.

"You little shit."

Another fist came Gabe's way and he ducked, sweeping with one foot at his dad's bad leg. His dad crumpled upon himself, hissing through his teeth with pain. He quickly tried to get to his feet, but Gabe already had the tip of Excalibur to his neck.

"Stop!" Gabe screamed at him, with all the rage that had built up over Sothea's father's death, over the fact that his own father was trying to kill the girl he loved.

"Do it then, you little prick!" his dad cried out. "I won't stop hunting her. She's a monster!"

Gabe's heart twisted to hear her described that way. He'd spent his life being called names by his dad. He would not allow him to start on Sothea. He stared into the older man's eyes. He wasn't sure his dad was still in there at all. He had been consumed by rage. But could Gabe really kill him? Was it what the man deserved? He didn't think so. He had spent years being the butt of the joke, the focus of all of his father's frustrations. But he also knew, deep down, that it had been brought about by the death of Gabe's mother. It didn't justify the behaviour, but it explained the cause – a terrible sense of loss, of loneliness, of guilt. Gabe knew exactly how his father felt, because he felt those emotions too.

Excalibur sang in his hand. The Sword of Truth. The sword that only Arthur had been able to retrieve because it had seen the intentions of his heart. Gabe twisted the sword back and his dad winced, but Gabe only showed him his own reflection in the gleam of the sword's blade. As his dad gazed into it, he was taken within his own mind, and Gabe saw the vision as if it was his own...

He dropped the ice creams and rushed to the water. He waded in, grabbing at his wife's body, a feeling of helplessness and sense of panic washing over him. He stumbled and forced himself deeper into the river, trying to secure her. He held her around the waist and dragged her towards the shore. His wife, Annabel. For a split second, he thought she would be okay. Maybe she'd just swallowed a bit of water. He'd seen enough movies to know that after a few chest compressions she'd cough up some river water and be right as rain after a hot cup of tea. But life wasn't like in the movies. She didn't wake up. Numerous people helped, all taking turns to perform CPR until the paramedics arrived. He pushed them all out of the way, pumping her chest again and again and again...

It was a sight no husband ever wanted to see. His beautiful wife, dead.

The vision suddenly shifted, and he was alone in the darkness, alone with the fierce rage of his frustration. It tore at him, the years that followed shown as fragmented memories. The countless cans of beer, the arguments with Gabe, the empty days and nights that followed her death. That terrible all-consuming loneliness. And he jumped when something brushed at his shoulder, anticipating seeing his son bringing down the sword he held. He lurched away, but as he turned, he was shocked to see that it was not Gabe, but his wife.

She stood in the clothes he had seen her in last – a summer dress she'd wanted to wear especially for their holiday. Her face was saddened and hurt, but calm.

"Annabel..."

He stood and reached out for his wife, but she pulled away, stepping backwards.

"You killed him in my name." Her voice echoed ethereally in his head.

"What did I have to lose?" he said. "When you were taken from me..."

"I never wanted that from you. What about Gabe? Only one of us died that day, but you carried on your life as if we both did. He needed you and you ignored him. Now you're here fighting a battle I never asked you to fight." She shook her head, and he saw that her sadness was not because she had died, but because of what he had become.

"Annabel."

She stepped back again as he tried to close the distance between them.

"Make it right," she said.

Then, all at once, she was gone. And Gabe was back in his own body looking down at his father, who was still staring at his reflection in the flat metal of the sword. His dad stumbled backwards, drawing away from himself.

"What have I done?" He raised his hands and stared, wide-eyed, at the blood that stained them. "I'm sorry, son. I'm so sorry. Forgive me."

Gabe withdrew Excalibur and sheathed it, taking a step away from him. The deed was done. Excalibur had revealed his dad's true reflection. Gabe's past self and Sothea were nearing the circle now. He frowned, looking back at his father. The man was in no state to move, let alone get up and kill Sothea. Had he changed the course of the future? What would happen to him now if events were different?

"I forgive you," Gabe said.

His dad nodded, smiling despite the tears, and then covered his face again.

Gabe suddenly remembered what Ama had told him. *Sothea must first face a fate of her own. She walks her own road, as do you. She has not yet come to peace with her shadow.*

The memory of Sothea entering the fae realm flashed before his eyes. She had split into two versions of herself, fighting a war within. Gabe's eyes widened and he suddenly knew what he had to do. He had no time to waste as he sprinted towards the stone circle. He saw his former self about to step in.

"No!" he shouted, but his voice did not carry.

He would not reach them in time. Gabe gritted his teeth and willed his limbs to move faster, forced himself to push past a limit he had never reached before. He screamed as his limbs protested, then all at once he broke through. All the pain and strain vanished, and he became unchained. A fluid grace coursed through him, and there was no longer any resistance. Gabe burst forward in a lurch of speed, his feet barely touching the ground, his movements as streamlined as a snake through water.

His past self stepped through the portal. He saw Sothea take a step, saw half her body disappear into a scatter of sparkling mana. Then he was there at her back. He grabbed her other arm and pulled. There was some resistance, but he knew what would happen next. He yanked Sothea back from the portal and into the mortal realm, grabbing her waist and hoisting her away.

She fought him, struggling, kicking, and lashing out with sharp elbows. Then he let her go and stepped in front of her. Her eyes widened, and she looked back to the portal in confusion before turning back to him. There was no time to explain. He dashed to the circle and drew Excalibur, slicing at the fabric of the mana that connected the two realms. He heard the boundary crack, then saw the shadow of his other self slam his fists against the veil.

He stepped backwards, breathing heavily.

"Gabe!" Sothea said. "How? When?" She looked between him and the portal again. "What are you doing here!? We were just about to—"

She was cut off mid-sentence as Gabe dropped Excalibur and pulled her in for a hug. He embraced her with all the emotions that had been trapped inside him.

"I thought I had lost you," he whispered into her ear.

"Gabe, if you don't explain what's going on right now..."

He stepped back, meeting her eyes. "It was me." He began to laugh. "Don't you see? It was me the entire time! I was the one who pulled you back."

Sothea looked at him in confusion, rubbing the fabric of his strange cloak between her finger and thumb.

He took a breath to calm himself down and tried again. "I spoke with Ama," he said, taking her hand. "She's okay. I saw her in Faery. Your dad is okay too."

She brought a hand to her mouth, visibly hit by several emotions at once. "What?"

"They are both okay. Ama told me that he is with your mother."

"Oh God, Gabe. Are you sure?"

He smiled, nodding, and raised a hand to brush the tears from her eyes. "It's all going to be okay."

She pulled herself close to him, burying her face in his chest. He closed his eyes and savoured the scent that blossomed from her hair. He was back with her, and the world made sense again. He kissed the top of her head, stroking her back, and then whispered softly.

"I had to stop you from going in. I saw something in you too. The other version of you. I saw it as you were walking through the portal."

"What does that mean, Gabe? I can't stay here! I can't stay here any longer! They're coming after me."

"Shh," Gabe soothed. "Don't worry. My dad's not hunting you anymore."

"He's not dead, is he?"

"No. We... made our peace."

She looked shocked and confused, and he smiled.

"I made you a promise, didn't I?" he said. "We will leave this world behind. But first there is something that we must do. Well, something you must do. But I will be by your side the entire time."

He felt her watching him as he knelt to pick up Excalibur, and as he sheathed it he met her gaze. She looked at him with sad eyes that seemed to know his dreams of waking King Arthur had died. He nodded in acknowledgement of her silent understanding.

"It's okay," he said softly. "His memory was all I needed. His memory led me to you. And his memory allowed me to believe in myself again."

He stretched out his hand and she took it. He led her to the top of the hill where the spring flowed. The stone doorway was still open, and the entrance was completely and unnaturally submerged in shadows. It did not bleed from a gradient of light to dark, but instead there was a stark line that marked the border, and on the other side was complete blackness.

He stepped inside, stopping midway so that half of him was still visible, and the other was wrapped in an impenetrable dark. Then he looked back and extended his hand.

"You have to face her, Sothea," he said softly. "It is the only way."

She shook her head.

"Ama was right," he continued, before she could protest. "There is a way for both of you to exist, a way without one of you destroying the other. A harmony."

"Harmony! How could you say that?" she asked. "You've seen what she is capable of. You've seen what she does."

He smiled. "When Ama first said it, I wasn't quite sure I

understood. She said you had to come to peace with your shadows. I thought that she was only referring to you, but now that I think about it, what Ama said applies to all of us. I saw it when Excalibur showed my dad the truth of himself. He was lost in his own shadows, just like you. And in the other side of his reflection, I saw myself. I saw the moment before I came to you, when I attacked my dad. Saw how my shadows took control and moved my body. I wanted to hurt him, but another part of me didn't. Like there were two sides of me fighting to take hold.

"We all have shadows. We all have a monster living inside us. And just like you, we all try to fight it. But our shadow is as much a part of us as our light. The sooner we see it has a place, the sooner we can learn how to accept it. It is the fighting within us that causes us harm. I think the trick is learning to live side by side."

There was a moment of silence before Sothea nodded. Then she took his hand and let him guide her into the dark.

CHAPTER TWENTY-SIX

Sothea found herself staring once again at a mirror. And just like last time, her other self stared back at her. Her arb was vicious and grotesque, repulsive and horrific, but calm. Mists trailed around her missing limbs, forming patterns that churned and lashed out against the empty darkness.

She could barely stand to look at the ugliness of her reflection. She almost turned away, but then she felt a hand placed on either one of her shoulders. Her mother and father appeared in the reflection beside her arb. Sothea's eyes went wide, and she dropped to her knees.

"Get away from me!" she shouted. "Get away! I don't want to hurt you!"

But her parents remained still. And, much to her surprise, the arb did not attack them. She breathed heavily through her tears, confused and shocked by what she saw.

"We are always with you, Sothea," her mother whispered. "Do not fear what you are. Remember the stories I used to tell you?"

"Mama..."

"She is right, darling." It was her father who spoke this time.

The stories of Princess Apsara. They came rushing back to her.

"What does the fear show you?" her mother whispered.

"The fear shows me myself," Sothea replied.

In that moment the mirror dissolved, and the vision of her parents started to disappear.

"Remember we are always with you," her father said with a smile. "And we will wait for you, until your time comes."

With that they were gone, and Sothea was left alone with herself. Her *other* self. Her arb drifted closer and spoke to her in ancient Khmer.

"We are not separate, Sothea. We were born from a sacrifice."

The words rung through Sothea's bones. The tale of Princess Apsara. In an instant, another arb appeared behind hers, then another, and another. Hundreds of them in a diagonal line. Sothea looked around her and saw that she was surrounded by another line of women, each bearing a striking resemblance to herself.

She recognised the one closest to her as her great-grandmother. Sothea had never seen or met her, but she knew within herself that it was true.

"We are all versions of one another," her ancestors said in unison. "Our kind has been misjudged, misunderstood through time. We were not born from a curse, we were born from a sacrifice. We were born from the will to protect our people and those closest to us."

"How can that be true?" Sothea replied. "All I have done is harm."

"That is because you fear the power you hold. You fear the power of your darkness, just as the world does. You have misunderstood your true nature, just as all around you have."

"What is my true nature then?!"

The hundred voices all answered her, including the arb reflections. "We have said it already."

Sothea frowned and recalled their words. "To protect our people... Our true nature is to protect."

It all came rushing to her at once, and with that rush came all of her ancestors, from the dawn of time. Their memories all became hers. Hundreds of lifetimes. She watched her ancestors kill, but the people they killed were cruel and unjust. The men they tore apart were rapists and murderers, corrupted and greedy.

"This power is yours to command," they told her. "The longer you fear it, the longer it will control you. The more you deny it, the more innocent lives will be taken."

She took in a deep breath, her eyes filled with thousands of memories, and then all at once she was alone again. Her arb was right in front of her. They were face to face, barely an inch away from each other. Deep pools of black stared back at her, and in those obsidian eyes she saw herself.

Sothea repeated the words of her arb. "You and I are not separate."

And in that moment, it all clicked into place.

She felt her skin falling away, her bones dissipating, and the power welling inside her. She bared her razor teeth and felt malice and power coursing through her form.

"I have always been this," she said out loud. She was no longer scared. She no longer feared what she was. "I was born from a sacrifice. I was born to protect my people."

She no longer had a fractured self. She was whole, and she was all her ancestors that came before her. She closed her eyes and took in a deep breath through her nose. She felt the sinews of her muscles reattaching, felt her bones and limbs grow back.

She and her arb were not separate.

"We are one and the same."

The words were uttered like a mantra, and as she spoke them the mirror appeared again in front of her. Sothea stared into the reflection of herself. Her face was no longer something static. It was a dynamic flux of her humanity and her shadow. She could choose who she was in any moment. Her being was not a defined thing set in stone. She was malleable, able to reshape herself at will. This was her truth and her power.

She walked towards the mirror, pausing for a brief second before stepping through and accepting every part of herself, shadow and all. The veil of the mirror's surface felt like cool mist against her skin. It stretched like thin fabric as she walked through it, pulling until the tension released and puffed into smoke. It wrapped itself around her body, forming a dress and cloak of smoke.

When she emerged on the other side, she found Gabe waiting for her, smiling his new light-hearted smile. But his expression turned to something like surprise, and then something more sombre, before he fell to one knee and bowed his head to her. Like a knight from one the stories he told her.

Confused, she turned back to the mirror to take herself in again. She was now adorned in the golden and red silks of the Khmer royal palace, thin like air, and a stark contrast against the moon-white features of her skin. On her head sat an ornate golden crown, with a smoky black gem that might well have been part of the mirror itself – or the dark eye of an arb – at the centre of her forehead.

She smiled and shook her head. Despite what she had just gone through, she did not see herself as a person worthy of such a bow – especially not from Gabe. He looked different now too, since he'd come back from Faery. For one, he was wearing a cloak. But he stood a bit taller as well, like he had regained a part of himself, and that part had given him a little bit of extra height as well as confidence. There was a glow about him, a glow she recognised as the magic of the land. The boy she'd first met was scared and unsure, but this Gabe... It was like he had been through a lifetime in mere moments.

She smiled to herself. Clearly, it was often those who did not believe themselves worthy that were most deserving of praise. Perhaps sometimes it just took the eyes of another to raise them to a higher status.

Sothea knelt in front of him and ran her fingers through his hair. Her nails had grown into points, a result of her merging together with the shadow of her other form. She grazed them delicately over his skin, but with the intent to hurt, they could shred flesh down to the bone.

"Thank you," she whispered.

Gabe raised his head and their eyes locked, thrumming emotions resonating between them in the empty air.

"If only we could have done it sooner," he said, smiling and bowing his head so that their foreheads touched.

The obsidian gem that now lay upon her brow touched softly against skin, and through its connection their minds were joined in a field of their own. Emotions ran back and forth between them in strange shapes and colourful waves of expression, unfiltered by the typical boundaries of belief.

He poured his emotions into her, and she mirrored with her own. Their emotional bodies merged in a place beyond physical bone and tissue, wrapping and folding together like spirals of water. Their hands joined together in the same fluid motion.

"It is time we set off," Gabe said.

"Are you sure you want to? I have nothing left here, but there may still be someone here for you." She could feel goodbyes that had not been said within his heart.

Gabe paused, but eventually nodded. "My father has always

blamed me for my mother's death. I said goodbye to him the day she died in that river. He let the shadow consume him. I have done what I can for now. One day, when the boundaries of this life bleed into the next... Maybe then we could speak again."

Sothea offered him an understanding smile, kissing him softly on the cheek where she knew old tears had fallen. "So, what is next?"

Gabe stood, and Sothea followed suit. He looked to the passage that led into the world of the fae.

"I haven't told you yet of all that awaits us there," he said. "But I can assure you that it is not all good magic and kind things. There are creatures there..."

"Creatures like me?" Sothea raised an eyebrow.

"Well..." Gabe started. "Not quite like you, but similar in more ways than one."

She smiled. "Lucky that you have someone like me to protect you from them, then."

Gabe smirked. "I thought the knights were meant to be the ones protecting the princesses?"

"Most stories don't have princesses like me." She winked and took the first step towards the staircase. Together, they began to climb.

When they surfaced, they found themselves high up on a mountainside. Waterfalls cascaded, mountain ranges gave way to rolling hills. Forests carpeted the landscape for miles and white-water rivers carved their own path through the valleys. The sky was not the soft blue of the mortal world, but rather a deep indigo, lit by a black and purple sun. Just beyond the stone circle and spring, alight with the illumination of runic symbols and carvings on the ground, was the sprawling land of the fae.

From up here they could see far across the land. It was not just a sight to behold, but a wonder like no other. They were in what looked to be the east of this strange realm.

"Well, this might take some getting used to," Gabe muttered.

Sothea smiled from ear to ear, letting go of his hand and beginning to twirl, dancing and laughing in the light of the purple sun. It was home.

She had never realised how much of an alien she felt in the mortal world. She thought Cambodia had been her home, but the feeling was nothing compared to being here. This realm, this place, it spoke to her in ways she had never known. Every cell in her body sung with the energy in the air.

This was where she belonged. Every part of her.

G abe watched Sothea dance and felt the mirror of her joy within his own body, although he did not join her. He simply stood and watched her magical movements, one hand resting on the hilt of Excalibur.

Should this not have been Arthur's reward? Gabe felt like he had stepped into his own dreams, and yet they had all been made possible on the back of a long-dead king. When had Arthur passed? Had his spell of sleeping failed from the start, or had it faltered with the magic of the world? How many ages did Arthur sleep through, only to die beneath the stone lid of his sarcophagus after all? Had he slept, or was the myth simply created in order to pass on an oath-filled baton?

He now knew Arthur had broken oaths, from what he saw in the mirror. The Lady Morrigan had even referred to him as "Oath-breaker". The knot of Gabe's own promise had already unravelled. He had seen it through to the end, despite all the hardship that had come his way. But as he stared at Sothea and felt the emotions that she drew from his heart, he knew that there would be new promises on the horizon. Ama spoke of fate and destiny like a force in the world that was as real and tangible as the wind. Where would that current lead him next?

It had been Arthur's mission to help humanity return to what they once were. The fact of the matter was that Gabe had no idea what humans had once been. All he knew was what humans were now. Arthur spoke of a time when kings were honest servant leaders, when people knew the language of the world, and lived together with beings of the fae. Could that time come again? Morrigan seemed to think it was out of the hands of a single man to change the course of an entire world.

Gabe's grip tightened around Excalibur. It was not mere chance that the sword had allowed him to grip its hilt. He had pushed that fact aside as he fought to save Sothea. But now it could not be ignored. Excalibur had allowed him to wield it. A sword that an entire world had tried and failed to pull from stone, and yet he had been able to do it. He looked down at the sword and swore he felt it reacting to him. Excalibur stood for truth. How would that guide his fate? Now that his dream of awaking a sleeping king had crumbled, what new dream would arise from the ashes?

Gabe had always viewed his life through the lens of the fabled King. But he could do that no more. He had to cast away his crutch and become his own man, had to find his own fate... Perhaps he already had, and he just didn't know it yet. The thing with fate was that it went unseen, unheard, and unfelt. It operated under the guise of free will, secretly pulling strings through pivotal moments in a life.

Sothea ceased her dance and looked at him. Her hair tossed as her head spun, and her eyes sparkled with the shimmer of magic that exuded from every inch of this world. She closed the distance between them and drew her body to his, so that her chest and pelvis were pressed firmly against him. Her hands drew through his hair, tracing spirals over his head. She looked up at him with a sharp and dangerous stare, that could only be a dare. A dare to venture deeper into the unseen parts of her. It was a question too. Was he brave enough?

Gabe released his grip on Excalibur and wrapped his arms around her, his palms tracing the curve of her back. Then, because he couldn't hold himself back anymore, he kissed her lips. Their emotions raged like the swell of deep ocean waves, rising and crashing against one another's shores. There could be no force, no shadow-dwelling creature, capable of tearing their bond apart.

In that kiss, they sealed their love for one another. Braiding it in ancient patterns, weaving their emotions into the shapes of the old knots from Celtic tales, blossoming as naturally as flowers in bloom.

Sothea's lips curled into a smile as they peeled away from one another, and Gabe felt his do the same as he basked in the light of their dream come to life. Slowly they walked to the edge of their vantage point on the mountain and stared properly off into the land below. Large roots and vines spiralled all the way down the rock face to the ground. Gabe hadn't thought about it yet, but he supposed they would need to find some way to get down eventually.

The land beneath them resembled Cheshire in some respects, covered with rolling hills – except there were many more lakes and rivers, providing the water for giant trees that must have reached at least fifty meters into the sky.

"This place probably already has a name, doesn't it?" Sothea said. "I thought it would be nice to have our own name for it too, though."

He smiled. "It has probably been called many things

throughout many times. I reckon a new name wouldn't do any harm. Did you have something in mind?"

"Well, there is this word in Khmer," Sothea said. "*Dei Sanyea*. Or 'Sanyea' for short."

As soon as she said it, the world seemed to shimmer. And Gabe felt tingles spring from the bottom of his gut and rise into his heart.

He laughed. "I think it's perfect."

Sothea smiled, hugging him.

"What does it mean?" he asked.

"Well, Sanyea is a promise," she replied. "To pledge yourself. And Dei means 'land'."

"So, the promised land?"

She nodded. "It fits, don't you think?"

Gabe gazed out over the realm below, bathed in dreamy amethyst light. "Sanyea..." he repeated. The words made his heart glow again. In response, the wind picked up, casting twirls of shimmering dust through the air.

"I think it likes its new name," Sothea said, hugging him from the side and nestling into his chest.

He smiled. "I think you're right."

EPILOGUE

They stood together for ages. Time did not work like it had in the other world, marked by the cycles of the shifting sun and the seasons. Time may not have existed at all, save for the imprint their minds made on the world around them. But as they stood in the light of their promised land, something trembled far in its recesses.

The odd creatures that lived nearby began to scatter, flying into the wind or scampering away along the ground. Deep in the heart of a world left to dream, something stirred, rumbling into wakefulness.

Completely unnoticed by the two figures stood high on their mountain amidst the clouds, the trees that stood below them began to shiver. Their leaves fell and their bark stripped away, peeling back like a dream meeting the waking world.

The gateway between worlds had been opened for the first time in many generations, and the entire realm began to shift and adapt in response. The act of crossing over from the mortal realm to this one had caused ripples. And what arose from those ripples had yet to be unleashed.

ACKNOWLEDGEMENTS

It takes a village to raise a child and a small army to shepherd a book to publication. I'm eternally grateful to everyone who has played a part in the conception, birth, and rearing of this unruly progeny.

To my screenwriting partner and friend, Ian Masters, for all the "Balkon" chats over the years, for being a gracious host in Phnom Penh (twice!), and for adding arbs to my catalogue of folk monsters. You planted the seed. This time next year, Rodders!

A doff of the cap to my editors Makenna Albert and Kate Nascimento. Makenna, your counsel on the first draft helped me focus on the story I wanted to tell and provided the necessary confidence boost to wade through the many rewrites and edits. Kate, your pin-point accuracy is both terrifying and enlightening. I love your unwavering positivity despite being presented with passages that must be the grammatical equivalent of nails scraping against a blackboard.

To the strangers (now friends) on Instagram who kindly agreed to read ARCs, provide feedback, and drive awareness of the book both pre- and post-publication. Thank you.

To my sensitivity readers Ines Sothea and Morn Vanntey. Thank you for your insight.

To Ronin, the "alpha" beta reader – standing room only on a train, two suitcases, numerous platform changes, trying to wrangle three hundred loose sheets of A4. Cheers, big man! To Neil Jackson and Anya Zazzi for beta reader feedback.

Most importantly, to Elena, for your gracious understanding when I retreated into the study to "write for half an hour". Night, after night, after night. Thank you for the sustenance, and for the love and unwavering support.

NOTE FROM THE AUTHOR

Hi,

Thanks so much for reading *The Arb*!

It was a lot of fun to write. I truly hope it was an entertaining read.

If you enjoyed the book, I would be incredibly grateful if you'd be so kind as to leave a review.

Reviews really help authors for a number of reasons, not least, providing feedback on what readers like and improving visibility of the book on online retail sites.

Thanks in advance and I look forward to reading your thoughts.

Jon

ABOUT THE AUTHOR

Jon Smith is the bestselling author of 15 books for children, teens, and adults. His books have sold more than half a million copies and have been published in seven languages. In addition to writing books, Jon is an award-winning screenwriter and musical theatre lyricist and librettist with productions at the Birmingham Hippodrome, Belfast Waterfront, and London's Park, Waterloo East, and Courtyard theatres.

A father of four, he lives near Liverpool with his wife and their two school-age children.

When he grows up he'd like to be a librarian.

www.jonsmith.net

X x.com/jonsmith_author

instagram.com/jonsmith_author

goodreads.com/jonsmith_author

amazon.com/author/jonsmith

facebook.com/authorjonsmith